DAMNED IF YOU DO

Also by Gordon Houghton

The Dinner Party

DAMNED IF YOU DO

Gordon Houghton

Picador USA
New York

Picador® is a U.S. registered trademark and is used by St. Martin's Press
under license from Pan Books Limited.

For information on Picador USA Reading Group Guides, as well as
ordering, please contact the Trade Marketing
department at St. Martin's Press.
Phone: 1-800-221-7945 extension 763
Fax: 212-677-7456
E-mail: trademarketing@stmartins.com

Illustrations by Joe Madeira

ISBN 0-312-26288-4

First published in Great Britain under the title *The Apprentice* by
Anchor, a division of Transworld Publishers Ltd

First Picador USA Edition: July 2000

10 9 8 7 6 5 4 3 2 1

Thanks to Sarah Westcott, my editor at Anchor; Jonny Geller, my agent at Curtis Brown; and to Kati, my partner – without all of whom, no book. Thanks also to Liz Greenlaw for her suggestions for Death's desert island discs; and belated thanks to Andy Bell, for inspiring Nigel's finest hour in *The Dinner Party*.

For the first eight, who didn't make it to the party,
and for K, their mother

CONTENTS

It could be you

Hades was dead – no doubt about it – and he wasn't coming back this side of the Last Judgement. They found his body one bright Sunday morning in July, lying face-down in a thicket by the river. His Agency badge was missing. His face was unrecognizable. He had been eviscerated.

No-one could agree how it happened. Death blamed War, of course; and War openly accused Pestilence. Pestilence, for his part, secretly suspected Famine – and Famine believed the other three were engaged in a conspiracy against him. An early-morning jogger, who witnessed the crime from behind a mulberry tree, and barely escaped with his life, swore that he saw three wild dogs crashing through the bushes and bounding back along the track towards town. Only one person knew the whole story, and he wasn't telling.

Whatever the truth, the fact remained – Hades was dead, and the Agency needed a replacement. An emergency meeting was held, a resolution was passed, and the traditional method for selecting a new recruit was agreed upon. In the converted attic of a two-storey town house overlooking the meadow, the Unholy Tombola began: Pestilence emptied a bag of coloured balls into a revolving wooden drum, Famine turned the handle, and Death removed the balls and read out the numbers.

'Seventy-two . . . Eighteen . . . What's this – a six?' He showed the ball to Famine, who tutted loudly.

'It's a *nine*.'

'Lucky bugger,' said War. He was slouched at the computer desk, typing in the numbers as they were announced, his manner increasingly irritable. 'Looks like it's a 'cking local. Just down the road.'

'Let's hope it's better than the *last* one,' Pestilence remarked.

'Couldn't be worse,' Famine concurred.

'Do you mind?' Death interrupted. 'OK. Eleven . . . Twelve . . . Thirteen – what are the chances of that?' Pestilence rolled his eyes and feigned a yawn; no-one else responded. 'And finally, the bonus number . . . Forty-*nine*.'

Everyone turned towards War, who entered the last number with a listless tap, then nodded and mumbled to himself as he scanned the on-screen information. 'Right . . . He's a Code Four male. Twenty-eight . . .' He laughed. 'Bloody typical – no name, no family, and no friends . . . Interesting case, though—'

'Just tell me where he's buried,' Death snapped.

War gave him his most apocalyptic glare, but spoke coolly. 'St Giles cemetery.' He paused. 'Has the Chief done you a contract?'

'Of course.'

'Have you got a *spade*?' Pestilence sneered.

'*Obviously*.'

'Make sure you find the right grave,' Famine added, weakly.

Death smiled at him, like an indulgent uncle with a Sabatier hidden behind his back.

MONDAY

DEATH BY FALLING FROM
A GREAT HEIGHT

The apprentice

I had been dead for countless years when I heard a knock on the coffin lid.

I didn't answer immediately. If I'd known what would happen over the next seven days, I wouldn't have answered at all. But, back then, my sole reason for not responding was a practical one – I wasn't sure if I was still in one piece. Depending on luck and the amount of time you've been buried, you can be as firm as a belly of pork or as loose as a thick pea soup. And you don't need me to point out that without lips, vocal cords and a tongue, the only role you'll get in *Hamlet* is Yorick.

So I wriggled, and fidgeted, and gave myself a quick pat and rub to check that the important bits and pieces were still available – which they were – and I was just about to test my voice by calling out a reply, when I heard a second knock.

I should explain something first.

Most people are afraid of burial. It's understandable: I even felt that way myself, once. But to a corpse, this fear is illogical. We can't be afraid of death because we know what it is. We have no use for air or light, so we don't miss them. Try as we might, we can't move very far, so a silent space six feet long and two feet wide is our definition of home comfort. The very fact which terrifies the living – being nailed into a cramped wooden box with six feet of solid earth above it – is to us a reassurance. We are protected here. We are *safe*.

Security is vital to the dead. Inside the coffin there are no risks. No-one needs or wants you. Someone, somewhere, may remember who you are, but they don't anticipate your imminent return. Outside, there is earth and sky, there are six billion people, there is danger. And there are strangers who rap their bony knuckles on your tomb and expect an answer.

My mouth opened before I knew what it was doing.

'Who is it?'

These were the first three words I had spoken since my death, and they sounded like the dry-throated croaks of a crushed frog. In comparison, and though it was muffled by the coffin lid, the response was firm, high-pitched, and excited.

'About time, too. I was beginning to think you were deaf. Or War had made *another* mistake . . . Can you hear me?'

'Who are you? What do you want?'

'You're all alike. Always the same questions. And you're *never* satisfied with the answers.' The intruder tutted. 'It's not as if it was *my* fault in the first place . . . Still, it can't be helped. Too many mistakes already. No point in making any more.' A third knock, this time above my head. 'Solid wood. Lovely job. You must have had some money tucked away. Don't worry, though – we'll soon have you out.'

And the first nail squealed free from the coffin lid.

I heard a juddering rumble as the lid was prised away from the coffin case, felt soft showers of soil fall onto my chest, sensed a distant thump as the lid was tossed out of the grave and onto the grass. I opened my eyes and stared straight ahead, but it was too dark to see clearly at first. (If you should ever pass by an open grave, don't be afraid: the corpse in the earth is as nervous as you are. Don't expect him to leap out and scream, because he won't – not unless you're unlucky.) At length I saw a faint shadow moving against the grey background, increasing in size until it consumed everything I saw. When the intruder finally spoke, his voice was louder, closer, more alarming:

'I *love* that smell.' He inhaled deeply. 'Now, where's your head?'

Before I could answer, two skeletal hands patted my chest, groped my neck, then gripped my cheeks. A moment later, an alien mouth was pressed against mine, generating a prickling warmth on my dry lips; a crackling, tickling feeling which fizzed through my body like a firework. The sensation intensified until it filled me completely, recreating and redefining the physical frame I had abandoned to decay. Veins burst with new blood, old bones stretched and stiffened, muscles leapt into life like snapping traps. My reanimated suit of skin was cold, and naked, and shivering with new impressions.

It was the most exciting moment of my death.

The stranger pulled slowly away from my face and climbed out of the grave. I could still smell his carcass skin, taste his fetid breath, feel the offal warmth of his lips; and as my eyes grew accustomed to the darkness, I saw him more clearly. He loomed over the high walls of the grave like a lighthouse perched on a cliff. His head was shaped like a giant butter bean with hair at both ends. Two crustacean black eyes peered from the cave sockets of his skull. The skin of his face and hands was pale, and seemed to shimmer like rocket flame in the gloom, now blending with the background, now a vivid contrast to the night sky. Above him, through the rustling leaves of a chestnut tree, a dozen white stars sparked into life.

'You can get up now.' When his mouth moved the jawbones pushed tight against his skin, like crabs in a sack.

'Is it time?' I asked.

'What do you mean?'

'The Last Judgement. Is it *time*?'

He raised his eyebrows. 'Look. I've got a job to do. I don't have all day.' He hunkered at the graveside. 'It's dawn. In a couple of hours it'll be Monday morning. People will come here, stare at this hole, and wonder why a zombie is slithering about in the soil. I suggest we spare them the surprise. There's a suit waiting for you at the office. You can shower there, too.'

I didn't understand what he was saying – but my confusion was overwhelmed by a sudden and powerful sense of recognition. He was very tall, especially from my inferior perspective. He had neither a hat nor a hood, and the coconut fringe of his short, black hair contrasted violently with the general pallor of his complexion. His clothes were more modern than I would have expected, too: a light grey scarf was wound tightly around his neck, and his hands were buried deep in the pockets of a long, dark herringbone tweed overcoat. But when I saw the scythe-shaped gold badge pinned to his lapel, I realized it couldn't be anyone else.

'Are you Death?'

He nodded impatiently. 'Let's skip the introductions. We haven't time. Right now I need you to stand up, get out, and follow me back to the office. We'll get acquainted later.'

Abandoning the security of a coffin is never a simple decision for a corpse. We are incapable of flexing the smallest muscle until we have the maximum amount of information. I understood Death's need for urgency, but I also had to ask:

'What exactly do you want with me?'

'Yes. Precisely.' He nodded, as though addressing a different question. 'It's a complicated situation, but you have the right to know, of course...' He tapped his forefinger against his chin. 'This is how it works. One of our Agents – you don't know him, he was my assistant – but, the fact is, he's been relocated. Permanently. And we have a procedure, back at the Agency, for selecting replacements. Basically, your number came up—'

'I don't understand—'

He held up his palm. 'You don't have to ... The thing is, we're offering you an opportunity. We're taking you on as an apprentice, and we're giving you a week to prove yourself. If you succeed – and there's no reason to assume you won't – you become a fully-qualified Agent, with all the benefits that guarantees: immortality, steady employment, freedom from boredom, and so on and so forth.'

'What if I fail?'

'You *won't* fail. Don't even *think* it.' He waved his hand dismissively. 'Besides, you can't lose. If things don't work out, we'll just put you back. *And* you get to choose the manner of your own death.'

That settled the issue. To a corpse, precisely how you died is everything. It's the first question your neighbours ask when you arrive; and your answer can mean the difference between dignity and honour, or shame and scorn. So, even if I didn't know what the apprenticeship involved, it didn't matter; and when Death reached down and offered me his hand, I took it.

How could I refuse?

My zombie brain

The fact is, back then I had no idea how I died. The only concrete images I could recall were of a woman tied to a bed, a wet rooftop, and an oil-soaked rag. But things are different now. I already remember so much more, and I feel ready to reconstruct what happened. Piecing it all together shouldn't be beyond me, either. I had a strong investigative streak in my former life: I was always watching, always listening, always asking questions.

I didn't always get the answers I was looking for, it's true – but I learned to accept that some mysteries remain mysterious.

Death's thin, white fingers reached under my arms and dragged me, with difficulty, onto the soft, dew-dampened grass. He turned my head to the right, inspected my neck, and grunted; then he knelt by me and brushed loose lumps of earth from my body, working silently, tenderly. I lay motionless, passive, watching his wiry hands smear some of the dirt into muddy streaks on my legs and torso. The top of his head fascinated me: crescents of black hair uncoiled from his crown like the curling arms of a spiral galaxy.

'Stand up.'

It was an encouragement rather than an imperative, and I obeyed. My senses crackled with the memory of life: the snake-hiss of wind in trees, the sweet smell of wet earth. Sharp air penetrated my mouth and lungs. A cold wind shrivelled the pores on my skin.

Death removed his coat and handed it to me.

'Put this on.'

As I buttoned myself in, I noticed that several parts of my body were missing.

*   *   *

My grave lay by the thick trunk of an old horse chestnut tree, in the fork of two gnarled and mouldy roots. The headstone, like those of my three closest neighbours, was so thickly blanketed with moss its inscription was indecipherable. I would have liked more time to say goodbye to my neighbours – just a few words to explain what was happening, and to reassure them. But Death, who had spent the last few moments searching distractedly for a sheet of paper hidden in his buff chinos, snapped his fingers impatiently and summoned me to a low stone wall bordering the cemetery.

'Right. Let's get down to business.' He unfolded the sheet and handed it to me. 'This is your contract. Read it, sign it, return it.'

He removed a thin, black pen from his back pocket and tossed it in the air like a baton before handing it over. I studied the paper briefly, but the print was too small, there wasn't enough light to read by, and my feet felt like two chunks of ice. The promise of a shower and a fresh suit of clothes took on a new appeal.

'What does it say?'

'It's a standard contract.' He snatched the sheet and followed the text with his fingers. 'Blah blah . . . Covenant between the Agency and the deceased, hereafter referred to, et cetera, et cetera . . . seven-day trial period . . . guaranteed employment . . . assessment at the end of the week, at which time . . . blah *blah* . . . failing which, the deceased must choose one termination from a short list of seven to be witnessed during his apprenticeship . . . all files to be returned to the Chief by Monday morning at the latest . . .' He handed the paper back to me. 'Just put your mark at the bottom. It'll make things easier for all of us.'

I signed without hesitation.

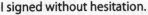

If you're wondering *how* I would have said farewell to my neighbours, and how the dead communicate with each other in general, the answer is simple.

Corpse code.

For example, the most basic response – a single knock on the coffin wall – means *No*, *Go away*, or *I'm resting*. Two knocks signify *Yes*, *Hello*, or *I'm ready to talk*. *Goodbye* is indicated by a long, slow scratch . . . And so on.

Don't misunderstand me: many corpses retain the ability to talk even when they are approaching the most advanced stages of physical decomposition. But there's no point in having a conversation when even your closest neighbour is separated from you by thick wooden walls and several feet of earth.

It's just not practical.

I returned the contract. Death thanked me, folded it three times, and slipped it into the top pocket of his polo shirt, where it competed for space with a pair of black plastic sunglasses.

'Can you walk?' he said.

'I think so.'

It was a small graveyard, perhaps only a hundred plots, most of them with worn, tilting, or mouldy headstones. Mine was one of the newer ones, and as we passed the open grave again, I wondered aloud if we shouldn't replace the huge mound of excavated soil.

'Forget it,' said Death. 'I can't be bothered.'

He skipped over the stray coffin lid, picked up the spade propped against the tree trunk, and headed for a narrow sandy path which bisected the cemetery. The path led from an iron gate in the south wall to a small, Saxon church dominating the northern end. The dawn illuminated clumps of trees on either side and the cluttered rows of tombstones sheltering beneath them. A few bouquets of withered flowers provided random splashes of colour. I was too focused on our journey to notice much else.

At the church we turned left and crossed a deserted main road before cutting into a narrow side street; then right, at the end, onto a long back road bordered by shops, houses, cafés, and a cinema. Finally, we turned left down a slope which curved towards a distant meadow. We saw no-one – not even a tramp, or a street cleaner, or a crook.

But the extraordinary experience of walking again, after lying still for so long, made me wonder how I could ever have enjoyed my time in the coffin. The powerful pull of gravity and the pressure of the pavement beneath my feet were like the sudden return of an exquisite memory. And as we reached the bottom of the slope, I was so preoccupied by the images and sensations of life stimulating my zombie brain that I tripped on the kerb, slipped face-forward, and landed on my chin.

Death picked me up, produced a black-and-white polka-dot handkerchief from another pocket, and pressed it against the wound. He squeezed my shoulder in an attempt at reassurance, then gestured to the building directly opposite.

'Welcome to the Agency,' he said.

The four car drivers of the Apocalypse

If you're imagining a Gothic structure with dark towers, flying buttresses, leaded windows and iron-bound wooden doors, forget it. There were no horses champing at the bit and foaming at the mouth, and no lowering clouds or flashes of lightning in the background, either. Death's office was simply a two-storey corner town house with a converted attic and steps leading down to a cellar. Three unremarkable cars were parked outside, and the sun rising in a clear sky behind us suggested it was going to be a pleasant day. I registered my dissatisfaction.

'Is that it?'

'What more do you want? A fanfare? A great multitude in white robes? The whore of Babylon?'

'I wouldn't mind.'

'It is what it is. No more, no less.'

We crossed the road and climbed a short flight of steps to the only visible entrance: a black, oak door studded with iron rivets. Death produced a ring of keys and selected the largest, oldest, rustiest one. He turned it in the lock, then hesitated.

'Before we go in . . .' he began. 'In the main office there are four of us: myself, Pestilence, Famine and War. And there's Skirmish, of course – he's War's assistant. He used to be an apprentice, like you. Don't take him too seriously.' He pushed the door open and entered a gloomy, stone-tiled hallway, where he propped the spade against the wall and tossed his grey scarf onto a hook. Above the hook were five bold, black letters: DEATH. I noticed two jackets on adjoining hooks, marked FAMINE and PESTILENCE, and an empty hook marked WAR. 'Our work here is different from what you might anticipate. Most of our practical business is sub-contracted to appointed Agents – former trainees like yourself.' He smiled, displaying twin rows of pointed, yellow teeth. 'What *we* do here is mainly administrative, though we're obliged to exercise our skills on the local population once a day.'

I nodded absent-mindedly. 'Keeping your hand in.'

'*Precisely*. Until the first blast of the Last Trumpet!' He waved his long, bony arms in a ridiculous flourish, like an orchestra conductor assailed by hornets; then his whole body slumped suddenly. 'Actually,' he confessed, 'I'm rather bored with the whole thing. Nothing seems to make sense any more ... My heart's not in it.'

At the end of the corridor there was a white panelled door. Death opened it to reveal a tall column of paper, wobbling precariously on a Formica-laminated desk: the top sheet almost touched the low, Artexed ceiling. He awkwardly side-stepped the pile and disappeared.

I followed him apprehensively. Things were happening so fast.

The office contained four similar desks arranged in a square: each faced a different wall, each bent to accommodate mounds of paper-work. There were sheets of paper scattered randomly on the floor, banks of paper leaning against the sides of filing cabinets, paper pyramids pushing against the windows and spilling from the sills, paper pinned to machines, paper blocking air vents, paper crushing shelves. The room was decorated from floor to ceiling with documents and files, contracts and memos, and in the midst of this paper world were three of the least normal people I had ever seen.

Death intercepted my approach and pulled me into the middle of the room. 'Morning, all,' he said breezily. No-one paid him the slightest attention. 'This is our new apprentice. He'll be helping me out for the next seven days.'

As if someone had flicked a switch, three heads revolved slowly and scanned me. This scrutiny was terrifying after the darkness of the coffin. It burned a hole through the thin layer of confidence I had created. It withered me. A wave of nausea spread from my stomach into my throat. I felt my jaw quiver, then drop – and I stood there with my mouth half-open, not knowing where to look or what to say.

*　　*　　*

Something about the intensity of their gaze reminded me of when I was alive, when I was a child.

I was often ill when I was young. My mother shielded me from contact with other children until I went to nursery school, and when she was finally, reluctantly, forced to let me mix with my peers, I spent two years reeling from one disease to another. Whenever I fell sick, she drew me back into the nest, and folded herself around me, protecting me until I recovered. For my part, I sought any excuse to return to her.

And though I remember one particular day and one specific memory so clearly, it could have been any one of a hundred such days and memories from my childhood. The picture is always the same. I am lying in my mother's arms on the sofa, dressed in my pyjamas, a soft, white woollen blanket wrapped around me. I can feel the warmth and softness of her skin against my head and feet. I have a fever, but the heat from her body penetrates the crucible of my disease. She strokes my head, so gently, so softly, that I never want to leave this moment, despite the sick feeling in my stomach. I never want to leave as she rocks me slowly in her huge, soft arms, her fine hair hanging over my hot face. I want to remain, frozen in this heat, as she lowers her head and – so tenderly – nibbles at my cheek and soothes me to sleep.

But I have a question which must be answered before I yield. I want to know when the fever will finish, when this pain and pleasure will end. I turn my face towards her, ready to ask; and she instinctively draws me closer, ready to listen. But as I look at her the question sticks in my throat. I cannot speak – because I am burned by the brightness of the light in her eyes, blistered by the terrible intensity of her power and love.

Immense power; unwavering love.

Standing alone while my new employers inspected me, something of that power and softness filtered through and brought me comfort even after death. But I remained gripped by a physical paralysis until the middle character in this eccentric trio shattered the awful silence.

'Could be worse,' he said, licking his lips. He was a tiny, bald, sickly creature with string arms, stick legs and a head that resembled a pock-marked skimming stone. He wore black boots, black socks, black jeans and a black T-shirt embossed with a single white emblem: a pair of scales. On his desk, beneath a dozen documents all stamped URGENT, was a black flat cap.

Death patted me on the back encouragingly. 'Considering how he died, we're lucky he's here in one piece.'

'What's his name?' This was spoken by the youngest member of the party: a pimpled teenager dressed in a sharp pink suit and matching leather tie. He had the physique of a plucked chicken, and his voice was squeaky and irritating, like a child's toy. It was obvious from the groans provoked by his question that he commanded little respect, and even less affection.

'Look it up.'

The teenager scowled but returned to his work. Exhausted, I removed a couple of sheets of paper from the chair by the door, then sat down and made myself comfortable. The office was hot, and I began to sweat beneath Death's coat. The sweat mingled with the smeared earth on my skin to produce a sharp but pleasant graveyard odour. I wondered when I would be shown the promised shower and suit.

Death looked around the room. 'Where's War?'

The answer came from the only member of the group who hadn't yet spoken. 'Busy.'

'Ah.'

'He *said* he'd be back on Wednesday.'

'Uh-huh.'

'For the meeting.'

'Right.'

I stared at the final stranger. He was dressed entirely in white: jeans, tennis socks, trainers, and a T-shirt featuring a small, golden crown stitched into the breast pocket. His arms were etched with scars: a geometric nightmare of ragged white lines and neat pink circles. His face was even more alarming: a mass of pustules and papulae, boils and blackheads. Buried under a mound of paper on his desk were several cosmetic items – foundation, face powder, acne gel. On the wall above his head was a framed statement: YOU DON'T HAVE TO BE MAD TO WORK HERE, BUT I AM.

'What are *you* looking at?'

He caught me off guard. 'I—'

'If you think my *face* is shocking you should see the bruise on my body.'

'Uh-huh.'

'Do you want to?'

'No, really. That's OK.'

'It's no problem. It's just here.' He pointed to his left breast, below the crown.

'I've seen bruises before.'

'Not like this one.'

And it was true. He lifted his shirt to reveal the largest and most disturbing contusion I'd ever seen. It stretched from his scrawny neck to the withered wall of his stomach, and from his left underarm to his right nipple – a giant sunflower of ruptured skin. Its colours shimmered as he breathed, cold and fiery like an eclipse, purple and blue-black at the dark heart, green and yellow at its border.

'I'm experimenting with a new disease. It has no apparent symptoms until the client wakes up one morning – and then BOOM!' He slapped his chest and laughed. 'Massive subcutaneous bleeding, swollen limbs, maybe some internal damage – I haven't made up my mind – and *maximal pain*.' He laughed again. 'I've got some other ideas, too—'

'I'm sorry,' Death interrupted quickly, turning to me. 'I should introduce you to everyone. This is Pestilence.' He gestured towards the bruised disease-monger. 'We call him Pes, for short.' Pestilence smiled sarcastically. 'This is Skirmish.' He indicated the pimpled teenager, who forced a sheepish grin and offered a tentative handshake. 'And this is Famine.'

'I prefer Slim,' Famine quipped, bowing his bald head.

No-one laughed.

'OK,' Death announced cheerily. 'Any mail?'

'The usual,' Pestilence answered, handing over a raft of envelopes. 'Your schedule for the next three days, as discussed on Saturday. The Chief's assessment of your reports from last week – it doesn't look good, I can tell you. And *precise* instructions for today's client: a rather easy number down at *quadri furcus* . . . Not even *you* can mess it up.'

Death gave him a sarcastic smile. 'Any postal chess?'

'Seven games.'

'Excellent!' His face brightened, and he brushed several sheets of paper from the desk in front of me to reveal a chess board in black and gold. Impatiently, he tore open one of the envelopes, read what it contained, then stared at the empty squares. For a few seconds he was utterly absorbed, recreating complex moves in his mind, tracing the paths of invisible pieces with his fingers. Finally, as if struck by the solution to a problem which had momentarily perplexed him, he nodded slowly to himself, dismissed the imaginary battlefield, and smiled kindly. Then, with an air of business-like efficiency, he tossed the remaining mail onto the board, removed my contract from his polo shirt and offered it to Skirmish. 'Stick this on the pile in the Chief's office, will you?'

Skirmish tutted, stood up slowly, and stuffed the contract grudgingly in his pocket. 'I suppose you want me to put it in a folder?'

'Of course . . . And after that, put the spade in the hall back in the Stock Room . . . And make sure you wash it first.' At last, Death turned towards me. 'Now. How about that shower?'

Terminations for special occasions

Death directed me back along the entrance hall to the first opening on the right. It was a flight of stairs leading upwards.

'As I said, it's mostly administration now. It used to be more of a challenge. We had stimulating conversations with the clients, several terminations a day, everything seemed fresh and varied. It was exciting back then. But now, the only thing I find interesting is the preparation.' We reached the top of the stairs: a long, narrow corridor, with a floral burgundy carpet. 'OK. A quick run-through. On your left, the Meeting Room; on the right, at the end, is the Lab. Behind us is the Stock Room . . .' He waited for me to turn around. '. . . and down there, straight ahead, is the bathroom. Come back down to the office when you've finished.'

'What about clothes?'

He barked a short, loud laugh. 'There should be a suit hanging on the back of the door.'

The suit was electric blue, heavily spangled, and at least two sizes too small. I also found a pair of dark green, floral boxer shorts, a tight, lime-green T-shirt bearing the words RESURRECTION – IT'S A WAY OF LIFE, a pair of light green knee-high socks decorated with smiling flatfish, and a pair of white, slip-on shoes. The shoes fitted perfectly, and were easily the most comfortable footwear I had ever worn, alive or dead.

The shower washed the corpse smell from me. I hadn't realized how accustomed I'd become to the sweet odour of dirt and decay until I stepped from the cubicle and dried myself. My new smell was alien, unwelcome. No cemetery in the land would have taken me in.

One more thing: as I dressed, I inspected my body more closely. I was missing three fingers (including one thumb), two toes, and one penis.

On the way back to the office I noticed a fifth door on the landing, just before the stairs. It was white, and shiny, and identified with a name on a small brass plate. I didn't stop to examine it though. I was too busy thinking about the other remarkable feature of my body: my legs, arms and torso were criss-crossed with thick, black, surgical stitches.

The office was empty, except for Skirmish. He was sitting at Famine's desk beneath the far window, alternately picking his nose and playing a hand-held computer game.

'Nice suit,' he said, without looking up. He grinned faintly, his fingers quivering over the controls. 'It's one of my old ones.'

'Really?'

'Yep. The one I was buried in.'

I changed the subject. 'Where is everyone?'

'Jobs.'

'What about Death?'

'Back soon.'

I sank into the chair by the door. I badly wanted to return to the coffin. I was surrounded by strangers. I didn't know the rules. I felt *exposed*. I gazed at the chess board on the desk again, and noticed that several pieces now occupied the previously blank squares. In an effort to distract myself, I studied the position carefully. I had been a keen player when I was alive, and it only took me a couple of minutes to realize that with a queen sacrifice black could probably achieve mate in three moves.

I was examining white's alternatives when I felt a presence at my shoulder. Startled, I turned around and saw Death looming over me. I hadn't even heard him enter. He was gazing at the crown of my head with alarm, and before I had time to wonder why, he pulled a comb from his shirt pocket and ran it quickly through my hair.

'You could use some of Pes' make-up too,' he observed. His gaze moved down to my jacket, registering an expression somewhere between mockery and sympathy. 'Then again, I don't expect anyone will be looking at your *face*.'

'Where are we going?' I asked.

'To meet our first client of the week.'

I followed Death down the corridor to another white panelled door on the left, opposite the stairs. 'I need a couple of files from Archives before we leave,' he said, checking his watch. 'Can you give me a hand?'

I nodded, wanting to be elsewhere.

The room behind the door was narrower and more sparsely decorated than the office. Apart from a naked light bulb and a wide bow window with a view over the street, it consisted entirely of ceiling-high filing cabinets, lining the walls and clustered in the centre of the room.

'Look in the A–Z index,' Death said. 'Under *Falling*. I'll get the Life File.'

He showed me a large filing cabinet to the right of the door. Five drawers, all unlocked. With difficulty I opened the second, marked D–G. It was choked with paper, each sheet so thin and fragile it was almost transparent. I carefully removed a document at random. The page contained around a hundred lines of minuscule type, beginning with:

DEATH:

Terminations for special occasions

Choking on a goat hair in a bowl of milk

(CLIENT: *Fabius*, 66275901748)

Drowning in a butt of malmsey

(CLIENT: *George*, *Duke of Clarence*, 4009441326)

Falling into a fireplace while attacking a friend with a poker

(CLIENT: *Count Eric Stenbock*, 28213124580)

due to an **Incredible sequence of unfortunate accidents**

(CLIENT: *numerous*)

Laughter at seeing an ass eat one's figs

(CLIENT: *Philomenes*, 0504567722)

as a result of **Stuffing a hen with snow**

(CLIENT: *Francis Bacon*, 6176160339)

by **Tortoise falling on head**

(CLIENT: *Aeschylus*, 79113751126)

'Have you found it yet?' Death was standing on a stepladder holding a pale blue document wallet.

'Almost.'

I flicked quickly through the other sheets until I located the document I was looking for. I removed it and read a random selection of headlines: FALLING DOWN A WELL, FALLING INTO AN UNENDING ABYSS, FALLING INTO A VAT OF BOILING OIL, FALLING OVER (GENERAL), FALLING OFF A CLIFF (VARIOUS).

'Which reference do you want?'

'Can you see *Falling from a Great Height*?'

I ran my finger down the page:

FALLING

from a great height

x-ref[1]: Diving, Dropping, Leaping (into, from), Plunging, Slipping, Tumbling

x-ref[2]: Aeroplanes, Buildings, Cliffs, Towers, Trees, Parachutes (Failure to Open), etc.

x-ref[3]: Accident, Murder, Suicide.

'Is this it?'

Death took the sheet and nodded. 'Just as I suspected. Completely useless.' He tossed it away. 'We'll have to improvise.'

He showed me the thick folder he was holding. It contained around a hundred sheets of biographical information about the woman he described as our 'client'. I scanned it briefly: age, favourite foods, changes in hair colour, sexual partners, medical records, likes and dislikes of all kinds.

'This is the Life File,' Death explained. 'Read as much as you can as we go along.' He smiled pleasantly and patted me on the back. 'It's a routine start to the week. A rather formulaic termination. But we can make it more interesting.'

I had no idea what he was talking about.

One of the cars parked outside the office belonged to Death: a rusty, beige Mini Metro. We climbed in and he pulled rapidly away, tyres screeching, burning rubber. As he raced up the slope towards a T-junction, he explained that most Agents now used inexpensive vehicles, that like everyone else he had to move with the times, and that a horse was no longer a suitable mode of transport.

I was too distracted to concentrate fully on what he was saying. Disappointed, too: *The four car drivers of the Apocalypse* just didn't carry the same weight.

If they only knew, back in the cemetery.

We drove towards the city centre along streets that were increasingly familiar. And this is where *my* story – the story of how I died – really begins.

We passed a large square which, for the first fifteen years of my life, had been the site of the old bus station. It was redeveloped in the 1980s: the bus station remained, but it was surrounded on all sides by new offices, restaurants and flats. Anyway, as we passed the entrance, I looked up from the file and caught a glimpse of one of the new residential blocks on the far side of the square.

And I remembered.

Sliding.

Sliding rapidly towards the edge of a grey slate roof, the steep, slippery slope accelerating the slide, the wind and rain whipping into my face; slapping my hands and feet against the wet tiles, trying to gain a hold, hoping to slow the descent; releasing a long, loud cry of terror.

Suicide and sherbet lemons

Death parked on a double yellow line outside the library, a depressing block of dirt-streaked concrete at the edge of the main shopping centre. He expertly applied a little rouge to his pallid cheeks, smoothed his hair with his bony fingers, then turned towards me. 'When we get out,' he said, 'look straight ahead, try not to shuffle, and keep your mouth *closed*. We don't want people seeing those teeth.'

We left the car and walked up a paved incline towards a distant crossroads. It was a warm, blue day and the city centre was alive with bodies. Against Death's advice I instinctively bowed my head, fearful that someone might notice the zombie amongst them, scream with terror, and rustle up a lynch mob. Even then, and despite my efforts to protect myself from this surreal carnival of humanity, details forced themselves upon me – details so vivid and so isolated, it was as if they were in colour while everything else was in black and white.

I saw shoes like strange fruit, in which thick laces burrowed and gorged themselves like worms. I saw clothes in colours and shapes which dazzled and nauseated me, flowing over the grey pedestrian precinct like a radioactive sewage spill. I saw faces with teeth like shining daggers; eyes like big, black stones; noses and ears like blobs of putty plastered into place; hair like a rash, or a rabbit's fur, or a raven's wing. I was exposed, everywhere: to the brightness and variety of skin colours and textures, to a constant crashing wall of sound, to the electric touch of living, breathing bodies, to the pungent smells of people and animals and food, and cars. And when anyone glanced, however briefly, at my face or clothes or body, I shrivelled to a speck and yearned for the comfort of the coffin.

The only way I could survive this onslaught was to focus my gaze on the gaps between the advancing ranks of living flesh; but as soon as I looked up and ahead, I noticed to my horror that Death had quickened his pace and had slipped into the crowd. I couldn't have followed him even if I'd known where he'd gone: when your muscles are withered and weak from so many years of inactivity, you forget what it takes simply to move, to ignore the body's complaints and keep pushing forward. Resurrection requires effort.

I knew that if I succumbed to panic my fear of discovery would be realized, and it took all my remaining strength to walk on into the unknown. Fortunately, Death hadn't gone far: I found him again at the crossroads, sitting on a public bench, behind a circle of people as bright and hideous as giant parakeets. The bench was one of several in a pedestrian area overhung by trees and overshadowed by an old church tower. He saw me, and patted the space next to him.

'Sherbet lemon?'

'Sorry?'

'Have one.' He opened his fist to reveal half a dozen sticky yellow sweets, covered in furballs from his pocket.

'No. Thank you.' I held up my three-fingered left palm for emphasis, and sat down. His presence calmed me a little; the oppressive mass of people seemed less threatening. 'So what happens now?'

'We wait.' He popped a sweet in his mouth and sucked loudly as he talked. 'We don't ask why, or what the point is, or what else we could be doing – we just sit here.' He glanced at his watch and sighed. 'Fortunately, she'll be along at any moment.' His eyes widened and he began to rise. 'In fact . . .'

I followed his gaze.

Our client was a small, fair-haired woman with spidery limbs and a wiry torso. Her file told me she had dressed in black ever since she was eighteen; she was very organized; she hated cats; she drank orange juice on Sunday mornings; she had had only three lovers, and had married the last; she washed her face before her anus when she showered; she had cut her fingers catching limpets in a tidal pool when she was five; her eyes were earth-brown with a sea-green corona. She had scheduled her suicide for lunchtime so that she could finish her morning's work in the office and no-one would suspect anything. She had once deafened a man for two days by slapping him on the right ear.

She was forty-one years old.

She stopped a couple of metres away from us and gazed up at the church tower, the breeze ruffling her long skirt. She looked like a robot raising its mechanical head to the stars.

'In some ways she's dead already,' Death remarked idly, as we watched her enter the tower and ascend the spiral staircase. 'She's covered in dead skin. Her brain cells are shutting down by the million. Her hair is dead fibre, all her organs are withering, her cell structure is falling apart.' He paused to suck his sweet. 'She's wearing the dead hide of a dead animal on her feet, dead wool from a dead sheep on her back, the dead product of a dead plant in her skirt. She's the ghost-image of a thousand ancestors, all dead. Her future is death, her past is death, her present is falling towards death . . . Makes you think, doesn't it?'

I took the question to be rhetorical. 'Shouldn't we follow her?'

He shook his head. 'She can't fall until it's *time*.'

I recalled her file again. In many ways, the pattern of her life echoed mine. She had experienced a happy childhood which had left her unprepared for the violent diversity of adult life; and after one catastrophic incident with a lover – I don't remember the precise facts – she had withdrawn so far into herself that she now found it difficult to engage with anyone. She existed, but she did not *live*.

'OK,' Death sighed, 'this will only take a few minutes. Then we'll get some lunch.' He bought a couple of tickets from a bat-faced man at the base of the tower, and opened the door to the staircase. 'Ninety-nine steps to the top – do you think you can make it?'

I breathed hard, and nodded.

He stopped at every window on the way up to reveal some trivial fact. More likely he was giving me a rest, for which I was grateful. At the first window: 'I remember when this was still a church.' At the second: 'They pulled down everything but this tower over a century ago.' At the third: 'The bell rings every quarter of an hour.' The fourth: 'Been here almost a thousand years.' The fifth: 'Great view from the top.' The sixth: 'It's seventy-two feet high – are you sure you're OK?'

We had turned seven circles in space, passing through alternating intervals of sunlight and shadow, before Death quietly announced that we had reached the summit. An archway led to a four-sided, crenellated parapet, with an old iron weather cock at its raised centre. The woman stood on the far side, gazing out over the low protective wall to the road below. The roof was deserted apart from the three of us.

The Life File offered nine basic reasons why she wanted to kill herself:

Her life had no focus.

At fourteen, she had imagined a future as a great poet and philosopher; failing that, she had wanted business success; failing that, she had wanted children. None of these conditions had been fulfilled.

Her parents had given her what she considered to be a stupid first name – one which had been a continual source of amusement to her enemies.

She considered herself to be unlucky in love.

She had always been attracted to the idea of a brief, intense life climaxed by a dramatic death. Her heroes had all suffered a similar fate. She couldn't claim to have enjoyed an intense life as such, but the dramatic death retained its appeal.

No-one had invited her out to lunch that day.

She had once read a book in which a character almost exactly like her had decided to throw herself off a tall building as a solution to all her problems. She shared the character's last name, and they were the same age.

She had an important meeting that afternoon for which she was unprepared. She had long suspected that most of the people in her department held her in low esteem, and that all of them laughed at her behind her back.

All of her close relatives were dead.

Personally, I thought none of these reasons justified suicide; and had I not been under contract, I would have suggested alternative solutions to her problems.

I felt a surge of despair, too. How could she so idly throw away something which all zombies yearn for and envy – life itself? When I was dead, this question would never even have crossed my mind; but as a zombie – as a newly enrolled member of the ranks of the *un*dead – it had a special significance. Fundamentally, though I sympathized with her reasoning, I couldn't understand her conclusion.

Then again, it was none of my business.

Death's lugubrious head filled the borders of my vision. He slipped another sherbet lemon between his teeth, then grasped my shoulders, and spoke in a whisper. 'Listen carefully. Time is a circle. We intercept the circle as it is being described, but the interception must occur at precisely the right moment. If we make a simple mistake here it could have terrible consequences in a hundred, or a thousand, or a million years from now.' He frowned. 'At least, that's what the Chief always says. Personally, I've never seen any evidence of it.' He shook his head to dismiss the thought, then handed me a scrap of scented lilac writing paper and the same black pen I had used on the contract. 'Anyway – I'll do the deed, you write the note.'

'What note?'

'The *suicide* note.' He put his hand on my shoulder. 'And keep an eye on the stairs – I saw a couple at the ticket booth who looked like they were ready to follow us up here.'

'What should I write?'

'You've read the file. You decide.'

He approached the woman cautiously to avoid signalling his presence. He needn't have bothered: she was single-mindedly preparing herself for the leap, and saw nothing but the image of herself falling. She eased herself gingerly onto the lower part of the parapet, into one of the crenelles, where she perched for a moment, swaying slightly. Her skirt flapped like a flag as she rocked back and forth, first leaning over the edge, then back towards safety. She removed her hands from the wall, stood up, and spread her arms.

I looked over the side.

I was sliding again.

My hand slipped from the window frame and I started to slide. I lurched forwards for the handle, but my fingers flapped uselessly against the greasy paintwork. For the thousand moments contained within that single first second, I felt I could stop myself; but my body slithered down the roof with increasing speed, over the grey slates, the steep slope accelerating the slide, the wind and rain whipping into my face. I slapped my hands and feet against the wet tiles, hoping to gain a hold, trying to slow the descent.

I let out a long, loud cry of terror.

She stood on the parapet, ready to fly, Death waiting silently behind her.

What should I write?

Everything that I had read and remembered in her file? The exhilarating urge for self-annihilation, the self-loathing, the horror? I knew of every blow she had ever received, every kiss, every handshake, every touch. Random images surfaced: her first lover suggested playing another game of Scrabble, and she wanted him to talk and to talk to him, and all he ever did was play games, and she had to play the game, let him control her, and follow his suggestions because she was terrified of losing him, and if she lost him the writhing hatred of her snake-pit stomach would destroy her, and she realized even then that he wasn't the one; and she was fifteen years old leaping in front of a car, and she said it had been an accident (but she knew that the lights had drawn her in), and the car struck her softly and tossed her aside and she felt no pain, but when she awoke so many people stared down at her that she felt ashamed and cried for herself; and they laughed at her when she couldn't climb the rope, her useless hands too weak to hold on, no technique, no skill, and the teacher shouted at her thinking it would push her upwards, but it only drove her harder into the floor.

The bell chimed the quarter hour.

She had never felt comfortable with being alive. It had always seemed like something that happened to her, against her will. She hadn't *asked* to be born.

But she could choose when to die.

My thoughts were disturbed by the echo of footsteps.

I listened. Steps, and voices, rising from the stairwell. I glanced towards Death. He was still standing behind the woman, who swayed as if she was about to faint. A murmur of attention rose from a small crowd gathering below. The people climbing the stairs would distract her, save her from herself. And a part of me wanted them to – but my instructions were clear. I tried to attract Death's attention by hissing. No response. I whistled quietly, using the sound of the breeze to disguise it. He might as well have been a gargoyle. I picked up a small rock and aimed it at his back. It flew over the parapet.

Someone in the crowd shouted: 'Don't do it.'

The voices from the stairs grew louder.

The woman hesitated.

And I was standing on a balcony overlooking a deserted paved square. A narrow balcony, with a low wall made of yellow Cotswold stone. A thin layer of concrete, then seventy feet to the ground.

A woman was standing close by, gazing at the street lights in the distance. She was the same age as me. I had known her for a long time, but she hesitated before she asked. I knew that she was afraid of the answer.

'Did you find anything?'

'Enough,' I said.

She turned away. 'I'm . . . disappointed. But thank you.'

I shrugged. 'It's why I'm here.'

She laughed bitterly and walked back inside.

It started to rain.

*   *   *

There was a short, loud cry of terror, echoed by screams from below. I looked over the parapet and saw the crowd surging towards the southern end of the tower.

The woman had disappeared.

'I thought she was *never* going to do it,' Death said gloomily. I hobbled wearily to where he stood and gazed over the edge. The woman had struck the pavement head first. Her body lay sprawled like a starfish on the seabed. Her head was cracked open.

'I heard voices,' I told him, indicating the stairwell.

'That's why timing was so important. If I hadn't pushed her—'

'You *pushed* her?'

He shrugged. 'I'm Death. I have no choice.'

We stared silently at the scene below until we heard people on the roof behind us. When we turned around we saw a young couple kissing by the eastern wall. They were completely unaware of what had happened.

'Have you written the note?' he asked.

I felt a surge of panic. 'I couldn't think—'

'Now would be a good time.'

I took out the pen, rested the notepaper on the sloping lead roof and quickly scribbled a message. At first I thought it was pointless, but the more I considered it the more appropriate it seemed. Death crunched his sweet, glanced at the note, then shoved it into his back pocket.

'Cute,' he said.

As we passed the couple on our way towards the stairs, my mind drifted again.

I was locked in a kiss. My lover and I were one person, joined at the forehead, nose and mouth, at the arms, hands and chest, at the groin, thighs and feet. We were consumed and controlled by the kiss, worshipping each other so completely with our bodies and minds that we became one spirit, one ecstasy.

And I remembered the taste.

Our mouths were like an orange. Our tongues were like the flesh. Our lips were like the soft, waxy rind.

We reached the foot of the staircase. The ticket booth was empty, but satellite groups of the larger crowd occupied much of the pedestrian area. Death instructed me to wait, pushed his way through the fringes, and melted into his surroundings like a chameleon. It was only afterwards that I realized he was planting my suicide note somewhere on the woman's body.

On his return he asked me a question:

'What was her name?'

'Her name?' I echoed.

He nodded.

'Laika,' I said. 'Like the first dog in space.'

Less than half a day earlier I'd been indifferent to everything but the security of my own personal environment. Now the fact that we had so quickly ended the life of a woman about whom I knew only a few random details, whose name we hadn't even mentioned until this moment, disturbed me deeply. When I thought of her I only saw the spreading pool of blood, the flattened head, the blank eyes, the shattered skull, the twisted limbs. To the Agency, she had no identity other than as a client; but she was more than this to me ... And looking back on this now, I see in this feeling something I was unable to articulate at the time: I was beginning to doubt the wisdom of having signed my contract.

I remembered the note I had written, and wished that I could have created a more meaningful message, something unique to *her*. But all I had managed was a single word:

Sorry.

Dead red roses

We ate at a grim first-floor burger joint a hundred yards from the tower, overlooking the road that led back to the car. Hunger is one aspect of existence I didn't miss as a corpse, and its tentative return at the sight of a greasy chargrilled steak was particularly unwelcome. Death said little during the four hours it took him to devour three T-bone specials, five portions of thick-cut chips, a chocolate nut sundae, a banana split, and countless coffee refills, but he did wonder why, before sampling it himself, I'd only consumed a tiny part of my meal.

'I've never liked TexMex,' I explained.

'What kind of a zombie *are* you?' he said.

Frankly, a poor one. Even amongst the undead, I don't make the grade. I am non-violent, relatively sentimental, and have no great lust for flesh – living or otherwise. But even if I had, I still wouldn't have felt like eating.

At the end of lunch, after the crowd, the ambulances and the police had disappeared from the scene, Death paid the bill (without tipping) and we walked slowly back to the car. He tore off a parking ticket fixed to the windscreen and ripped it up before accelerating rapidly away.

After a quick trip to Office World to collect five packets of plain white copier paper, a laser cartridge and a novelty pen, we returned to the Agency. Apart from his insistence on humming a particularly mournful tune, and his observation that the reason he ate so much at lunch was that he ate so *little* at breakfast and dinner, Death seemed content to travel in silence.

He reverse-parked in front of the house between a white 2CV and a black Fiesta, turned off the engine, stopped humming, got out, shut the door, and walked away. It was all done with a fluidity and speed born of long practice; but he seemed preoccupied. I remained in the car for a moment, then followed him.

It was early evening and the sun was hidden behind the house. I guessed that it must be late summer, but having been underground for so long I couldn't be sure. A corpse, of course, doesn't notice the passing of the seasons – because for him all the days and months and years are the same.

The sound of laughter led me to the office, where Famine, Pestilence and Skirmish were listening to Death's description of the day's events. As I walked through the door Pestilence failed to stifle a snigger.

'What's the joke?' I asked.

'Nothing,' he replied. He let his jaundiced eyes wander the length of my shining blue suit, then smirked.

'How's the bruise?'

He seemed genuinely pleased by the question. 'Growing by the hour – and spreading round the back.' He began to lift his shirt. 'Would you like to have a look?'

'Later, maybe.'

Death tossed his car keys to Skirmish, with the simple explanation: 'I've got some paper in the boot. Take one for yourself.' Skirmish tutted and shook his head, but obeyed. He scuttled out of the room, knocking over a coffee cup as he left. Death picked it up and put it on his desk, next to the chess board. Then he turned to me and asked if there was anything I needed.

I needed reassurance that I had performed my work adequately; I needed a translator to help me understand my new world; I needed to know exactly how I had died – but above all, I needed to rest, and this is what I told him.

He nodded. 'I'll show you to your room.'

We headed for the doorway but Pestilence intercepted us, a sickly grin splitting his pimpled face. 'Don't forget we have to collect the goods from the Lab tomorrow. *Before* we head downtown.'

'We'll be there,' Death replied.

We walked back along the main corridor, turned right after the stairs into a narrow passageway, followed the passageway to another long corridor, turned right again and headed for the last door on the left.

Death removed a golden key from his pocket and turned it in the lock. 'The key is the Chief's idea,' he explained. 'For the first few nights we'll shut you in. Make you feel more at home.' The door opened into a medium-sized corner bedroom, with two windows facing the side and rear of the house. The furnishing was sparse: a threadbare Barca lounger in the near left corner, a two-tier bunk bed against the left wall, a writing desk beneath the side window ahead, a wardrobe in the far right corner, a table with a stand chair beneath the rear window, and a menacing candelabra cactus to the right of the door. 'As you can see, you'll have to share. We're one room short, I'm afraid.' He smiled and gave me a comforting pat on the back. 'Anyway, breakfast is about eight tomorrow. Come to the office when you're ready.'

On the writing desk stood an old Bluebird typewriter. Next to it was a white vase filled with dead red roses.

As a corpse I had had no need to distinguish between good and bad taste, between rubbish and quality. I lost all sense of discrimination, considered all things equal. As a result, when I looked at the Artex ceiling, the white, shagpile carpet, the red-and-black diagonally-striped bedclothes, the floral wallpaper with matching curtains, and the Formica table with its portable television and blue glass ornament in the shape of a swan, I was incapable of deciding whether or not I liked my new home. It was more exciting and more unusual than the coffin – and it gave me a powerful sensation of something familiar from my past – but, fundamentally, it wasn't *me*.

I was vaguely aware of Death closing the door and turning the key in the lock. It was a nice touch: that simple sound gave me an immense sense of security. I walked over to the rear window. A canal and a railway line separated me from the long, low meadow and the evening sun.

I returned to the bed and lay down on the bottom bunk. I knew this town, of course – but I couldn't remember its name.

As I sank into sleep, alone and safe once more, I floated back to the warm, slow days of my childhood, and to my parents' house. I climbed the stairs to the first floor, staring at the soft, floral-patterned carpet beneath my feet as I counted the steps; I passed the old grandfather clock on the landing, listening to the lazy swings of the golden pendulum; and I turned the wooden handle on the door to my father's study, and crept inside. It wasn't that I was forbidden to enter, but to walk boldly into such a sacred place seemed somehow irreverent.

I was an only child, and the study provided the perfect space for me to make my own amusement. It contained an old writing desk in which my father kept the tools and scraps of his hobby wrapped in a blue velvet cloth: he used to repair watches in his spare time. There were pictures and painting kits, too – and scrapbooks and photo albums, newspapers and notebooks, curios and potted plants . . . And there were dozens of board games permanently piled high against one wall. I remember spending the whole of one summer teaching myself to play chess.

But, best of all, the entire room was lined with bookshelves from floor to ceiling, containing hundreds of books in all sizes and colours. I spent many hours immersed in solitary silence, browsing through volume after volume of fact and fiction, absorbing anything that came my way: science or art, story or trivia, essay or anecdote. Sometimes, if my father was out working late, I would climb onto his desk and reach up to the highest shelves where he kept his crime novels. I think he put them there as a precaution, because of the adult world they described; but I was far less interested in the secrets of adulthood than in fraternizing with the criminals and helping the detectives solve their cases.

It feels now as if most of my youth was devoted to creating and inhabiting an interior landscape of mystery and suspense. I shared arcane knowledge and indulged in melancholic reflection with Sherlock Holmes, exchanged hard-boiled wisecracks with Sam Spade and Philip Marlowe, hung out with the comic hoods on Damon Runyon's Broadway, drank tea from china cups with Miss Marple . . . I could never get along with Hercule Poirot, though. Even as a child, I found him far too smug.

And now, long after my death, I see that I was never happier than in those hours I spent alone, with a pile of unread books before me; listening to the slow ticking of the grandfather clock, waiting for my father to come home.

I awoke to a succession of loud grunts and the rattle of the door handle. It was as if some irate primate had been released in the corridor and was desperately seeking an exit. I sat on the edge of the bed, collecting my thoughts. The room was dark, and pleasantly cool. Through the window I saw stars, and heard the barking of dogs. I was about to speak when the rattling stopped, and the angry grunts were replaced by receding footsteps.

I had just remembered fully where I was when the footsteps returned, this time accompanied by petulant complaints. A key was inserted in the lock, the handle was twisted, and the intruder stood in the doorway.

I heard a sigh.

War's little helper

The silhouetted figure gave a token knock.

'Who is it?' I said, squinting against the light from the hall.

'Skirmish.'

'Come in.'

He did so, switched on the light, locked the door behind him and said, 'I see you've settled in.' He was carrying a tray with a plate of salad, a wobbling brown dessert, and a glass of water. He saw me studying the food. 'It's a goat's cheese salad with walnuts, olives and sun-dried tomatoes. Very healthy – I don't want to end up looking like War.' He pointed at the dessert. 'That's a low-fat creme caramel. Pes stole the last of the rice pudding. D'you want some?'

I shook my head. He placed the tray on the table, turned the chair around, sat down, and took a long, slow drink from the glass.

'You don't say much, do you?'

'I'm out of practice.'

He grunted an acknowledgement. 'It's hard coming out of the coffin.'

He ate his meal noisily and very quickly, shovelling the food into his mouth as if he hadn't touched anything since breakfast. When the last flabby gobbet of dessert had disappeared, he sank into his chair, rubbed his belly in a circular motion, and belched loudly.

'So,' he began. I waited for him to continue. Instead, he stood up, walked over to the Barca lounger, twisted round and sat down. He eased the lounger into recliner mode and started to pick food from his front teeth.

'So what?'

'So . . . how was your job today?'

I was standing at the top of the tower again, gazing down at the woman's broken body. I imagined Death pushing her, and watched her fall earthward. For one brief, glorious moment she was graceful, like a diving bird of prey, then she thumped onto the pavement below. The thought made me feel sick.

'It was OK.'

'Uh-huh.' He ran his tongue around the inside of his lips. 'You're on a standard contract, aren't you?' I nodded. 'So it's . . . shape up or ship out?'

'If I fail,' I said carefully, 'I get to choose any one of the deaths I witness this week.'

Not that I had any intention of throwing myself off a tall building on Sunday evening. Suicide was far too low down the list of respected deaths in the corpse community to be my first choice. I couldn't decide what it *meant*, either. To the woman, it was a final decision produced by years of despair and an act of revenge on the living. To the watching crowd it was a shock, or an entertainment, or simply a story they would never forget. To my employer, it was a reluctant obligation.

'What was your original termination?'

'I can't remember it.'

He laughed. 'I remember *every*thing about mine. I was kicking a football around with some mates in this loading depot downtown, and the ball went under a truck, and I went in after it. And I started pissing about pretending I was trapped under the wheel – it got big laughs. Jack the bloody lad. Anyway, long story short, the truck started up, went straight into reverse, and backed over my chest. *Splat* . . . Funny thing is, exactly the same thing happened to a cat I once had.'

Skirmish finished picking his teeth and climbed onto the top bunk. I removed my shoes and jacket and returned to the lower tier. We were silent for several minutes, until he leaned over the edge and said:

'Has anyone explained why you're here?'

'No.'

'They haven't told you about Hades?'

I shook my head.

'No-one has mentioned anything at all about an assistant?'

'Not really.'

'Typical.'

He looked at the wall with an expression of disgust before retreating to the upper bunk. Faint strains of Mozart's *Requiem* echoed across the corridor from the room opposite. I was exhausted, and confused, and ill-at-ease with my new surroundings – and I would much rather have turned over and fallen asleep – but one question wouldn't leave me alone.

'Who's Hades?' I said.

TUESDAY

DEATH BY CHOCOLATE

Breakfast of the damned

I awoke feeling happy.

This was unusual. Happiness is useless in the coffin; so is despair. Emotions as a whole never really concern the dead because they are incapable of experiencing anything to any great degree. Ask a corpse how he feels and he's likely to respond:

'What do you mean?'

Assuming he can still talk, of course.

The wardrobe I shared with Skirmish was stocked with a supply of clothes for six more days: a rainbow collection of T-shirts, a stack of floral boxer shorts, and half a dozen fresh pairs of socks. To reflect my mood I selected yellow socks embroidered with a dancing crab design, boxer shorts decorated with yellow roses, and a yellow shirt bearing the slogan ZOMBIE POWER! I was not offered a choice of suits or shoes.

After dressing, I remembered Death's instructions from the previous evening and followed the corridor to the office. My door was already unlocked. Skirmish – who had deferred answering my question about Hades to a more suitable time – was nowhere to be seen.

'How are you this morning?'

The office was unoccupied except for Death, who was sitting at his desk by the door. He was opening letters with the kind of knife normally associated with a ritual sacrifice. A portable CD-player to the left of the paper column was belting out a guitar solo from the Grateful Dead's 'Live Dead' album.

'Happy,' I shouted.

'Enjoy it while it lasts,' he said glumly. He turned down the volume and handed me a single sheet of blue notepaper. 'Take a look at that.'

Written on the paper were four numbers – 7587 – and a signature.

'What is it?'

'Correspondence chess. My opponent has moved the knight she had on g5 to h7. She's trying to recreate one of the matches from the Ninth Correspondence Olympiad. Penrose-Vukcevic, 1982–85. Probably using a computer.'

He took the note from my hand and slipped it into a document wallet bulging with similar offerings. I seized the opportunity to ask a question which had occurred to me before.

'Why do you play chess with the living?'

'It's an obsession,' he said waving his arms manically. 'I can't resist the challenge ... It's like dancing – a passion and a weakness.' He smiled briefly at the thought of these twin indulgences, then assumed a serious air. 'It's tradition too, of course. If my opponents win, their reward is to go on living. If they lose – and they invariably do – they die ... I'm playing around two hundred games right now. This one's a woman, about thirty years old, and she's just had a freak heart attack. As far as she knows she may live, she may not, so I threw down the gauntlet and she picked it up. Actually,' he added dolefully, 'she would have recovered anyway.'

I smiled in sympathy.

'Do you play chess?' he asked.

'I used to,' I replied laconically – and I would have added that I wasn't a bad player either, but my mind was distracted by an idea I couldn't pin down, and my cadaver's instinct for self-protection forced me to deprecate my abilities: 'I knew the rules, but I never really explored it to any depth ... Like almost everything I did, I preferred to watch.'

A typical Lifer.

Lifer, incidentally, is the term used by the dead and the undead to refer to the living. In general, Lifers are warm-blooded, agile, emotional and inquisitive. They have colourful, soft skin. They eat and excrete.

The dead – the patient mass of corpses waiting for Armageddon – are an entirely different species, and one which included *me* until very recently. They are cold-blooded, lazy, socially inept, and indifferent to almost every subject but their own security. Their skin, even when intact, is waxy and pale. They are eaten and excreted *by* other creatures.

The undead – zombies – straddle the abyss between the two. Our blood is cool and flows slowly; we can stand upright, but find it easier to fall over; we desire life and feeling, without really comprehending either; we *want* to ask questions but hardly ever find the right moment or the right words. Our skin is ashen and unyielding, but readily disguised. A zombie eats and excretes, but his diet is usually limited to living flesh.

This plays havoc with the digestion.

Death and I headed down the hall towards the breakfast room, the last door on the right. When we arrived Pestilence and Famine had already found places at the oval dining table, and were reading the morning newspapers. Famine was wearing black silk pyjamas with the traditional scales emblem embroidered on the jacket pocket, Pestilence was wrapped in a white quilted dressing gown. They lowered their papers to exchange brief smiles as we entered.

'Take War's place,' Death suggested, indicating a chair between himself and Pestilence. 'He won't be back until tomorrow.'

There were five seats in all, three unoccupied. I sat down in silence and glanced across the table towards Famine. His head was hidden by the *Guardian*. A small headline caught my eye: *Spate of grave desecrations signals 'decline in moral standards'*. Pestilence had apparently discovered a similar story. He was reading the *Sun*, where the full-page article facing us was titled: *They Nicked My Stiff! Claims Sex-Op Vicar*. Death either didn't notice or didn't care that he was in the news – he simply clapped his hands and announced a hearty good morning. When no-one answered, his enthusiasm waned as quickly as it had waxed.

Breakfast was already served. I'd been given a bowl of cereal, a glass of orange juice and a banana. Pestilence appeared to be eating a selection of mouldy cheeses and a rotten apple. Death had a bell-shaped metal cage containing three live mice. Famine's plate was empty.

'Aren't you hungry?' I asked him.

'Always,' he said.

I glanced down at the table with a vague feeling of embarrassment. The napkins were black, decorated with waving white skeletons. The crockery was bordered with a miniature coffin motif. The cutlery had bone handles.

I heard a squeak, and looked up to see Death opening the cage door. He plucked one of the mice from its prison, broke its neck swiftly, and slipped the entire body into his mouth with a quick slurp. After some energetic and prolonged chewing, he spat out a tiny white skull and swallowed the rest. The remaining two mice scurried around the cage excitedly. I pushed my bowl away.

'Would you like a bite?' asked Pestilence. I turned and saw that he was offering me what appeared to be a wedge of Brie that had been left in a warm, damp room for three months.

Before I could answer, Death intercepted: 'Leave him alone.'

'Why not let him try?' Pestilence persisted.

'Because it's not why he's here.'

'You are *so* protective.'

'And you are a meddler.'

'D'you think you could stop arguing?' Famine interrupted. 'You're ruining my appetite.'

The white walls of the dining room were bare apart from four framed slogans beneath four pictures. The slogans read: A MEASURE OF WHEAT FOR A DAY'S WAGES; HE WENT FORTH CONQUERING, AND TO CONQUER; POWER WAS GIVEN TO HIM TO TAKE PEACE FROM THE EARTH; and (less impressively) MOVE WITH THE TIMES. Three of the pictures were obvious likenesses of Famine, Pestilence and Death, but they sported ostentatious fancy dress, carried rather gruesome weapons and rode horses of varying colours. Accompanying Death in his portrait was a short, squat, flabby man astride a disgruntled donkey – I wondered briefly who this could be, but didn't like to ask. The final picture showed a red-faced giant against a backdrop of violent combat. I took this to be War.

'Aren't *you* hungry?' Famine threw my own question back at me. Although everyone else had finished, I had barely touched my breakfast.

'Yes,' I told him.

He stared, expecting more. I stared back, adding nothing.

Skirmish appeared from the adjoining kitchen wearing a natural cotton pinafore and pink Marigold gloves. He gathered the plates, the bowl and the cage (which now contained a solitary white mouse skull), then retreated through the saloon doors. After a brief clash of crockery he came back.

'Did you put them in the dishwasher?' Death asked.

Skirmish went back into the kitchen with an expression of extreme ill humour. We heard the rattle of further crockery collisions and the slither of sliding drawers before he returned.

'Did you switch it on?' Famine continued.

Skirmish repeated his previous manoeuvre, this time with even less grace, and reappeared to the sound of a low, mechanical hum. He ripped off his gloves and tossed them onto the table, before settling into the remaining unoccupied chair. He pointedly, and irritatedly, clucked his tongue against the roof of his mouth.

'Is there something wrong?' said Pestilence.

The Lab

After breakfast, I accompanied Death and Pestilence to the first-floor landing. They bickered all the way up the stairs and paused only when we reached the last door on the right. It was made of polished steel studded with rivets, and featured a large, plastic plaque at eye level: WARNING! DISEASE! AUTHORIZED PERSONNEL ONLY.

'Ignore the sign,' Pestilence reassured me. 'It's just a little joke.' I failed to see the humour in it, and felt a fish-out-of-water feeling wriggle through me. 'Now. Who's got the keys?'

'Don't look at me,' Death said. 'I thought you had them.'

'If I had them I wouldn't be asking,' Pestilence replied.

'If you had them you wouldn't need to.'

'Well I don't have them and I *am* asking.'

'And I'm telling you I haven't got them.'

'Well who *has* got them?'

'I *don't know*,' Death said in resignation. 'But Skirmish should have a spare set. Unless he's thrown them down a drain.' He retreated, and I realized that he was about to leave me alone with Pestilence.

'I'll come with you,' I offered.

'No. You stay here. I'm sure Pes will be happy to discuss today's schedule.'

He disappeared down the stairs. When I turned around Pestilence was already opening his dressing gown.

'It's bigger than yesterday,' he boasted.

He needn't have said anything. I could see for myself that the sunflower bruise had doubled in size. The black heart now spanned almost his entire torso from neck to navel, and from nipple to nipple. The yellow circumference extended to the elasticated waist of his white pyjama bottoms, curved around his back and under his armpits, and illuminated his chin like the reflection from a bunch of buttercups.

'Is it painful?' I asked.

He smiled, his thin mouth framed by a ring of cold sores.

'*Everything* is painful.'

He adjusted the gown until the bruise, and his rashes of budding pimples, ripe boils and erupted pustules, were no longer visible.

'You know, you're very lucky,' he added. 'We're only allowed to release a radical new disease every few decades. The Chief has the final say – but it's a rare event.'

'Uh-huh.'

'This one is particularly interesting. Once the client has ingested the first batch – that's where you come in, by the way – it mutates into a viral infection transmitted by direct physical contact. However,' his hands moulded into fists and he focused on a point to the right of my head, 'the most fascinating part occurs pre-contact. The virus acts in such a way that it *encourages* the host to approach potential targets, and continues to promote positive signals until a physical connection has been established.'

'Right.'

'Naturally, it's also immune to the mild antiseptic protection provided by saliva and tears, and gastric acids have no effect whatsoever. The tricky part is introducing it without infecting one of *us*.' He laughed excitedly, exposing a crescent of sore, red gum. 'Once the virus has penetrated the outer defences, its next objectives are the membranes surrounding the interior organs, particularly the heart and stomach.

After that . . .' He drew his flattened hand across his neck and grimaced.

'I see.'

'The end can come in a matter of days, or the client can continue to suffer severe and random bouts of pain for years . . . But the most impressive fact of all is its capacity for infinite variation.' He looked me directly in the eye. 'It's a *stunning* achievement, even if I say so myself.'

'I wonder where Death is?' I said.

After staring at the carpet for a couple of minutes, I was relieved to hear Pestilence announce that he was going to get changed and that he would be back *pronto*. I was glad to see the back of him. I waited for quarter of an hour, twiddling my one remaining thumb, and tried to remember what I could about my old life.

I was born in a town somewhere a few miles south of here. I don't remember what it was called. Place names have little value to a corpse, so we bury them deep almost as soon as the blood stops pumping. But I clearly remember the hospital where I was born, the old church in the town centre, the ruined abbey by the park. I even remember relaxing in a boat on the river one hot summer afternoon – I can see splashes of light glittering on the ripples, hear the slapping of the blades, smell the newly mown grass of a nearby field. And I see my father grinning, as his hard arms pull against the oars.

My father was a detective in the police force, but he hardly ever spoke about it. I knew him better as the kind, patient man who loved to assemble and dismantle watches. I remember waiting in his study for him to come home, running my fingers over the blue velvet in which he kept his instruments and spare parts, tracing the outlines of tiny wheels and cogs, squeezing the springs between my fingers.

Whenever I wasn't reading, or watching television with my mother, I spent as much time as possible with him. I loved to watch as he picked up delicate cogs and wheels with his silver tweezers and slotted them carefully into place; I loved to listen to him describe how one part connected to another, and how all of them combined to make the finished instrument. If he caught me touching anything he would – albeit rarely – grow angry and send me away; but his anger didn't last, and I would soon be standing by the desk again, asking him simple questions:

'What's that?'

A miniature disc, like a tiny revolving saw-blade.

'A spring barrel.' The secret terminology of his answers was a shared intimacy: *escape wheel, bottom train plat, winding crown.*

I pointed to a small black cylinder with a fine metal tip.

'What does *that* do?'

'It's an oiler.' He stuck out his tongue, as he always did when he was concentrating. 'It lubricates everything.'

'What does that mean?'

He looked up, removed his eyeglass, and sighed with feigned impatience.

'It means if you don't stop asking questions I'm going to tie you to this bench and see what *you* look like inside.'

He loved to tell jokes. Short, unsophisticated, surreal jokes. There was one in particular that I found hilarious when I was young:

Q: Why did the monkey fall out of the tree?

A: Because it was dead.

Happy days.

My earliest memory is of my mother. It's from 1969 – so long ago now! – when I was only two years old.

I can still see myself resting, half-asleep, on her lap, watching black-and-white images flicker on the television screen. The blurred pictures show a space ship that looks like a huge, fat insect, and two ghosts running slowly over a desert of volcanic ash. The ghosts look like they are talking, but their lips don't move and their voices crackle and hiss, like an old record. Their speech is punctuated by high-pitched beeps.

'I can't believe it,' my mother says. 'They're walking on the moon!' She strokes my thumb with her fingers, softly, absent-mindedly. 'They're actually walking on the moon.' And she kisses me on the crown of my head, letting her lips rest there.

I am not interested in the pictures, or the sounds they make. I don't care about the science or the spirit which drove three men across two hundred thousand miles of black space. I am unmoved by their effort and their achievement . . . I just enjoy staying up so late, absorbing my mother's sense of wonder, feeling her mouth on my head, lying half-asleep in her arms.

I never felt such peace again until the coffin.

What more can I say? I spent an uneventful childhood acquiring all those trophies which seem so useless when you're dead. I learned how to swim, and climb, and play games. I ran a successful ant farm, and cared for a dozen different pets. I knew how to tie knots, and how to start a camp fire with two dry sticks. I learned to ride a bike. And though I was never an outstanding student, I got an education, qualifications, and certificates of all kinds.

And, like many people, I believed in God. A God of mercy, justice and control. A God who, without thinking, could push me from my mother's womb in 1967, and escort me to my death twenty-eight years later.

What a life!

Pestilence returned first, dressed in a white jacket, a white shirt (with a white tie), white flannel trousers, and white pumps. He looked like Hopkirk from *Randall and Hopkirk (deceased)*, or like Elvis before the fat hit him.

'No sign of Death, then?' he asked redundantly.

As I shook my head, we heard footsteps on the stairs.

'I thought you had been sucked into a tar pit,' he continued. 'But wishes don't always come true, it seems.'

Death ignored the sarcasm. 'I couldn't find Skirmish anywhere. Turns out he was moping around outside.'

'Doing what, exactly?'

'Nothing. Just moping. When I grabbed hold of him he couldn't remember where his keys were. Started to have a tantrum.'

'*Hmm.*'

'That's what I thought. Still sore about the promotion.'

'But you got what you wanted.'

Death rattled a ring of five keys before us.

The Diseases Department was an L-shaped room which bent around to the right. It had three small windows, one to our left, the remaining two ahead, allowing enough light to see by but not enough to work in. The floor was covered in linoleum the colour of embalming fluid, the walls were painted blood red. My developing sense of taste told me that these two colours did not match.

'Welcome to the Lab,' Pestilence announced.

'Switch on the lights,' Death suggested.

A dozen small spotlights illuminated the room. The sudden bright-ness made it even less pleasant, but its true purpose was more clearly revealed. It looked and smelled like a school chemistry lab: heavy wooden work surfaces incorporating cupboards and enamel sinks, a confused array of scientific equipment, several Bunsen burners, gas terminals everywhere, enough rubber hose for a dozen joke snakes, and a pervading odour of sulphur. There were also three large chest freezers against the far wall.

'Have you got the note?' Death asked.

Pestilence patted his jacket pocket and removed a flimsy, crinkled ball of paper. He unrolled it carefully and read the message to himself.

'What does it say?'

'Let's see . . . We're looking for batch zero-eight-stroke-ninety-nine . . . Transmission by ingestion. Handle carefully until release. Ensure identity of specified targets. The usual details.'

'Right. When do we infect?'

'We've got three hours yet. That'll take us to –' he glanced at his gold wrist-watch '– one o'clock. We can have lunch in the café first.'

'Good. Now, where is it?'

'In one of those,' replied Pestilence, pointing to the far wall.

I took the right-hand freezer, Pestilence the left, with Death in the middle. The lid was heavy, and I struggled to open it. It yielded slowly, creaking and juddering, a thick, cold cloud of white water crystals bellowing from its open mouth.

'What am I looking for?'

'A large plastic bag,' Pestilence replied. 'Brown plastic, with a sticky label attached. The label should have the batch number on it. And whatever you do, *don't* open it.'

The freezer was stacked with piles of white jumble. Boxes, canisters, bags, plastic envelopes. I scraped the frost from the lid of a small wooden crate, revealing the title VARIOLA MAINTENANCE. Inside were three tiny, metal cylinders bound together with a rubber band and marked *Smallpox 28*, *Smallpox 29* and *Smallpox 31*.

'What happened to Smallpox 30?'

'Disappeared,' replied Pestilence. 'One of Skirmish's less successful practical jokes. No-one knows where it is.' He stopped rummaging, and glanced at Death. 'And it's not the only thing that's gone walkies ... If you ask me, he shouldn't have been given the keys in the first place.'

To the right of the crate, several bundles of plastic bags were crammed into a large cardboard box. They contained diseases I had never even heard of with release dates far into the future. To the left, a dozen tiny ampoules were vacuum-sealed onto a cardboard tray. The package had no identification, no label to suggest what disease it might be or to what uses it could be put – but one of the ampoules was missing. I was about to look underneath when Death claimed victory.

'I've found it!'

'Let me see.' Pestilence snatched the bag from Death and studied it closely. 'I'm not so sure. We have to be *very* careful—'

'Look, it's the right batch number. It's clearly marked. It's a virus ... And I'll take full responsibility.'

'Fine.' Pestilence handed the bag to me. 'Look after this disease as you would look after yourself.'

Since I had lived carelessly, died mysteriously, and did not even know my own name, this was a strange request.

The colour, shape and contents of batch 08/99 were very familiar to me. The packet contained a family-sized assortment of chocolates which I had often shared with my parents at the cinema, when I was a child. My personal favourites were the round orange ones, partly because they were so easily confused with the coffee variety, which I hated with a passion.

The name on the bag said it all: *Revels*.

A catalogue of desire

When I left school at eighteen, I shaved off the pathetic pubic chin fuzz I'd been growing for five years and, like my father before me, joined the police force. I didn't know what else to do. I was exactly six feet tall, I was vaguely attracted to the idea of justice, and I wanted the uniform. So I signed up, found myself a flat, and left home . . . I had fallen in love for the first time, too. I had it all mapped out: I would marry my childhood sweetheart, we would live in the flat and have one child, we would agree on everything, and I would repair watches and read books in my spare time. I was so ignorant.

But my mother knew. I'll always remember her parting words to me as I stood on the threshold, a suitcase under one arm, a portable stereo under the other.

'Come back whenever you need to,' she said.

My chosen career was a mistake. I spent the next three years making coffee, being mocked by students and tourists, and getting bruised outside night clubs. But most of all I hated the atmosphere of authority and obedience: it was so suffocating, so *humiliating*. It surprised no-one when, on the third anniversary of my joining, I handed in my helmet along with my resignation.

The whole experience left me feeling useless, stupid, and vulnerable. I believed that I had failed my parents and myself. I believed that I would fail at everything I did from now on.

In the same year that I quit, my first love ended. Life slaps everyone hard, but it reserves special tortures for the naive; and I simply couldn't cope when my lover moved out of the flat. So I didn't: I cancelled the lease, sold everything I owned, and lost contact with my family. My mind went into meltdown soon after.

I became a zombie long before my death. For six months I drank and begged my way through existence, unseen and unacknowledged. I existed in a world of voluntary amnesia: I couldn't remember who I was, where I came from, what I wanted. I forgot how to feel and how to speak. All I recall are the words of others, disconnected from time and place. *Get a fucking job ... He must be so cold ... Sponger ... Cheer up – it might never happen ... Do you need help?* And I still don't know how I crawled out of that nightmare. I must have had assistance – you don't escape from quicksand without a branch, or the firm grip of some-body's hand.

But the experience had changed me irreversibly: I had shrivelled to one small knot of despair. This knot was all I had to offer, so I protected it with all my strength. And it made me feel too ashamed and too worthless to return home.

For the next half-decade I took jobs which provided me with anonymity. I was a lavatory attendant for a while, cleaning up an unending trail of shit and piss, gratified to have work which mirrored the feelings in my gut. I became a road-sweeper, patrolling the streets at night, disconnected from living, breathing people, but still cleaning, still trying to wipe away the unending stains. I was an office cleaner for two years, picking up the unwanted fragments of other people's lives, digesting them, disposing of them ... And gradually, agonizingly, the knot of despair unravelled, and I inched away from the darkness back into the light. For the first time in many years, I made a positive decision: I found a job as a waiter in a restaurant my parents used to visit. I chose it in the hope that a miracle would happen: that they would find me and accept the shrivelled husk I had become.

And in the month of my twenty-sixth birthday, at the end of a long, slow evening, I heard my mother shout my name. I glanced across the room and saw her approaching cautiously. I was terrified. The grief which I had imprisoned in my stomach flooded into my veins, sending a spasm through my whole body. I stood paralysed as I wondered whether to stay or run – but a violent storm blew from the frozen wastes of my past and knocked me to the ground. I lay on the floor of the restaurant and wept, for the first time in many years; and my mother sat by me, and grabbed my hand, and gently rubbed my thumb.

When I finally summoned the strength to look up, there was a mixture of such anger and compassion in her eyes that I couldn't speak, and I waited for her to break the long silence between us. My father stood behind her, so much older now, his face a hard, emotionless mask.

'I thought you were dead,' she said at last.

My father's face softened.

'I've just . . . been away,' I said.

They didn't judge or condemn me, as I had often feared they would. They simply brought me back home and promised me a small amount of money to do anything I desired. I felt obliged to repay their generosity with action, so I took advantage of it immediately. I used some of my father's contacts, rented an office with a frosted glass door, placed an advert in the *Yellow Pages*, and waited for the phone to ring. I tried to tell myself that I was still cleaning up the shit, and patrolling the streets, and helping people. I convinced myself that my choice had been a logical one, and that I could still hide when I needed to. But, as with many of my decisions, I had simply decided to try something on a whim, and because I could think of nothing better.

I became a private detective.

*　　*　　*

72

Few people tell the truth, so I was rarely unemployed. I was hired by husbands to spy on their lying wives, by wives to spy on their cheating husbands, by bosses to spy on their swindling employees, by executives to spy on the rivals that were spying on them – and by solicitors to spy on everyone. It was an ideal career for someone who needed to be alone.

Some cases were about money, but most were about sex. This was fine by me because, as I've already said, I liked to *watch*. What did I see? I saw people shag in showers, screw in shopping malls, make love in lavatories, hump in hay-lofts, grind in graveyards, fornicate in forests, fuck on fake fur rugs, copulate in car parks, and bang in bed.

I felt like a character from a Jerzy Kosinsky novel. Of course, I was nothing more than a voyeur, albeit with a licence. But don't knock voyeurism until you've seen it for yourself.

And I grew familiar with sex again, both in my personal life and at work – so familiar that it became nothing more than a dry catalogue of desire whose contents were like a mantra. *Analingus, bestiality, bondage, buggery, coprophilia, cunnilingus, ejaculation, fellatio, fisting, masturbation, necrophilia, paedophilia, sado-masochism, scatophagy, urolagnia.* Some of these acts were illegal in practice, others could not be legitimately portrayed in films, books and digital form. The inability or unwillingness to differentiate proved incriminating for many of my clients.

So. Sometimes it was money, sometimes sex – and occasionally, as with the last case I investigated, it was both.

This is the scene.

It was a windy Friday in September. I can still see the leaves blowing on the pavement beneath my window. I was in my first-floor office on the High Street, leaning back on the swivel chair, alternating between reading my favourite trivia encyclopedia and firing elastic bands at the coat rack. No-one had requested my services in four days, and I was regularly hitting each hook in sequence and setting all kinds of records, when the telephone rang. I was on such a streak that I briefly considered leaving it on answerphone.

I picked up the receiver. It was a woman's voice, and we exchanged the usual pleasantries. Her tone was familiar, but I had buried the memory of it so deep that I couldn't attach a name or a face. She didn't sound distressed or alarmed, but she refused to discuss any details whatsoever over the phone. This was unusual. Normally a potential client would at least say *It's my husband* or *I think she's cheating*, or whatever, and you'd have some idea. But all she gave me was a description of herself, and a place and time to meet that same evening.

Our rendezvous point was a corner café in the new bus station square, and out of habit I arrived late. She was later – and since it was evening, and still warm enough to sit outside, I took a table beneath the green-and-white striped awning, ordered a coffee, and waited. I briefly tried to recall where I'd heard her voice before, but the information refused to crawl from the black pit of memory. So I just carried on waiting for almost an hour, staring out into the square. I drank two more cups of coffee, the sun's red glow faded to dark purple, the air grew cold. At last, realizing that she wasn't going to turn up, I picked up my document wallet and prepared to leave.

Someone tapped me on the shoulder.

'Sorry I'm late . . . Remember me?'

I dropped the wallet. I turned. I saw the half-moon reflected in her eyes.

74

Nightmare on Walton Street

'What I like about disease,' said Pestilence, 'is that you don't know what's happening until it's too late. It sneaks up on you, takes hold and won't let go. It doesn't apologize. It says: this is what I am, take it or leave it. It's both an honest and a dishonest method of termination.'

We were standing on the pavement in front of the Agency. It was a bright, warm morning with a few faint streaks of white cloud. The Revels were safely stored in my inner jacket pocket. Pestilence was applying a great deal of make-up to my face, and frowning periodically. He was having difficulty disguising my features to his satisfaction.

'The end result is still the same,' Death replied.

'But the approach is different. It has style, and stamina. Lifers continue to treat it with drugs, machines, immunization. But the disease will always win because it can adapt.'

Death rubbed his beard between forefinger and thumb. 'Don't you ever question what you're doing?'

'Of course not. I'm *far* too busy,' said Pestilence, brushing a final touch of rouge into my cheeks.

Famine emerged from the Agency's front entrance and descended the steps, carrying a mixed basket of fresh and cooked food: fruit, raw chicken, vegetables, a couple of pork chops, and two bottles of water. My stomach churned with hunger.

'Is any of that for me?'

He looked at the basket with horror, his watery fish-eyes revolving in their scaly sockets. 'No,' he said quickly. 'No. Everything's been modified. Powerful emetic. Designed so that the more you eat the more you want, and the more you want the more you throw up. In the end, the body rejects more than it's consumed.'

I fell silent, and we looked at each other with embarrassment until he staggered off towards his black Fiesta. He rested the basket on the rear bumper, shaking his head.

Death asked me if I still had the package, I said yes, Pestilence repeated the question, I repeated the answer, and we all climbed into the Metro. I sat in the rear seat as we sped away, the Metro's tyres squealing and spitting gravel. Death raced out of the side street without looking, roared away up the hill, and overtook three cars at 60mph in a 30mph zone. We shot along the back road towards town at 80mph, ski-jumping three sleeping policemen, before Death slammed on the brakes and executed a perfectly controlled skid into a No Parking zone outside a coffee house. We had travelled less than half a mile from the Agency.

As he stepped out of the car, I asked him why he always drove so dangerously.

'I'm immortal,' he said.

The Jericho Café, on Walton Street, held many memories for me. It was where my first love ended after three short years, and it was the setting for all the important moments in the relationships which followed my breakdown.

These later affairs always began, for me, from a position of security, inside a carapace of humour and small talk. We shared trivia over cups of coffee, and talked about everything but our feelings for each other. Without emotions, we were safe. We had a future.

But emotions can't be contained – and the drips of feeling which seeped into our conversations became a trickle, and then a flood. This was the second stage: a time of risk. We competed with each other to protest our mutual love and admiration, using words of all shapes, ideas of all sizes, statements and declarations and intentions of all kinds. These feelings were so powerful that nuances of behaviour were magnified until they became reasons to live and die; and our most indulgent fantasies became a test of our love.

But I soon felt vulnerable outside my shell. I knew that the more I exposed myself to feeling, the more painful the final separation would be. So I moved quickly into the third phase: I encouraged situations which would allow me to retreat. I began to find the trivia irritating, I made my fantasies too demanding, I ran out of friendly words. The air between us grew stagnant, and I withdrew into the safety of my carapace again.

My life became a repeating nightmare.

The interior of the café was much as I had remembered it. A dozen polished wooden tables neatly arranged in a narrow space around the service area. Areas of gloom offset by powerful spot-lighting. Pictures by local artists hanging on the walls. I had sat at the table by the window a thousand times it seemed, maybe more. In the two years before my death, I had passed an hour here on many evenings after work. No-one recognized me now, of course. The living hardly ever notice the dead, and a zombie is not much more remarkable than his cousins in the soil. We make nothing, achieve nothing, inspire nothing – so we are safely ignored.

Death ordered a black coffee at the bar which I imagined still held the imprints of my elbows.

'Did anyone bring the Life File?' he asked.

'We don't need it,' Pestilence reassured him. 'I had a look last night. I have all the details here.' He tapped his forefinger against his temple.

'Who are we looking for?'

'A couple. He's twenty, medium height, dark hair, glasses. A pseudo-intellectual student. She's a year older, shorter, unnatural blonde, and for some reason she hangs on his every word. No accounting for taste ... We give *him* the disease, he infects *her*, they both spread it around.' He smiled. 'And, thank you, I'll have an espresso.'

They both turned towards me, as if driven by remote control.

'Cappucino,' I said.

I sat at my favourite table without prompting. Pestilence took the seat opposite, completely silent, evidently considering something weighty as Death waited for the drinks. Outside, the pavement was alive with dozens of people, a sea of soft bodies criss-crossing each other's paths, ant-like in their whirling motion. As I watched them I felt an overwhelming nostalgia. I yearned for their health and the colour in their cheeks. I felt a flashing memory of the novelty and freshness of their existence. I envied their life, their wholeness, even their mortality ... But not for long. Pestilence interrupted my thoughts in his usual oily manner.

'You know,' he began, 'you should really be in Diseases. There's always work to be done. Plagues, random illnesses, minor ailments. And you get the pleasure of creating your own workload.' He smiled smugly. 'You get the highest return, too. Of course, some of us just deal with individual cases' – he waved a hand dismissively at Death – 'but with a disease you start at the bottom and can't go anywhere but up. The figures speak for themselves.'

A fat, bearded man looked through the window and smiled at a woman inside. He entered, sat down, placed his hand on her shoulder. Pestilence waved his arms with increasing animation.

'The key is *planning*. Achieving maximum impact with minimal resources. Look at the Black Death. *Pasturella pestis* was designed specifically for fleas, so that the plague could be transported across continents on the backs of rats. We *thought* about it. When we released it in China we knew that all we had to do was sit back and watch it spread. It found its way to Europe and in one year' – he held up his right finger to emphasize the point – 'it had wiped out half of England. Three centuries later, the population of London is still down by a quarter. It had a mortality rate of ninety-nine-point-nine-nine per cent. Now that's success.'

The woman kissed the bearded man, and pulled a photograph from her bag. The photograph showed two children at a swimming pool.

'We're hoping that today's release will be just as effective. A new *style* of disease.' He laughed shrilly. 'The Chief wants a time-bomb for the new millennium. One of those coincidences that convinces Lifers there's something more to existence than existence itself.' He pressed his hand against mine. It was cold and greasy. 'But high-infection, high-fatality, high-profile illnesses are just the leading edge. We're discovering new methods to promote mutation or recreate favourable environments for the established diseases, too. Malaria has been a success for years, but we're also working on smallpox, diphtheria, cholera, tuberculosis, and so on. The point is *variety*. Apart from the killers, we're constantly experimenting with non-contagious diseases and non-fatal contagious diseases. Gingivitis, pinworm, the cold, neurotic disorders – they all need careful planning and expert execution—'

'Why are you telling me this?' I interrupted.

He removed his hand and glanced over his shoulder. Death was trying to fit three cups into two hands. 'Because you're not the first apprentice to fill Hades' oversized boots, and you won't be the last. You should consider a transfer before it's too late.' He leaned over and added in a whisper, 'But keep away from Famine.'

I was about to ask him who Hades was, and why I should keep away from Famine, when Death returned with our drinks. For a few seconds, the questions fizzed around the inside of my skull. But my brain just couldn't make the connection between desire and action – and before I knew it the moment had passed, and the conversation had whirled away from me.

An hour slid by, in much the same manner as it might have done when I was alive. With nothing to distract me, I ate most of an Emmenthal, tomato and mayonnaise sandwich. Pestilence selected a ripe Cheddar which he repeatedly maintained was 'too fresh'. Death requested half a pound of roadkill as a joke, but settled for another juicy steak – this time bleeding between the two halves of a crisp, white baguette. Between mouthfuls he passed comment on everyone who entered and left the café, identifying precisely how long they had left to live, why they had to die, and which Agency department would be responsible.

'That one, for example, is our client on Thursday evening.'

He indicated the bearded man, who was leaving hand-in-hand with his friend. They were both laughing.

I pushed the rest of my sandwich to the side of the plate.

Pestilence dominated the conversation for the remainder of lunch, pontificating through a second hour about 'the illusion of choice', and using the bag of Revels (which I was required to produce) as an example. He pointed out that although every chocolate was different in shape and content, and each one appeared to offer something different, they all carried the same, equally deadly virus. His elliptical metaphorical excursions only ended when Death abruptly announced that he had spotted today's clients. I turned and followed his gaze. Through a dense crowd of cars and pedestrians, I glimpsed two people queuing outside a cinema. They fitted Pestilence's description perfectly.

The Seventh Seal

Death barged his way through the queue, not from habitual impatience, but because he had already reserved tickets for the matinée
by phone. After paying for them in cash, he bought a half litre of Cola
and a large tub of toffee popcorn, into which he greedily stuck his
long, white fingers at irregular intervals. The three of us waited by the
entrance as the crowd flowed slowly through the foyer.

I remembered the cinema too, of course: the Phoenix Picture House.
The sign had been redesigned, the walls repainted, the advertising
boards overhauled – but it was still showing the same art-house films.
Today's presentation was *The Seventh Seal*, some black-and-white,
angst-ridden gloomfest which I'd once endured with a girlfriend for an
hour on late-night television. I'd reached the point where some actor
got bumped off up a tree, and then I'd fallen asleep. I wasn't looking
forward to repeating the experience.

'This is one of my favourite films,' Pestilence declared to anyone who
was listening. 'It displays a profound understanding of existence.' He
dipped his hand into Death's popcorn and munched his way through
a sticky handful before continuing. 'The plague scenes could be
more authentic, and the animal theme is a little heavy-handed, but it
contains some of the most striking images I've ever seen in Lifer art.' He
nodded in complete agreement with himself.

'I prefer *Bill and Ted's Bogus Journey*,' said Death. 'The actor who plays
me is infinitely more amusing. Bergman is such a bore.'

'And you're such a philistine.'

'Well, you're such a snob.'

'My favourite film,' I interrupted. 'When I was alive, I mean . . . It was
The Maltese Falcon.' They stared blankly. 'But now, I suppose, it should
be *Night of The Living Dead*.'

'Would you like some popcorn?' said Death.

*   *   *

Our clients collected their tickets and we trailed them through a set of glass double doors, down a narrow, sloping corridor into the lower cinema. The lights had already been dimmed. The audience wasn't huge, and we found spaces in the back row directly behind the couple. Death and Pestilence bickered about the seating arrangements as the adverts rolled, swapping places half a dozen times in the process, and didn't settle their differences until the opening credits. Even then they both leaned over to ask (again) if I had the bag, and I said (again) that I had; and the film, with its grim subtitles, and its opening scene where Death plays chess with a medieval knight returning from the Crusades, began.

At the first sighting of a hawk hovering oppressively, I sighed and glanced down at our clients. They were both staring blankly at the screen. Images from the film were miniaturized through the man's glasses. He rested his left hand on the woman's thigh, stroking it occasionally. After a couple of minutes he opened his rucksack with his right hand, reached inside, and produced a large bag of Revels. I felt a surprising surge of affection and regret.

Half an hour or so passed, during which I almost dozed off three times, only to be roused on each occasion by loud barks of laughter from Death, who was finding the whole experience hilarious. Realizing that I wasn't likely to get any sleep, I allowed my mind to drift.

It meandered again to the woman standing by my table at the bus station café; to her bobbed black hair and brown eyes; to the white crescent of moon reflected in her black pupils.

Her name was Amy. She was my first love, and the only one who really mattered. We had lived together for almost three years in the flat I rented in the east end of town, and for a while we floated happily on a calm sea. But it didn't last. I wanted what my parents had: stability, and a family, and a clearly defined future. But Amy had a zest for life and for experimentation which I didn't share. She wanted to explore every experience she could, to break through every barrier she encountered – and she soon discovered that the limits of my own territory were very narrow indeed.

So she left; and in the five years of numbness that followed I only allowed one painful memory of our relationship to surface.

We were lying in bed together one Saturday morning in winter. It was almost over – maybe two or three weeks before the end. But we were in a calm period. We hadn't argued for a few days, and we had even rediscovered some of our old affection. Amy was lying on me in her night-shirt, stroking my head and nibbling my cheek softly. I grew excited, and she felt me, and she rolled off.

'Not yet,' she said, grinning. 'I've got a surprise for you.'

I tried to pull her back but she was too quick. She crossed the bedroom and hurried into the kitchen. I lay there for a few minutes, listening for clues, but all I heard was the opening and closing of drawers. I began to feel increasingly apprehensive.

When she returned she was holding a plastic shopping bag and a large elastic band. She returned with these to the double bed, removed her night-shirt, slipped the bag over her head, and pulled the elastic band around her neck. She sucked the plastic into her mouth as she spoke.

'Fuck me,' she said. 'Take it off before I pass out. But fuck me first . . . *Do* it.'

I didn't reply. I just lay there, frozen. After a moment she removed the bag and the elastic band and tossed them aside.

'Christ – you're so fucking boring,' she said.

*   *   *

And it was true: I was. I have the luxury now of finding the incident funny, though a little sad; but back then, I simply couldn't understand why she wanted to play games with mortality. And because I couldn't express this feeling, my inaction was humiliating for both of us.

It's no wonder she left.

After she had gone, I reduced myself to nothing and started again. I threw away all the moulds which had shaped me: my parents, my fear of experimentation, my history. I recast myself in my own image, and grew a hard outer shell . . . So when my mother found me and shouted my name across the floor of that restaurant, I had become a different person. And when I collapsed on the floor and wept, I wept for the corpse of my past.

The nature of my sexuality had altered completely, too. Like Amy had once done, I now wanted to explore the limits of my free will. I wanted to punish the innocence which had caused me so much suffering. I wanted to expose myself to new desires, so that nothing would ever hurt me again. At first, my appetite was conventional. I wanted a woman to dress up, or to undress slowly, or to masturbate in front of me. I wanted to watch her having sex with her other lovers, or to video us together so that I could replay it when I was alone. I wanted to tie her up, and to be tied up, and to feel the threat of pleasure and domination. But gradually, with each new relationship, the borders of my desire expanded. I could never cope with physical pain – nipple clamps, wax play, body piercing, whipping and maiming were a no-no from the start – but I developed a taste for PVC and leather, for sex toys and games, and for danger. Things I had once regarded as perverse were now drawn inside the borders of the normal.

I had created an adult version of my childhood inquisitiveness. How do you know what you want until you've tried it? But the more I experienced, the more I wanted – and the less I was satisfied.

Until I turned around at that table in the bus station café though, I never became emotionally involved with my work. Despite the temptations, despite what I photographed, filmed, tape-recorded, and noted down, despite the most intimate knowledge, I crushed any incipient feelings. But the sight of the crescent moon reflected in the deep, black pools of Amy's eyes was irresistible. It stimulated too many memories. It was as if someone had thrust a giant blow-torch into my face, and illuminated the darkness that shrouded my past.

'Of course I remember.'

I nodded, and shook her hand, and she sat down. We spoke awkwardly for a couple of minutes, exchanging information and blandishments, and then she fell silent. She played with the buckle on her alligator skin bag, perhaps repeating words in her mind which she had rehearsed a thousand times already, perhaps thinking of something else entirely. I had no way of knowing what was going on inside her head; I never had. She only released the information when she was ready. So I simply waited for her to speak, studying her face for clues. She looked pale and tired, but in everything else she was composed, and smartly dressed in a crushed linen jacket and matching trousers. A heavy gold wedding ring mirrored the galaxy of ostentatious jewellery on the rest of her body.

'I have to be rid of him,' she said at last. 'I *need* to. But if I tried to walk out, he'd kill me. He'd track me down. And he'd do it without thinking.' She opened her purse, removed a passport photograph and placed it face down on the table, as if she couldn't bear to look at it. 'He's a shit. I hate him.' She twisted her head in disgust. 'He makes me *do* things.'

I pointed to her wedding ring. 'Are we discussing . . . ?'

She nodded. 'And if I don't do it he dishes out threats. It's not just me – I've heard him talking about other people. He gets crazy.'

'Why haven't you gone to the police?'

'His word against mine.' She laughed bitterly. 'Besides, he never leaves a mark.'

It was impossible to know exactly what had been happening, or even what her motives were in hiring me – but I didn't push for more information. She would produce it when she wanted me to hear.

'How can I help?' I said.

She looked into my eyes for the first time since sitting down. 'I need evidence. I *know* what he does. I can smell it on him when he comes home at night; I've seen it on his clothes.' She shuddered. 'But I need proof. Real proof – as much as you can get.'

I still needed her, even now. I'd known it from the moment she sat down. I wasn't angry with her, despite the circumstances in which we had parted. Too much had happened since then. I wanted my past, and my parents, and to run my fingers over the velvet on my father's desk again – but most of all, I wanted *her*.

'I want you to get me something that he'll be afraid of,' she continued. 'And I need somewhere to keep it safe.'

And even as her story unwound, I resurrected a sentimental cliché so out of context with my recent history that it hijacked my judgement. I remembered us walking barefoot in the meadow after a spring shower, wrapped around each other, needing the touch of each other's skin, wanting the atoms of our bodies to fuse together. I saw the sun sinking slowly behind us, one of a hundred different sunsets we would share, a thousand different skies.

And love began to infect me again. It swam in my bloodstream and infiltrated every extremity of my body, fire-cracking in the tips of my toes, hammering against the pads of my fingers, whirling around inside my head. It shorted every synapse and pierced every cell wall. It consumed me.

And instead of refusing the case, as every instinct screamed I should, I reached across the table and turned over the photograph.

Pestilence nudged my elbow and gestured towards the seat in front. I was still staring at the photograph in my daydream, and it was several seconds before I noticed that our male client had opened his packet of Revels and was offering one to his partner.

'What do I have to do?'

He looked at me as if he regretted ever having advertised his department to such an imbecile. 'Swap the bags. Obviously.'

I watched carefully as the woman deliberately selected three of the flat, plain chocolates from the packet, and the man grabbed an indiscriminate handful. I took the poisoned Revels from my jacket, broke the seal, removed a corresponding number and placed them in my lap. The chocolates hadn't melted: a zombie may have life, but he doesn't have warm blood.

As I waited for the right moment, questions fired inside my undead brain. How could I cause the death of people I didn't even know? Was it easier to kill someone for whom you felt no sympathy? Did I have any right to even consider it? With the woman's assisted suicide, there had at least been some sense, some desire on her part. But this was so random, and so meaningless. It depended on nothing more than luck.

At the sight of his namesake appearing on screen, Death released another long, loud, laugh. Our male client carefully placed his bag of Revels on the armrest and turned around slowly, his eyes wide with the annoyance of a professional aesthete whose weekly culture banquet has been poisoned.

'Please. If you can't control yourself . . .'

Like many irked intellectuals he failed to complete the threat, but his anger provided a window just large enough for me to exchange my packet for his. Ignoring all my doubts, I fulfilled my obligation.

And then I did a rather foolish thing. Perhaps I wanted to see what it was like, and to feel what the living must feel. Perhaps it was because I hadn't eaten much all day, and the atmosphere in the cinema caused me to lose concentration. Perhaps I was too pleased with my first active contribution to my new employer, or simply confused by the pointlessness of it all. Whatever. Without even thinking about what I was doing, I reached down, picked out a Revel from the pile in my lap, and popped it into my mouth.

The worst thing was: it was coffee-flavoured.

Zombie in la-la land

This is how the disease spreads.

It begins with an introduction, a polite enquiry, a suggestion that we meet. Neither of us has anything to fear. We are free agents, without obligation or pressure. So we meet, and the encounter passes without incident. But at the end, as we are about to part, the disease asks if it might stop awhile. I refuse, of course. It asks again a moment later, when it considers me to be a little more accommodating – but I sense its trickery, and I refuse again. It asks a third time, immediately after, catching me off my guard. This is how diseases work. They are insidious.

And I say, 'OK. Stay. But you leave when I say so.'

And it replies. 'That's fine by me.'

Of course, it's lying. Of course, it takes control. It doesn't leave until it's exhausted you with its sick little games.

This is what diseases are like.

'How are you feeling?'

I looked up to see a thin, pasty-faced beanpole in a black polo shirt and pale chinos. His rubbery lower jaw was limber as an eel, and his pale lips shimmered as he spoke. Flecks of popcorn nestled in his black beard.

'Who are you?' I asked.

'Is he all right?'

The beanpole's companion was shorter. He had yellow, glazed eyes like a dead cod. His neck was stained golden and black like an eclipse of the sun. His skin was cratered with spots, as if he were some new species of leopard.

'I don't think so. What do you suggest?'

'Just let it run its course.'

'Who are you?'

'Friends,' said the beanpole.

'I have to leave now,' I told them. 'I have work to do.'

I was lying on the soft, blue carpet of the foyer. A crowd queuing for tickets regarded me as the supporting feature. I stared at the two people closest to me: a snow-haired middle-aged man, and a younger, snow-white woman. I thought I recognized her, but she stared as if she was afraid of me – or as if she needed help. Looking closer, I saw that she was not so pure after all. The whiteness of her face had been spoiled by a black bruise on her right cheek, and a red cut on her lip. And when I returned her stare she looked away quickly.

'We should all leave together,' agreed the leopard.

I reached up to touch him, but he pulled away, protecting his precious leopard hide. I began to wonder if he was my friend after all. I much preferred the idea of the snow people; they were infinitely more interesting. I said hello to them. They ignored me, but I was not to be deflected. I repeated the greeting – a little louder this time, since it's often the case that the first attempt at communication is simply misheard. The snow-haired man looked at me for a long time with deep, black eyes.

'Try to keep him quiet,' said the beanpole. 'He's attracting attention.'

I looked around the room to see if I could guess who they were talking about, but there were no obvious candidates.

'What do you suggest?' the leopard replied.

'How should I know? It's your disease.'

'Oh. So it's *my* disease now, is it?'

'What do you mean?'

'I think you know exactly—'

'Excuse me,' I interrupted, 'but I'm trying to talk to my *real* friends.' I smiled at the snow couple. 'Thank you. Now, if you would kindly keep quiet while we make our introductions . . .'

'Just relax,' the beanpole said.

'Calm down,' echoed the leopard.

I tried to rise but felt my face was aflame. When I lay down again the fire was snuffed out.

'How long does he have?'

'I don't know. An hour. A day. A month. It differs from one host to the next.'

The virus fizzed and coiled inside. A gang of snakes had built a nest in my stomach, and a box of fireworks had been lit inside my skull. I felt as if I was about to vomit, then explode.

'I think we should give him the cure immediately.'

The leopard looked puzzled. 'What cure?'

'What do you mean?'

'I mean: what cure? I didn't bring a cure.'

The beanpole was outraged. 'Well, where is it?'

'Back at the Lab.'

I extended a hand again, but they darted away like frightened fish. I would have repeated the attempt, but someone was stuffing my arms and legs with sea urchins.

'We'd better get him out of here.'

The leopard nodded.

'Can I have some water?' I asked.

'A whole pitcher full,' said the beanpole, smiling kindly. 'Just follow me.'

I rose very slowly, with plenty of verbal encouragement, noting that my two helpers remained at a safe distance. My limbs were generating enough heat to melt Pluto, and my spine was a perch for a maniac woodpecker, but the promise of refreshment spurred me on. I felt a brief and uncontrollable urge to say goodbye to the snow couple, but could no longer see them. The rest of the crowd retreated from my approach – some with the aid of the beanpole's elbows – and I staggered onto the street without incident.

The outside world was a cauldron of searing heat. The pavement burned like molten steel, the road flowed like lava, the buildings shimmered and melted in the burning air. And I was assaulted by a kaleidoscope of blinding colour. Red shirts, green blouses, pink T-shirts, blue singlets, black summer suits, blue cotton jackets, khaki shorts and lemon trousers, peach skirts and purple dresses, brown sandals, orange deck shoes, white slip-ons, black pumps. I squinted for protection and inched forward, following the leopard, followed by the beanpole. I wanted to touch everyone, to embrace all these hues, to share my scorched skin; but my companions were watchful, and they pushed aside anyone who advanced on the borders of my viral kingdom.

We crossed the road and headed for a giant, cream-coloured stag beetle sheltering from the sun. The leopard approached its thorax and pulled one of the insect's forewings aside, exposing a leathery interior. He held the wing back and beckoned me with his spotted paws.

'Please. Just get in. And don't touch either of us.'

I did as he requested, squeezing inside the beetle's shell and settling in its soft abdomen. If the leopard or his tall friend had asked me to leap from a high tower, or a suspension bridge, or anywhere, I would have obeyed their command.

They were beautiful people.

I remember nothing about the short flight home which followed, except for this conversation:

'I trust you haven't told him yet?' the leopard asked.

'What about?' the beanpole replied.

'About the small print.'

'The Chief's instructions are very clear.'

'But you seem to be growing a little *soft*.'

'I think he has a right to know, that's all.'

'On the contrary. The dead have no rights.'

The rest of the time I swam quietly in the blue sparkling coves of my own mind, trying to shelter from the sun which had fallen from the sky.

The beetle landed by an immense two-storey nest, with a converted attic for the queen and a basement for the drones. Three other insects waited patiently outside: a black scarab shimmering in the heat, a white termite motionless as an unseasonable mound of snow, and a sleek and shining dung beetle, redder than a wet tongue.

'Is that War's new BMW?' the beanpole asked.

'Hmm,' the leopard grunted.

'He's back early.'

'Don't expect we'll see much of him tonight, though.'

'Are he and Skirmish . . . ?'

'As usual.'

The leopard pushed aside the stag beetle's left forewing and stepped onto the molten steel pavement. He firmly invited me to get out. I offered my hand, still driven by the promised glass of water, but he rudely refused it, and I had to crawl free from the insect's belly on my own. He compounded his discourtesy by leaving me alone with the beanpole, skipping up the steps to the entrance to the nest and disappearing inside.

I felt very sick, as if I'd eaten a piece of hell. My stomach was flipping like a pancake. I didn't know where I was. I didn't know who I was.

'Water,' I whispered.

'Come on,' said the beanpole. 'Let's find a cure.'

'How does that feel?' Death asked.

'My head,' I explained.

'Does it hurt?'

'It's spinning. It won't stop.'

I was lying in a dark corner of the Lab, drinking a glass of cold tap water. Pestilence had found a bottle of white pills for me in one of the wooden cabinets. 'It's still in the experimental stages,' he had told Death. 'And it's designed for the living rather than the dead, so I can't be sure of the side effects. But he should be fine.'

And now my head wouldn't stop spinning.

Worse still: I felt an insistent pressure in my groin. The food I'd consumed yesterday had travelled the length of my torso and been processed by my resurrected stomach and intestines. I realized that I needed to urinate for the first time in many years. Death escorted me to the bathroom (still refusing to touch me in case any residual infection remained), and closed the door behind me.

I removed my trousers and boxer shorts and sat down on the lavatory, vaguely observing the avocado colouring of the bath and toilet. I was obliged to sit: my tiny stump of a penis was useless for directing the stream. At last I felt the pressure on my bladder easing, and a painful rush of liquid flowing the short distance down my truncated urethra. I heard the noise of my waste emptying into the bowl, and looked down briefly.

My urine was dark yellow, thick, and streaked with blood.

The journey back to my room felt like a rough ferry crossing. The first-floor landing heaved as I left the bathroom, and descending the stairs was like riding the down-curve of a sixty-foot wave. I stumbled at the foot, and the ground floor rose to meet my outstretched arms.

'Careful,' Death said pointlessly.

'I *am* being careful.'

We turned right into the main hallway, right again into the narrow passage, right once more into the corridor where my room was. Death opened the door, and I staggered inside and collapsed onto the lower bunk. He remained in the doorway.

'Would you like anything to eat?'

'Not just yet.' The thought sent my stomach into a fresh series of back-flips.

'OK. Scream if you need anything.'

The door closed. The key turned in the lock.

Safe again.

Revelation 6:8

I remembered everything that had happened to me since I'd swallowed the poisoned chocolate, but the memories were dislocated, as if they belonged to someone else. I felt ashamed of what I'd done, and wouldn't have been surprised to discover myself back in the coffin by morning. I felt so groggy, this wasn't an unattractive prospect.

I sat up slowly, and surveyed the room. The television was switched off. The vase of dead roses and the typewriter still stood on the writing desk. The blue glass ornament in the shape of a swan had been turned around. For want of anything better to do, I stood up, walked to the desk and opened the left drawer. It contained an old Bible on top of an unopened packet of plain A4 paper. I removed the Bible and stroked the packet with the three good fingers on my left hand, momentarily mesmerized by its blinding whiteness. In the right drawer I found two more books. The first was entitled *Coping with Death: A Handbook for the Recently Deceased*, the second *The A–Z of Termination*. I didn't bother opening either of them. My brain was wobbling like a decelerating gyroscope.

Sitting up had been a bad idea. Standing had been worse. I returned to the bed and lay down.

When I awoke it was dark, and there was a note on the carpet by the door. The writing was spidery and child-like: *I'll be back later with something to eat – Death*. I had no idea what the time was. I removed my crumpled jacket and felt something rattle in the left pocket. Emptying it onto the bed, I discovered half a dozen Revels. The sight of them rocketed the sparse contents of Tuesday's menu to throat level. I scooped them up with one hand and threw them in the bin.

They helped confirm what I'd been pondering all day: this particular mode of death was deeply unsatisfactory. Amongst corpses, certain diseases guarantee unquestioned respect, but if I was to fail in my apprenticeship (as now seemed likely), I couldn't bear to repeat what my brief illness had exposed me to. The shame of it, the humiliation . . .

It just didn't *feel* right.

Coincidentally, those are the precise words Amy used when she ended our relationship. She sat by the window in the Jericho Café and repeated what she had said only an hour earlier. 'It just doesn't feel right. Not any more.'

I nodded. 'It hasn't felt right for a long time.'

Funny, the things you remember when you're dead.

Three short, firm knocks interrupted my thoughts.

'Who is it?'

'Death.'

'Come in.'

He unlocked the door and entered, making sure he secured it again before approaching the bed. He was carrying a plate piled high with salted crackers which, briefly, uncomfortably, and inexplicably, reminded me of sex. He left them on the table by the window before settling into the Barca lounger.

'How are you feeling?'

'Better.'

He nodded. 'I brought you some food. Pes says you won't feel like eating for a while – but just in case.' I thanked him. 'We have a meeting tomorrow morning. Late. You should come along. See how things work.' I smiled weakly. 'There's no rush for breakfast.' He stared at me in silence for a moment, then sat up and prepared to leave.

'How did I do today?'

He paused before answering. 'We're not sure if any infection actually took place. You were writhing around so much after your accident, our clients moved seats and left the bag behind. It'll be a couple of days before we know for sure.'

'Sorry.'

'Shit happens.'

He stood up.

'Where's Skirmish?'

'Out on the town with War. Probably trashing some restaurant.'

He walked towards the door, unlocked it.

'Who's Hades?' I asked. The question escaped before I knew what I was saying.

Death turned casually, and pointed to the battered Bible on the writing desk. 'Look him up,' he said. 'Revelation. Chapter six, verse eight.'

Fat man, red beard

I see nothing.

I'm in a warm, dark, vibrating place. I hear a low, muffled hum.

My whole body is aching. My hands are tied behind my back with rope; my legs are tied to my hands. My mouth is stuffed with a rag that tastes of oil and grease, sealed in place by insulating tape. The tape winds three times around my head, biting into the skin on my face and neck, tearing my hair when I move. Sweat rolls into my eyes, runs down my cheek, drips onto the warm, dark, vibrating surface beneath me.

And I am screaming. But with the rag, and the tape, and the low, muffled hum, no-one can hear.

I might as well be a prisoner in a medieval oubliette.

I opened my eyes.

I saw a soft, white pillow, and a deep, white carpet, its thick threads almost level with my line of sight. I had a fleeting sense of the familiar once again. I released the pillow reluctantly and rolled onto my back, gazing sleepily at the wooden slats of the upper bunk. I rubbed my eyes and focused on the Artex ceiling: spatterings of stalactites frozen in mid-drip, white stars clustered in crazy constellations. I saw animals, and food, and faces, and the chaotic spinning of suns.

I saw nothing.

When I stood up my head was still weak from Pestilence's dubious remedy and I lost my balance on the way to the wardrobe, tripping over a particularly thick patch of shagpile and falling against the writing desk. The collision dislodged the vase of roses: I heard it roll, then watched it fall onto the carpet by my feet. I crawled over to the wardrobe and climbed it like a cliff face; but I opened the door too eagerly, and the edge struck my forehead just above the nose.

Groaning, I selected an orange T-shirt with the words FRIEND OF THE SEVEN-EYED LAMB™ across the chest, a random pair of floral boxer shorts, and some tangerine socks embroidered with red lobsters.

Zombie fashion!

After dressing I made my way to the dining room, unaware of the time, uncertain that anyone would be there. Having eaten very little the day before, I needed breakfast now. My stomach was riding a motorbike through a fiery hoop.

The door was closed, but I clearly heard Death's melancholic tones: 'The things we do, I'm amazed that any of us can sleep at night. But I'm even more amazed that the Chief expects us to enjoy it. Why do we go on with it?'

The respondent's voice was loud, aggressive, and unfamiliar: 'Things would be a damn sight 'cking worse if we didn't, that's why.'

Hunger, and a mild curiosity, pushed me through the door.

Death was sitting in his usual place at the head of the table. He was wearing a light grey kimono and black velvet skull-embroidered slippers. Next to him, in the chair I had occupied the day before, sat a sunburned giant with Ronald McDonald hair and a bushy, red beard.

Death turned around as I walked in. 'Feeling better?'

'Still groggy.'

'How did *that* happen?'

'Sorry?'

'Your head.' He waved his hand in my general direction. 'Above your nose. The red patch.'

'It's nothing.'

He nodded, and indicated the fat man with the red beard. 'This is War.' He pinched his ear and added confidentially, 'He's a little deaf.'

The stranger paid him no attention; he seemed more interested in studying every aspect of my appearance. I returned the compliment. His fingers were the colour and thickness of traditional pork sausages. His eyebrows looked like dead caterpillars. He was dressed entirely in varying shades of red: a scarlet polo shirt with a large, golden sword embroidered on the breast pocket, wide crimson jeans with a salmon-coloured belt, maroon ankle socks, and bright ruby plimsolls. He filled every expanded inch of his clothes – a stockpile of muscle, blood and bone inside thick walls of flesh.

Death cut short our mutual scrutiny by introducing me: 'This is my new apprentice.'

War looked me in the eye. 'Don't you have a name?' he bellowed.

I shook my head.

'Each to his own.' He continued to feast on the vast platter of cold meats spread before him.

I sat in Skirmish's seat, where a bowl of cereal and fruit were laid out for me. After sampling the first mouthful I couldn't prevent myself assaulting the rest. It was a strange experience. The sensation of solid food squeezing down my throat and creeping spasmodically through my intestines was still uncomfortable after so many years of digestive inactivity.

'So what was the body count?' Death said, continuing a conversation the beginning of which I'd missed.

'Thousands.' War slipped a slug of spicy salami down his throat.

'Sounds like a good day's work.'

'One of the best.'

'Going back?'

'No need to. The wheels are in motion. All the Agents know what to do. I might pop in for a special guest appearance in a couple of weeks, but that's just maintenance. I'm not due anywhere until Monday.'

'But you can still help me out on Friday?'

War nodded. 'No rest for the wicked.'

Death had already devoured two of his customary trio of white mice before I'd entered, but he delayed the third for several more minutes. As I finished off the last of the fruit, he opened and closed the cage door repeatedly and tapped his fingers against the bars. It appeared to give him some pleasure; but the mouse squeaked with fear.

'Where's Skirmish this morning?' I asked.

'Wasn't he in your room?'

'Not when I got up.'

'Skirmish!' War interrupted. Gobbets of boiled ham flew from his open mouth like missiles. '*Skirmish!*' The second call nearly deafened me. Death continued to tease his prey, preoccupied with his own thoughts.

Within seconds I heard heavy footsteps racing down the stairs and along the corridor towards us. Skirmish burst into the dining room looking as annoyed as anyone can in a pink, ankle-length night-shirt. His irritation relaxed into servility when he realized who had called him.

'What is it?'

'Come here, you 'cking bugger,' War commanded. No sooner had Skirmish negotiated his way around the table than War stood up, leapt upon him with a speed I would not have thought possible, and wrestled him to the ground. It was the most unequal contest I'd ever seen, and it was ended by the pair laughing loudly and slapping each other on the back.

'Now that you're here,' said Death, flicking the roof of the cage, 'there's something you could do for me.' He opened the door and dragged the mouse out by its tail. 'The Chief has a message for today's meeting. I'd like you to collect it.'

Skirmish rolled his eyes and pointed at me. *'He's* your apprentice.'

'But I'm asking you.' Death slipped the mouse into his mouth, crunched on the bones, sucked loudly, and spat out a small, white skull. It bounced along the table and came to rest by my left arm.

Skirmish stared at him angrily, then dropped his gaze and left without another word. A moment later Death rose, and bowed politely.

'I'll see how he's getting on,' he said.

I was alone with War. His physical presence intimidated me more than that of anyone I had met since my death, but I have long since learned to disguise my responses. As he shovelled half a dozen slices of beef into his mouth, I quietly picked at the remnants of my breakfast. At last he looked up.

'Nice suit,' he said.

'Thank you.'

'Apart from that, you look like shit.'

'Oh.'

'Like it here?'

I nodded.

'Watch out for Pestilence,' he whispered.

Startled by his bluntness, I stared through the window and said the first thing that came into my head. 'Is that your BMW?'

He turned around, chewing noisily. 'Yep. You can't turn up at a battle looking like a sodding dog's breakfast.'

'What was wrong with the horse?'

He pointed at the framed slogan on the wall beneath Death's portrait: MOVE WITH THE TIMES. 'Too inefficient. I need to be anywhere at a moment's notice.' He folded his hands across his ample belly, pleased with himself. 'Besides, have you ever *seen* apocalyptic horse shit?'

*   *   *

Death re-entered the room, sat down, stared at me. He had changed into his day clothes: Timberland boots, pale jeans, a cream T-shirt, and a black-and-white check lumberjack shirt.

'The meeting is in five minutes,' he announced. 'A prompt start will give us more time this afternoon.'

'What've you got on today?' War asked.

'Accidental death,' he sighed. 'Unfortunate business.'

'Always is.'

Death nodded. 'It's rather apt, though. Our client's whole life has been a catalogue of accidents. He's got scars from shaving, from shark-fishing, from hacking away at frozen ice cream. Scars on his head and neck, scars on his knees. He spends his time lurching from one small tragedy to another.' He breathed deeply. 'He even bumped into *me* a couple of weeks ago.'

He stared at the table with a look of such compassion, I was reminded of my mother's face when she found me again at the restaurant, five years after I had disappeared.

We left the dining room as a threesome and climbed the stairs to the first floor. The corridor was empty but I heard laughter from the first room on the left. War marched in without knocking and was greeted unenthusiastically. I turned around to see Death closing a door marked THE CHIEF – the same door I had seen on Monday, after my shower. I briefly caught sight of an iron spiral staircase leading upwards.

'You can't trust Skirmish to do anything properly,' he said.

Behold a pale horse

The Meeting Room: a long, Formica-laminated table surrounded by six chairs, a flickering fluorescent light directly overhead, a coffee machine on a wooden stand in the far left corner, a photocopier in the far right. Death sat at the head of the table, Skirmish opposite him; to his left were Pestilence and Famine, to his right myself and War. The walls were bare but painted a lurid crab red, a shade which clashed violently with War's outfit. Since his outfit already clashed with itself, this caused no great anxiety.

The desk was covered with paper.

'Morning, everyone,' said Death. He looked around the room for a response. No-one seemed interested. 'Any questions before we begin?' Blank stares. 'Then I declare this meeting open.' He coughed theatrically. 'Today's session will cover the following subjects: updates from Pestilence, Famine, War and myself; a proposal for the new filing system; a review of our field Agents; any miscellaneous additional matters arising from the discussion; and a message from the Chief. Let's start with the updates – Pes?'

'Well, there isn't much to tell.' Pestilence's tone was calm, confident. He established eye contact with everyone in the room, including me. 'Batch 08/99 had a problematic release, but if it succeeds we're anticipating global contamination within three years. The contusions are slightly more enigmatic: after a promising initial spread the bruising seems to have dissipated. Most disappointing. I've reorganized the testing regime and expect more positive results soon.'

Famine picked up the thread. 'I've put into practice all the recommendations discussed at Saturday's meeting. Currently researching emetic foodstuffs. First tests carried out yesterday. Nothing came up.' He chuckled, but his pun was received with icy silence.

'I,' began War self-importantly, 'was supposed to be helping

Weapons Research with some sodding statistical survey, but I didn't have time.' He sighed. 'Actually, I couldn't be arsed.' He sniffed, rubbed his belly, belched loudly, and looked at Death. 'How about you?'

'Apart from the usual fatalities – the details are lodged in Archives – I've been dealing with our new apprentice.' All eyes turned towards me, and I felt a snake of fear writhing in my gut. 'I'll have more to tell you on Saturday, but everything is running smoothly so far. Wouldn't you agree?'

'I don't know,' I replied. It was an honest confession, but the horse-shoe of eyes wanted more. 'I don't know what it's like when things *don't* run smoothly.'

The question had taken me by surprise – as usual, my mind had been elsewhere. It's hard to shake off the habits of the coffin.

In particular, I'd been thinking about the words I'd read the previous evening, about Hades. As soon as Death had closed the door, I'd staggered over to the desk and opened the Bible. With an immense feeling of excitement and anticipation I quickly located the passage. It said: *And I looked, and behold a pale horse. And his name that sat on him was Death, and Hades followed with him.* I'd scanned the rest of Revelation 6, and then the whole book, but there was no more helpful reference than this.

'Obviously,' Death continued, 'we'll be in a better position to judge at the weekend, so I'll submit a more complete report then, along with the financial summary.' The arc of piercing eyes turned away from me. 'Now: the reorganization of the filing system. The Chief is currently effecting the transferral of all documents presently to be found in Archives to the office on the second floor, ready for digital encoding. The estimated window for completion is about two years, after which time all Life Files will be processed by the Chief before use, with additional information appended where necessary. From now on, all Termination Reports will be transferred directly to the Chief on completion and will form part of the appropriate Life Files. No documents will be issued without prior authorization from the Chief, and all files currently in circulation must be returned within the next ten weeks. The practical results of implementing this system should include a huge reduction in paperwork, greater efficiency in terms of time and resources, a tangible reduction in errors, and a more manageable workload for us all.'

Like everything else, the afterlife has its moments of utter tedium, and a zombie's attention span is shorter than most. Looking for excitement, my brain led me back to Amy, and to the bus station café . . . where I turned over the photograph.

I don't normally like generalizations, but I'll make an exception this once: Amy's husband *looked* like a criminal. A passport photo can make a mug out of anyone (particularly if you're dumb enough to choose the plain white background) but in any light he would have been a triple-strength bozo with a frothy spiv topping. He had the square jaw, the meatloaf neck, the Brylcreemed hair. He had a scar running from his left ear to the corner of his mouth. His eyes were frighteningly small, impenetrably black, primitively deep-set. He had the stubble, the tan, the broken nose. He even had a gold tooth. I was jealous of him, of course: Amy had chosen him, and rejected me.

'I'll need some more details,' I said, fighting the urge to mock. 'Name. Age. Where he works. Who his friends are. What time he goes out.'

Amy nodded. 'Anything you want. And his name's Ralph.'

Ralph, for Christ's sake. Ralph and Amy. Chalk and cheese. What had she seen in him? A man whose name was a euphemism for vomit. I offered her the photograph but she fended it off with her palm. I placed it in my inside jacket pocket, where it remained until my death seven weeks later.

'One more thing . . . You should decide how much information you want. The truth can be more uncomfortable than you expect.'

She laughed. 'Nothing can be worse than what I already know.'

Amy provided me with names and a few basic details, and we arranged a follow-up meeting to finalize the deal in seven days' time. As we parted, she smiled and shook my hand. Her grip was feeble, like a child's, but her touch was like a match flame against my skin.

For the next week I left the elastic bands and the trivia encyclopedia alone, and threw myself into pen-pushing and key-pressing. I dug up some dirt from my father's police contacts, trawled through the national criminal databases, scoured back issues of newspapers for information about relevant individuals and companies. At first, it seemed that he was nothing more than an amateur, an international milk thief. He'd bought property in the town centre despite being on every credit blacklist in the country. He was a partner in a wine importing business – wine being the cover for more profitable and distinctly illegal merchandise. His name was associated with half a dozen minor companies in London, none of which had seen a tax return for the last ten years. But despite the overpowering musk of corruption with which he marked his territory, I only found two firm convictions.

The first involved hazy connections with the local mafia, a half-baked association of hatchet men with interests as wide and laughable as a kebab van protection racket and an extortionate student loan scheme. As a minor player, he'd got two years. The second was a pathetic attempt to hold up the NatWest on the High Street with plastic guns and a water bazooka, and that had led to a five-year stretch. He was released early for good behaviour, and for the last couple of years appeared to have been a model citizen.

So much for research.

We met again the following Friday. As Amy sat down, I noticed she had applied make-up to her left eye to disguise a tiny cut – it could have been anything, and it wasn't my business anyway. I handed her a dossier containing the information I had gathered and said nothing. She sipped a cup of tea as she read it, nodding when she discovered a detail she recognized, but mostly unmoved. After quarter of an hour she placed the report on the table, pushed back the hair from her face, and said:

'We have a deal.'

I gathered up the papers. 'From here it's a financial arrangement. A cheque at the end of every month, until you get what you want.'

And the thought zipped through my head: Did she still want me?

'Whatever it takes. He's paying.' She flashed both rings on her right hand, then finished the rest of her tea and stood up.

'Is there anything in particular you'd like me to work on?'

'What do you mean?'

'You mentioned that he . . . *did* certain things to you.'

She smiled briefly, inscrutably. 'I'd rather not. Unless you think it's necessary.'

'It could be important. If I don't find anything else.' She nodded, and I wondered how reluctant she really was. 'I won't be there, of course, but I'll need to set up the equipment. Whenever it suits you.'

'Give me a week. I'll call you.'

She was wearing a short black skirt, black suede shoes and a white shirt. When she turned around to leave I noticed the tanned skin of her

neck above the collar, and remembered the time when I had run my
fingers over it, as I had done with the velvet cloth in my father's study.

A hard ball of emotion caught in my throat, and I forced my attention
back to the banal, business-like atmosphere of the Meeting Room –
where everyone, for some unknown reason, was staring at Skirmish.

'So where is it?' Death asked.

'I had it a minute ago,' Skirmish replied. Panicking, he swept aside
the notes in front of him, some of which leapt from the table and
floated gracefully to the floor. Stooping to pick them up, he banged
his head on Famine's chair. Reorganizing his files, he caught sight of a
folded sheet of paper which had strayed towards War. 'Here it is.' He
unfolded it slowly, ceremoniously. 'The Chief's message says: *It has
come to my attention that certain of our Agents are interfering with
standard termination practice. I would ask those Agents to reacquaint
themselves with the Agency's clearly stated terms of employment: impro-
visation of any kind is expressly prohibited, and any deviation from
established procedure will result in a severe reprimand and ultimate
suspension. Keep up the good work.*' He looked at Death and smirked.

'Thank you.' An awkward silence followed. Death chewed his lower
lip and sank into melancholy reflection. Then, as if dismissing the
Chief's criticism, he continued with forced breeziness. 'Moving on to
miscellaneous additional matters: I've made several requests for new
costumes, equipment and supplies, which I've passed on to the Chief.'
He chewed his lip again. 'And if you haven't found them already, your
work schedules for the next four days are on your desks in the office.
Any further questions?' The only response was an embarrassed hush.
'In that case, I call this meeting to a close, and I'd like to remind

everyone of the next one – this Saturday, same time, same place.'

Ten seconds later all the documents had been cleared away, all the Agents had left, and I was sitting alone in an empty room.

Hanging around

In the time between my second encounter with Amy and her subsequent phone call, I discovered a darker side to Ralph.

In those two weeks I spent the days in research and the nights on stake-out. Amy had given me the registration number of Ralph's Mercedes and told me where he parked it: in the pay and display beneath the bus station square. From the safety of my second-hand Morris Minor I watched that car for thirteen evenings in a row, noting the minor scratches in paintwork, the immaculately clean plush leather interior, the electric sun roof, the tacky wheel trims. It was boring work. On one occasion he drove for a pizza, on another he visited a friend, on a third he went to the supermarket and bought a box of Ritz crackers. None of these is a criminal offence. He hired *The Long Good Friday* and a couple of porno flicks from the video shop, then paid a call to his mistress on a barge on the canal – compromising perhaps, but hardly blackmail material.

And then, on the ninth evening, just before midnight, I found exactly what I needed.

As usual, Ralph appeared at the bottom of the steps with his hands in his jeans pockets, whistling a tune so badly that I was sure I recognized it. He scanned his surroundings carefully before unlocking the Mercedes, revving the engine, and turning his CD-player on full-blast.

I followed him only when he had disappeared up the exit ramp, and tagged him at a safe distance as he drove over the canal bridge towards the railway station. He checked his mirror only once – when he stopped at a set of traffic lights – but I had spent many years acting invisible, and he didn't pay me any further attention. Just before he reached the railway viaduct, he turned left into an unlit side road and headed for an industrial estate consisting of around thirty single-storey warehouses. I drove by, doubled back, turned off the lights, and trailed him along the road in the shadow of the railway embankment.

He parked the Mercedes about half a mile further down, outside a depot distinguished from the rest by a huge, red number 9 fixed above the entrance. I immediately turned off my engine and waited. As Ralph climbed out I noticed another car to the left of the building: a Land Rover with the message LONDON ZOO – CONSERVATION IN ACTION printed on the side. I felt a powerful rush of adrenaline which left me momentarily light-headed; then a second wave, which sharpened my senses and alerted every muscle. I didn't think I was about to witness a discussion on animal welfare.

I took my camera, zoom lens and micro cassette recorder from the back seat and left the car. It was a cold, dry, autumn evening, with a clear sky and a full moon; after six hours of sitting on my backside, the icy air was refreshing. Apart from the distant hum of traffic, the deserted estate was as eerily silent as a ghost town. I hastened stiffly along the base of the embankment then quickly crossed the road to the depot, praying that whatever business Ralph had inside wouldn't be finished too soon. I needn't have worried: when it came to business, he liked to take his time.

The warehouse was shaped like a small aircraft hangar, with a sloping corrugated iron roof and walls of red brick. I could only see one entrance – a sturdy steel door with a plastic plaque attached – but I wasn't about to walk in and start taking photographs. Sitting in the car I had noticed three large windows in the roof, and after a brief scout around the building I found an access ladder which began about eight feet up the back wall and ran straight to the top. I reached upwards to the bottom rung, pulled myself slowly up, and began to climb. The metal was cold against my fingers, and my breath condensed in front of my face.

The angle of the roof was shallow, which was a relief. I have never been comfortable with heights, and even though the lowest edge was only thirty feet from the ground, the thought of falling made my guts ache. I felt much happier once I'd completed the precarious manoeuvre from the top of the ladder to the apex, and I could feel a firm sheet of corrugated iron beneath my body. Slowly and carefully, fearful that at any moment the roof would give way, I slid on my belly towards the nearest window.

As I peered through the glass at the scene below, a train roared by on the embankment. The sudden noise startled me: I slipped a couple of feet down the roof and almost lost my grip on the camera. When I looked up I saw seven carriages, stroboscopic streaks of yellow against the deep, black night.

My brief was not to find reasons but to gather evidence. I didn't know why Ralph had come to this deserted warehouse. I didn't know the name of his companion, or the precise nature of their relationship. And I had no idea why the two of them had brought a tall, thin, smartly dressed man to this place, tied a rope around his wrists, and suspended him from a roof beam.

I screwed on the zoom lens and took the first photograph: a picture of Amy's husband driving his fist into the man's stomach; the accomplice standing a couple of yards away, smiling; the victim's head bowed. The camera distanced me from the scene I was witnessing below. I told myself I had a job to do.

But as soon as I put the camera aside, I felt sickened – by the victim's pain, by Ralph's violence, by my own powerlessness. So I focused on the details of the scene, trying to maintain a sense of equilibrium, registering bald facts. A powerful overhead lamp described a circle of light on the warehouse floor, creating a small arena on the concrete. Ralph stood in the penumbra on the edge of the circle, smoking a cigarette. His accomplice, a much shorter and stockier man with a balding crown, orbited his captive, pausing only to gesticulate or to throw a punch. He held a bright green document wallet in his right hand which he tapped with his stubby forefinger and waved sporadically in the victim's face. Muffled echoes and the movements of his head told me that he was shouting, but I heard nothing clearly; my tape recorder was useless. At last I saw him toss the wallet aside, its contents scattering over the concrete like a sudden splash of white paint. Then he removed the man's shoes and socks, disappeared into the shadows, and returned with a heavy iron bar.

The second photograph: the accomplice swinging the iron bar against the naked feet of his captive; the victim arching his back and lifting his head in agony, revealing the gag taped over his mouth.

Ralph appeared inside the circle, laughing. I felt a rising tide of horror and humiliation and fear. I took the third picture a moment later: Ralph stubbing his cigarette on the back of his victim's left hand.

I took a dozen photographs, changed the film, and took a dozen more. I didn't allow myself to watch what was happening unless it was through the lens of the camera. I needed that barrier against the suffering.

I discovered that the human body was more vulnerable than I had previously believed. I observed that its limbs can be bent as easily as plastic, its bones can be broken with the simplest of tools, its teeth can be removed by the blow of a fist. I learned that it is so soft, a knife can cut it with no more effort than the downward motion of an arm; so sensitive that the slightest excess of heat will send it into spasms. Subjected to enough force and will, it can be manipulated in almost any way you choose. Its life can be drained by a single stroke.

And I could not keep the pain outside me. It was too strong. It flew upward from the victim, pushed through the window, seeped through the lens, found a crack in my shell, and crept insidiously into my soul.

Where it remains.

Three heads are better than one

Death was waiting for me on the landing outside the Stock Room, holding what appeared to be a sado-masochist's wildest dream: a long leather leash with three studded collars attached.

'What's that for?'

'Follow me,' he said mysteriously.

'Hold on,' I interrupted. 'I need to know something first.' He turned around, raised his eyebrows. 'Tell me honestly: how do I look?'

He frowned. 'Not great,' he said.

We descended the stairs, reversed direction down the narrow passage, then turned right towards my room. At the end of the corridor there was a wooden door with a stained-glass window, incorporating a grinning skull motif. It opened onto a short flight of steps and a long, overgrown back garden. The steps doubled back to the cellar, mirroring the arrangement at the front of the house, but we continued along a narrow gravel path through the grass, towards what appeared to be a small shed in the distance. Death stopped me at a tall iron gate, which divided the garden from the road leading to the meadow.

'Wait here,' he said. 'And whatever you do, don't scream and wave your arms. He gets a little excited.'

117

He shimmied around an oak tree and disappeared into the under-growth.

A dog barked. Then another. A third dog took issue with the first two, snarling, growling, snapping. I heard Death trying to pacify them. They continued to squabble violently.

The grass ahead rustled and bent forward, as if some powerful animal was pushing its way towards me.

An eerie silence followed.

I tested the gate. It didn't move.

'It's locked,' said Death.

I turned around to see him standing at the edge of the tall grass, brandishing a small, silver Yale key in his left hand. In his right, he held the leash – and at the end of the leash, was the most terrifying animal I had ever seen.

It was a dog, but bigger and stranger than any dog I'd encountered sneaking around the gardens of the corporate rich. It wasn't a breed I recognized, either. Its body was sleek, black and muscular like a Rottweiler, but its legs were powerful like those of a Dobermann, and its facial characteristics had all the dumb appeal of a Golden Retriever. It was half as large again as the tallest Irish wolfhound, and it pulled on the leash as a suspension bridge strains against the wound steel cables supporting it. But the oddest and most monstrous feature of all, the fact which I had been denying because it could not possibly be true, was also the most obvious:

It had three heads.

'This is Cerberus,' said Death, rubbing the animal's rump. 'And he's going to help us complete today's assignment. Aren't you, boy? Yes you *are*.' The dog raised its two outer heads to Death's outstretched hand and revealed a pair of slobbering red tongues dangling between thick black lips. The third head studied me and growled; then barked loudly. 'Ignore him. He's soft as a kitten inside. Watch this.'

As if he had read my mind and selected the Thing-I-Didn't-Want-To-Happen-Next, Death detached the leash from the collars and released his pet. I acted like a corpse, and froze. The dog scampered towards me, crashed into my legs and rebounded against the gate; it scurried back towards the grass, claws scraping on the gravel, then switched course in mid-air and bounced first against the tree and then against the wall, like a crazed pinball. Its chaotic path ended at Death's feet, where it sat obediently, scaly tail thrashing against an exposed root, heads panting in syncopated time, tongues pulsating like fantastic red jellies. Death reattached the lead and rubbed each skull in turn.

'He used to belong to Hades – a long time ago. More recently, he's been Skirmish's responsibility. That's *right*, isn't it boy? Skirmish. *Skirmish*.' The dog grinned three times over, then resumed the slobberfest.

'And how is he – *it* – supposed to help?'

'Cerberus is but a small part of the puzzle,' Death explained, with rare affection. 'There are many other parts but his role is perhaps the most vital.' All three heads turned and barked.

As is often the case with people who can't think of a sensible response to an inane statement – and zombies are as guilty of this as anyone – I opened my mouth without thinking.

'Don't you think Cerberus is a stupid name for a dog?'

Cerberus, three jaws slack, turned around and slobbered.

'Look after him for a minute.'

A light rain began to fall. Death handed me the leash and unlocked the gate. The hellhound took my criticism of his name personally, straining against the leather and choking on his collars in a futile attempt to escape. As we left the garden and walked around the side of the house the drizzle grew heavier, and he pulled even harder. By the time we reached the cars at the front, big soaking drops were splashing on the pavement, Cerberus was writhing madly, and my arms felt as if they were being yanked from their sockets.

'He doesn't like the rain,' Death explained. He opened the Metro's boot, removed the parcel shelf and flattened the back seat. 'Here, boy.' To my relief he took the leash and encouraged the dog into the car. Once inside it calmed a little, reverting to its dual state of vapid curiosity and spittle production. He gave it a final pat on its huge panting belly before closing the door.

Death suggested I get in, then skipped up the steps to the front entrance and disappeared inside. I opened the passenger door slowly and sat down, watching the three sets of predatory teeth nervously. The outer heads studied me eagerly, happy to drool and grin without prompting; the middle one evidently had some kind of attitude problem. It kept its jaws firmly shut, but exposed its teeth and gums through curled lips, snarling quietly but menacingly. It felt like half an hour before Death returned wearing his herringbone overcoat and carrying a cassette box. He settled into the driver's seat and slipped a tape into the cassette player. When he turned the ignition, some mournful classical tune I didn't recognize pounded through the speakers.

'It's the finale from *Don Giovanni*,' he shouted, putting the car into reverse. 'The moment when he descends into hell. Cerberus loves it.'

I nodded and turned to the front. Almost immediately, two long, wet tongues began to lick the back of my neck.

Death drove calmly and carefully, explaining that he *didn't want to upset the dog*. He was transformed into a model motorist, driving just within the speed limit, stopping at junctions, signalling at every turn. He even waved pleasantly at an elderly couple on a zebra crossing – but he could simply have been greeting them in advance of an imminent meeting.

We drove away from the town centre, crossing over the canal and passing under the railway bridge before turning onto a minor residential road. Death parked at the end, opposite a large municipal cemetery, and left the windscreen wipers running. He turned off the music then spent a couple of minutes checking his watch and verifying that there was no-one else in the vicinity. At last he opened the door and a cool blast of air filled the car. Cerberus shuffled across to the passenger side, the head nearest to the incoming rain whimpering pathetically.

'What now?'

'See that building across the road?' He pointed to a glass-fronted shop which looked like a cross between a stone mason's and a massage parlour. I could just distinguish, in florid script above the door, the title *Funeral Director*, but the rain obscured the name of its owner. 'That's where he works. But first, we're paying a visit to the cemetery.'

He climbed out, pushed the seat back and pulled on Cerberus' leash. The dog resisted, but Death was stubborn and soothing by turns: claws scraping, jaws snapping, necks twisting and turning, it was finally dragged onto the tarmac. I unlocked my door and followed the pair of them across the road towards the cemetery. The animal was almost uncontrollable, leaping against Death's legs, licking his hands, chewing on his coat, pulling ahead, racing behind, turning around, barking, growling, slavering, grinning.

'He's a little distressed,' said Death as we reached the cemetery gates. 'Apart from the rain, which always irritates him, we haven't fed him for a couple of days. In fact, he'd probably eat anything right now – except for poppy and honey cake, of course.' At the mention of this particular item of home baking, Cerberus growled and barked with all three heads.

'What's wrong with . . .' I stopped myself. 'That type of cake?'

'Didn't you learn *anything* when you were alive?' He looked incredulous. 'Cerberus had three mortal enemies before we adopted him.

Listen . . .' He leaned over and whispered the facts in my ear, so that the dog wouldn't lapse into a frenzy. He explained how a muscle-head called Hercules had humiliated the poor animal by dragging him from the Underworld and letting him find his own way back; how some half-wit called Orpheus had lulled him to sleep with a lyre, causing him to forfeit his food rations for a week; and how some shifty bird called Sibyl had fed him on the aforementioned cake and knocked him unconscious. Any mention of these names – or the merest whiff of poppies or honey – had him foaming at the mouths.

'Normally,' he continued, 'I wouldn't subject him to this kind of treatment. But for today's purposes it's essential that he's hungry, and that it rains. Otherwise the plan won't work.'

And the rain fell. Water ran into my eyes, dripped into the pockets of my jacket, drenched my T-shirt, penetrated my spangled trousers, soaked my slip-on shoes and saturated my socks. I had forgotten how wonderful it could feel, how astonishingly different individual experiences could be.

Death appeared equally content in his long coat, happy to dispense advice as it suited him.

'Keep back,' he said. 'Once we get inside, I'm releasing him.'

We passed through the gate into the cemetery. Ahead and to the left, a path ascended through a clump of trees to the graveyard; to the right was a modern, red brick church with a small lawn and a rash of ivy spreading over the porch. It didn't feel like home – my real home was a coffin somewhere north-east of here, and the thick, warm walls of earth surrounding it – but I did give a fleeting thought to the bodies buried in front of us, out of the rain. I wondered what they were saying to each other, what the local news was. And I experienced a moment of nostalgia, a fleeting yearning to return.

It disappeared as Death closed the gate behind us. He walked a few yards ahead then unfastened the leash. I expected the dog to bound into the distance like an escaped tiger, but it sat still, red tongues dangling.

'Go on, boy,' Death encouraged it. 'Go *on*.'

Cerberus sniffed at the gravel car park.

Death crouched down next to the dog, stroked its head and whispered something into its ear. It grinned with all three jaws and raced away up the hill.

'What did you say to it?'

'Woof. Woof woof *woof*. Woof woof,' said Death.

We left the cemetery and crossed the road to the funeral parlour, which occupied two houses at the end of a long terrace. A collection of rough stone blocks and carved headstones lay in the paved front gardens, with a few crude tags indicating prices and possible inscriptions. The left-hand building was dominated by a large plate-glass window, through which I dimly saw a display of coffins, a few of them as opulent as the one I'd been buried in. On the right, the house front was relatively normal, with a living room, a kitchen and a couple of windows upstairs. The narrow concrete path leading to the front door on this side was stained with a thick and greasy patch of engine oil, in which heavy drops of rain were creating multicoloured eddies.

'Looks like he's a home mechanic,' I observed.

'*He* isn't,' Death replied. 'But his neighbours are.' He rapped his knuckle against a green water-butt to the left of the path. 'Full. That's good.' He walked to the front door, turned around and scanned the horizon. 'No obstacles, no people. *Very* good.'

'What happens now?'

'We go inside.'

In the distance, Cerberus barked.

Death produced a ring of skeleton keys from his overcoat pocket, selected one, unlocked the door – and noticed my hesitation.

'It's fine. He's not due back for another five minutes.'

I followed him in. A long, narrow hallway ran the length of the house. Immediately to our right was a small kitchen, to our left a flight of stairs.

'Come and look at this.'

I went into the kitchen where Death was bending over the hob and sniffing. 'It's gas, just as the Chief said it would be. And there's a telephone in the hall. Did you see it? There should be another one upstairs.' He pressed his heel into the linoleum, about a yard away from the sink. 'The floorboards are soft here. Very soft. A little pressure and they'll give way. We shouldn't need them, of course – but if Plan A fails . . .' He looked up. 'And they're directly below the smoke alarm.' He clapped his hands, pleased by the preparation even if the execution itself held little appeal. 'I think it's going to work.'

'What's he like?' I interrupted.

'Who?'

'Our client.'

He paused. 'Short, bald, glasses—'

'No, I mean: what's he like *inside*?'

'All I know is what I read in the Life File this morning. He's forty-nine years old. He's an undertaker.'

'Nothing else?'

'Nothing very relevant. He's gloomy, a loner, an outsider. He smokes thirty cigarettes a day. He's poor company, on the whole. And he's accident prone – which is why we're here.'

'What kind of accidents?'

'Oh, dozens of them. Hundreds, maybe.' He puffed out his cheeks. 'For example, he wears glasses because he suffered from trachoma as a child. It's extremely rare in this climate, but he managed to catch it. *Very* bad luck. Between the ages of three and fifteen he fell and cut his head nine times. You'd think he was cursed. He's broken his left arm three times, his right arm once, and both legs twice. He's been knocked down by cars on six separate occasions. He's caught three colds every winter for the past forty years. But that's not the end of it. He was once struck by lightning twice in the same evening, and on his way to the hospital the ambulance was hit by a truck. Yesterday morning he narrowly missed being electrocuted in his bath. The first time he went ice skating he broke his nose. He was dropped on his head as a baby.' He sighed. 'The list goes on and on.'

I looked through the kitchen window. A small, bald man in a funereal suit slowly approached the house from the adjoining street. He was carrying two shopping bags filled with food. He rolled along the pavement like a huge, sad, marble.

'Is that him?'

Death glanced through the window and nodded.

'Shouldn't we find somewhere to hide?'

He shook his head. 'He's extremely short-sighted. The Chief said if we stay at this end of the kitchen, he won't even notice us. I'll believe *that* when I see it.'

In the couple of minutes before his arrival, Death told me that our client's major concern was whether or not he had led a good or a bad life to this point. Specifically, he only had three concrete reasons for considering himself good:

He experienced sporadic bouts of affection towards strangers. Sometimes this resulted in resentment and rejection, but mostly it made him feel happy to be alive.

His professional life was a success. He always paid due respect to the solemnity, formality and ritual of burial, and was often thanked by relatives of the deceased for his care and attention.

As an adult, he had never killed anything.

Against this, there were five reasons why he considered himself to be truly evil:

As a child, he had separated frogs from their legs, flies from their wings, ants from their heads, fish from their fins; and newts, gerbils, tadpoles, rabbits and cats from their tails.

He drank, smoked, gambled and ate too much.

He had used what he called the *f-word* as a limited-strike weapon against the following people: his mother and father, his aunts and uncles, both of his friends, his landlord, his underlings, people in the street, churchmen, door-to-door salesmen, tramps, farmers, bankers, lawyers, and almost everyone who appeared on television. He had also once severely abused a rock that had caused him to stumble, on a walk with a woman he admired.

He was notoriously avaricious. He had only ever bought a drink for his colleagues on one occasion, and that was due to a verbal misunderstanding. He often sat in his car in public car parks to use up the time remaining on his ticket. He refused to give money to any charity. Unless he was indulging his vices, he withdrew a maximum of ten pounds from cash tills.

He lied often and without good cause.

'And this rather minor Good-to-Evil Ratio of 3:5', Death continued, 'has been enough to convince him that he leads a life of sin second only to Satan. As a result, he regards his accidents as just punishment.'

Our client ambled along the path to the front door, narrowly avoiding the oil patch but bouncing off the water-butt. The rain had stopped but his suit still glistened and steamed, and his glasses were spotted with raindrops. He put down his shopping bags and searched for his keys. He found the front-door key but dropped the whole bunch as he lifted it to the lock. They landed an inch away from the drain. Trying to pick them up he edged them closer to the grate. Realizing that disaster was about to strike, he carefully plucked the keys from their precarious resting-place and cautiously opened the front door. He tripped as he entered the house.

'There are other ratios you might be interested in,' Death continued. 'For instance, the ratio of the dead to the living is approximately 1:1. The ratio of people who lose their keys down a drain after dropping them to those who don't is 1:343. The ratio of clients who die as a result of an incredible sequence of unfortunate accidents to those who die from natural causes is 1:2401.'

The ratio of stories written by the living to those written by the undead is approximately 10,000,000:1. However, the advantage this tale has over its rivals shouldn't be underestimated.

It's all true.

The unluckiest man in the world

He was an accident waiting to happen.

He stumbled through the front door and swayed into the kitchen. Unbalanced by the shopping he narrowly avoided a collision with an open drawer, but managed to swing the bags high into the air and onto the work surface. Humming quietly to himself, he took a sheet of kitchen roll and cleaned his glasses. Replacing them on his face, the earpiece slipped through his fingers and the glasses fell to the floor, cracking the left lens.

'Bugger sodding hell.'

Undeterred, he removed a frying pan from a cupboard beneath the sink, poured oil into it and turned on the gas. The gas escaped as he searched for matches: I heard the hiss, smelled its sweetness. He rummaged through three drawers, looked on the dresser, lifted up a newspaper, tapped his chin, checked his jacket pockets. The gas escaped. He peered into a bread bin, looked vacantly at a couple of shelves, explored a recess by the washing machine, puffed out his cheeks, inspected a plant pot. The gas escaped. He searched the herb rack, examined the draining board, patted his trousers, tapped his teeth, studied the microwave oven. The gas escaped.

He turned off the gas.

His face was illuminated by a sudden recollection. He burrowed into the nearest shopping bag and removed a box of Swan Vestas. He struck a match, took it to the hob, turned on the gas and created a ring of cool blue flame. The oil began to heat. He removed a long string of sausages from the second bag and placed it on the work surface, then grabbed the first bag and carried it to the fridge.

As he reached the fridge, he snagged the bag on one of the open drawers. Attempting to remove it, he tore a hole in the plastic. Frustrated, he pulled harder. The handle snapped.

The contents fell to the floor.

Eggs, cracked; bacon, soiled; milk, spilled. Broken glass from a jar of honey. Honey, spreading.

'Christ.'

He bent down to clean up the mess and banged his forehead on the open drawer.

'Hell*fire*.'

He leaned backwards and slipped on the milk and honey. Trying to soften his fall he caught his outstretched fingers on the broken glass. His other hand landed on the only unbroken egg.

'Shit shit *shit*!'

He disappeared from the room nursing his wounds, his suit smeared with dairy produce. I heard him running up the stairs.

He hadn't turned towards us once.

'He's gone for a bandage,' Death explained. 'I'm afraid we have to turn the heat up on the oil before he comes back.'

'Isn't that interfering?'

'Of course it's interfering. 'We *have* to interfere.'

'How can you just accept that?'

'I have no choice.'

He shrugged, and twisted the knob full on. The fat in the frying pan began to smoke.

Five minutes later our client wandered casually downstairs, his hand bandaged, his clothes changed. He was wearing black tracksuit trousers, a black sweatshirt and black sneakers with hooks instead of eyes. The laces were undone.

As he crossed the threshold into the kitchen the snakes of smoke rising from the pan activated the smoke alarm.

His curses were nullified by the shrill, repeating beep.

He ran into the hallway and returned almost immediately with a stool, placing it directly beneath the alarm. He turned off the heat, scrambled onto the chair, tutted, hopped off again, grabbed a screwdriver from the open drawer and climbed back on. Leaning backwards, he removed the screws from the alarm casing, let the plastic fall into his hand and slowly levered the battery free from its housing.

The beeping stopped. He sighed with relief and tried to turn around.

He had been standing on his laces.

He stumbled, pitched backwards towards the cooker, struck the frying pan handle with the back of his head and landed roughly on his buttocks. The fall knocked the wind from him. The frying pan, disturbed by the collision, flipped over and emptied hot smoking fat onto his bald crown.

He screamed, leapt to his feet and raced for the doorway. His shoelaces were flapping – but, miraculously, he didn't trip.

'Follow him,' said Death. 'Intervene if you have to. But be careful.'

I felt sorry for our client. It's true that he was about to enter a more comfortable stage of existence, and he would find it much easier to fall into the coffin than to climb out of it – but I couldn't help myself. I pursued him through the front door, ensuring I was behind him at all times, and if there was some hope within me that his ordeal would end soon, I tried not to let it interfere with my work. I simply watched as he swerved right, just missed the pool of black engine oil, and groped blindly for the water-butt.

And I fought hard against the urge to guide him.

His fingers thrashed against the edge. He seized the rim with both hands and plunged his stinging skull into the cold water. He shook his head wildly. The water churned and splashed onto a nearby tomb-stone. He pulled himself free and rapidly swallowed three lungfuls of air. His skin was spotted with small, pink blemishes, and his glasses were missing. I stepped quietly around him. He rubbed his eyes and staggered back towards the house.

'Christ *Jesus*.'

Still groggy from his encounter with the hot fat and myopic from losing his spectacles, he stepped on the oil patch, lost his grip, slipped sideways and landed heavily on his left arm. The oil soaked into his sweatshirt.

He groaned and raised himself upright. I followed him as he shuffled through the front door and back into the kitchen.

He was holding his arm and whining miserably.

He gazed blindly at the chaos on the kitchen floor and cursed everyone he had ever known; then, calming himself, he opened a drawer by the fridge and removed a half-empty pack of cigarettes. He slipped one into his mouth, located the matchbox, withdrew a match, struck it, and lit the cigarette. He inhaled and surveyed the destruction surrounding him, cursing again. He covered his eyes with his hands, forgot that he was holding the match and singed his right eyebrow. He yelled and dropped the match. The lit cigarette, freed by his scream, fell onto his left arm.

The oil-soaked sleeve slowly, but inevitably, caught fire.

He ran from the kitchen again and repeated his flight to the water-butt. His arm blazed like a torch; the flames lapped at his head, licked his body, caressed him. Death watched him escape, grabbed the matches, opened the cupboard beneath the sink and tossed the box into the bin.

I followed the man outside again. His arm was immersed up to the shoulder in the water-butt, his face contorted with pain and relief. His whole body shivered with fear, with cold. I felt a powerful urge to comfort him, as my mother had once comforted me when I was ill. But my duty dictated otherwise.

When we returned to the kitchen, Death had disappeared. Our client was weary. He sat down on the stool from which he had fallen only a few minutes earlier and rested his feet in the spreading pool of milk, eggs, honey and fat. Disgusted with his bad luck, he stripped off his sweatshirt, threw it aside and began to wash his arms, hands and head in the sink.

Groping for the tea towel to dry his face, he made three fatal mistakes:

He left the tap running.

He accidentally turned the gas on.

He knocked the long string of sausages to the floor.

And the phone rang.

'Who the fuck is that?' he wailed.

I watched him from the kitchen doorway.

'Who is it . . . ? Is anyone there . . . ? Look, if this is your idea of a joke you've picked the wrong fucking time. Really . . . I'm putting the phone down in five seconds . . . Four, three, two—'

He slammed down the receiver and returned to the kitchen. The smell of gas was already strong. He failed to notice it, his attention diverted by the running tap. He rushed over to turn it off before the water overflowed, slipping slightly in the pool of liquid food, and catching the hooks of his untied right shoe in the string of sausages.

The sausages held fast to his foot and followed him until his death.

The phone rang again.

'For fuck's *sake*—'

The man and his trailing string of sausages hobbled to the phone together.

'If it's *you* again . . . Oh . . . *Hello* . . . No, I just thought you were— No, no problem . . . Yes . . . Uh-huh . . . Fifty quid on the three-thirty? Yes, of course . . . No, nothing . . . I've just had an accident, that's all . . . Yes . . . Hold on, I think I can smell gas—'

He hobbled back to the kitchen, the sausages thrashing in his wake like an enraged viper. He turned off the gas, left the kitchen door ajar and threw open the front door to assist ventilation.

On the other side of the front door was Cerberus the dog.

Cerberus was hungry. He liked sausages.

Three red tongues dripped slobber.

Death descended the stairs in time to see his pet attacking a string of pork sausages with a small, fat, screaming man attached.

'Who rang the second time?' he asked.

'I don't know,' I replied. 'Who rang the first?'

He allowed himself a melancholy smile.

'Who the hell are you?' Our client was staring at both of us with a mixture of panic and terror. He shook his leg violently in a vain attempt to free his foot from the dog's three sets of tightly clamped jaws.

'I am Death,' said Death, offering his hand.

The man fled across the road, wailing. Cerberus followed him, growling ominously, signalling his determination to hold on. The meat, the innocent party in all of this, was trapped between the unlaced shoe and the dog's slavering maws.

'Looks like rain again,' Death observed. It was more of a summer shower, droplets spattering the gravel car park inside the cemetery gates, spraying our client's battered head and his monstrous assailant alike, sprinkling the freshly mown grass, filling the shimmering air with thousands of glittering lights.

At the cost of a sausage the man had finally freed himself from the dog's death-grip and was streaking up the slope towards the grave-yard. Cerberus decided that this was inadequate reward for his efforts and pursued him vigorously; they met again by a tomb at the summit. The leg-shaking and growling dance continued: a whirling, shuddering ritual punctuated by inhuman shrieks. We trailed them slowly in the rain.

'Does he have to suffer so much?' I asked.

'I don't make the rules,' said Death. 'It's the way things are.'

'But this could have ended much earlier.'

He turned aside. 'He's just unlucky, that's all.'

The trio of client, sausages and hellhound jigged and jerked and growled and cursed along the brow of the hill. A couple of times they retreated together and circled around us like planets caught in the gravity of twin suns; then, as if freed from our attraction, they sped off into space, chaotic bodies in constant motion. Death maintained a pensive silence until he saw that the man was pirouetting close to a fresh grave.

'It's time,' he said.

The open grave had no headstone, but a spade rested on the lip. Cerberus' growls deepened as he employed one final, canine scheme to seize the sausages: he shook his heads vigorously from side to side. The strength of the movement unbalanced his opponent, who stumbled backwards towards the gaping hole in the earth. The excavated soil was greasy with rain.

He slipped.

He regained his balance by taking a step back.

He tripped over the spade and tumbled earthwards, twisting.

But there was no earth to support him – only a black pit six feet deep. He caught his head on the walls of the grave as he fell. His body landed with a soft squelch, spraying water out of the hole and onto his nemesis, the dog.

Cerberus watched from the graveside, unperturbed. A pink string of pork sausages hung from his grinning mouths.

'He slips, he trips, he dives, he dips,' Death observed gloomily, patting the middle of the dog's three heads. We perched, vulture-like, on the edge of the hole. Our client lay face down in the mud below, apparently unconscious.

'Is he dead?' I asked.

'Soon. He's drowning.'

Cerberus guzzled two sausages in quick succession. Death teased the animal by threatening to remove the rest. Without knowing why, I buried my face in my hands.

The apartment

Amy rang ten days after our second meeting, and arranged for me to visit her the following Wednesday afternoon. This was about three weeks after the first phone call. Her apartment was located in the block directly above the bus station café where our initial discussions had taken place. More significantly, considering what was to happen a month later, it was the penthouse suite.

In the intervening period I hadn't been able to stop thinking about her, with one memory in particular returning again and again:

It's snowing. We are walking by a river at the northern end of a meadow, on the fringes of a dark wood. Black trees burst from the white ground like the spikes inside an iron maiden. The snow is shallow and crisp underfoot, untrodden, untouched. Golden evening light dazzles in the gaps between the trunks, sparkles on the ice in the swollen river.

'I just can't see how it's going to work,' she says. 'It doesn't *feel* right. Not any more.'

'How is it supposed to feel?' I reply.

'Better than this.'

'We can change it.'

'That's not what I want.'

Recently, we have begun to speak in code, avoiding words which might reveal precisely how we feel. At first it was a game, but the game has grown beyond our control and is smothering us.

'What *do* you want?' I ask her.

'Anything but this.'

We are on the edge of a dark wood by a swollen river. Her sharp features are frozen there in an expression of despair. Her teeth chatter, briefly, comically. Her black hair falls in front of her eyes and she brushes it aside.

'*Anything.*'

Her black hair falls, and she brushes it aside.

She is young. She has medium-length hair the colour of a raven's wing. She has a long, pointed nose that once belonged to a witch in a fairy tale, thin red lips open like a knife-cut, brown eyes piercing me, daring me to answer. But I turn around, and see a hole in the trees ahead where the snow rises in small drifts – and beyond it, a bridge. We need to return home and forget, but the path we are about to take will lead us back to the Jericho Café, where we will have a discussion that leads to our separation.

And I'm still standing there now, frozen in time, watching again as her black hair falls across her face. She was twenty-one; we had lived together for twenty-eight months.

She was beautiful in the snow.

I wondered how she had come from that moment to this; more specifically, what had induced her to marry Ralph. She was an only child from a poor family, but poverty and solitude are as much prerequisites to a lifetime commitment as they are to a career in ballroom dancing. I suppose I wasn't surprised she'd ended up with a criminal: when she lived with me the uniform had a certain appeal, and it's not so hard to make the switch to the other side of the law. But perhaps she never allowed herself to dwell on what he did. Perhaps he had been the wild lover who also sent her roses, the man who wanted children but respected her independence, the caring, sensitive type who knew exactly when to behave like a shit.

I had been none of these things. During our years together I had been little more than a clown. I had often made jokes to disguise my true feelings, laughed when I should have remained silent.

I rang the buzzer, Amy replied with an ambiguous 'Is that you?', and I struggled with my equipment up fourteen flights of stairs to the seventh floor. I had a phobia about lifts. Amy met me at the door, smartly dressed as usual, and explained quickly that she only had half an hour to spare.

The apartment was divided into seven areas. The short hallway led into a large, square living room, furnished in what the gossip magazines used to describe as *palatial elegance*, but which was equally identifiable as *criminal ostentation*. The remaining areas were satellites of the main living space. In clockwise order from the door: a coral bathroom decorated with a shell design, a narrow stone balcony overlooking the square, a round tower with a skylight and a collection of videos housed on a wide, free-standing bookshelf, a cramped kitchen and dining area, and a double bedroom with a four-poster. A thick black carpet clung to the floor throughout, like a stray oil slick.

Amy spoke rapidly, nervously, pacing the living room like a trapped animal, checking that everything was safe, seeking reassurances that Ralph wouldn't find out, that I was being careful. At length she led me into the bedroom and pointed to the dressing table.

'He hardly ever goes near it. But I've taken some things out in the last couple of weeks so he won't get suspicious.'

I installed the miniature camera in a drawer from which she had removed the handle. The hole provided just enough space for the lens, and the rest of the drawer was large enough to accommodate the recording equipment. When I'd finished, and checked twice that everything worked, I gave her my usual speech.

'It won't be perfect, but it should do it. Give me a call when you're ready to hand it back. Or stick the video in the post.'

'What do I have to do?'

'Just switch it on.' I showed her the button. 'When you feel it's necessary.'

Looking around the room, at its gaudy opulence; watching her folding her arms, trying to remain in control; listening to the fear in her voice as she thanked me and hurried me through the front door, two questions still remained.

What did she want from me?

And what did *I* want?

Cactus ex machina

We ate a very late, and very long, lunch at an Indian restaurant opposite the railway station. A vegetarian curry for me, a range of meat dishes for Death – and I passed my first stool since resurrection. It was early evening when we returned to the car, and it had stopped raining. Cerberus was still sleeping peacefully on the back seat where we had left him, and he didn't stir until, back at the Agency, Death dragged him from the boot and escorted him to the kennel.

I excused myself and retired to my room – where I was startled by noises I hadn't heard since I was alive.

I paused, then knocked hesitantly on the door.

'Who is it?'

'The apprentice.'

'Come in.'

The curtains were drawn against the evening sun, but I saw Skirmish slumped on the Barca lounger, watching a television programme I vaguely remembered. This was the source of the strange sounds.

'Inspector Morse,' he explained, without taking his eyes off the screen. 'My favourite episode. The one where the driving instructor goes bananas.'

I hopped across his line of sight and sat on the edge of the lower bunk. I couldn't claim to know the particular episode he was referring to, or to be as interested in it as he was, but I maintained a respectful silence for the next two hours until the programme finished. Quite coincidentally, this idle time also revealed the answer to a question I'd been pondering since Monday morning. As I watched, I began to recognize landmarks from the last three days, places I had visited, even the cemetery where I was buried; and long before one of the characters mentioned the name of the city, I remembered, at last, where I was. Oxford.

This was a relief, but there were more pressing questions. In particular, I still wanted to know what had happened to Hades. As the closing credits rolled I wandered over to the table by the rear window to collect my thoughts. Skirmish switched off the television and yawned. I turned around, and was just about to speak when Pestilence's remedy launched its final and most vicious assault.

I convulsed, tripped against the table leg, lurched forward, tried to steady myself, lost my balance completely, and fell against the cactus in the corner.

How unlucky can you get?

THURSDAY

DEATH BY MACHINES

Have brain, will travel

Thursday's outfit:

The usual sparkling suit and white slip-ons, blue forget-me-not boxer shorts, sea-blue socks embroidered with smiling crayfish, and a sky blue T-shirt bearing the enigmatic if rather bland statement: DO NOT DISTURB. I watched myself dress in the mirror on the back of the wardrobe door, and felt comfortable with my new identity.

I was the coolest zombie in town.

The dining room was crowded. All the Agents were present, and their miscellaneous breakfasts blanketed the table like multicoloured pond weed. The only free place was a low stool in the far corner where, after avoiding a collision with Skirmish on one of his frequent trips to the kitchen, I sat down.

'How's the cactus?' Pestilence asked.

'Better than I am,' I replied.

Skirmish disappeared through the saloon doors and returned with a bowl of cereal and some fruit for me, before resuming his assault on a natural organic yoghurt. He had been equally helpful the previous night, spending almost an hour patiently removing over a hundred spines with a pair of tweezers. I had passed the rest of the evening in the bath, soothing the discomfort, removing the variety of cadaverous odours I'd acquired in the past couple of days, and contemplating the suitability of accidental death. If nothing else, the episode with the cactus had confirmed my opinion: should my apprenticeship end in failure, I would not be slipping and stumbling my way back to the grave. As curtain calls go, it was too spontaneous, too uncontrollable.

'How's the bruise?' Death asked Pestilence.

'I told you yesterday.'

'Did you?'

'In the meeting.'

'Ah.'

Silence.

'So how is it *now*?' War shouted, spitting prosciutto.

'Smaller,' Pestilence replied.

'Eh?'

'SMALLER.'

'Hmm.'

Silence.

'Where d'you go from here?' Famine continued.

'I try again,' Pestilence answered.

'New ideas?'

'Yes.'

'Right.'

Silence.

Sitting there, chewing on a banana, watching my employers, I had an unusually complex thought for a zombie. I wasn't sure what the thought meant, or even if it was interesting, but this is what my brain was telling me:

The Agents' conversation was like many I'd had when I was dead. It functioned like a smooth, efficient machine: the words created a simple mechanical rhythm and worked tirelessly to produce useful output from minimum input. It is the same in the coffin. To a cadaver, words mean precisely what they say; if they didn't, the explanations would last until Judgement Day. So: a *shell* is a hard outer layer protecting a vulnerable core. A *machine* is an apparatus using mechanical power to drive movable parts. A *coffin* is six walls of wood dividing the dead from the soil. There is no room for metaphor or misunderstanding.

Corpses take things at face value. This is why they are never invited to parties.

'What's on your agenda today?' Famine asked me.

We're off to the fairground,' Death answered with forced joviality. 'In *disguise.'*

'Lucky buggers,' War interrupted. 'Me and Skirmish are spending tonight doing PR in the city centre. Knife-fights, minor riots, that kind of crap.' He scanned the table for sympathy. 'Obviously, I'd rather be in at the sharp end.'

'Obviously,' Famine agreed.

'But if the Chief says there are no flashpoints, there are no flashpoints.'

'It's beyond our control,' Pestilence reassured him.

'It drives me 'cking mad sometimes.'

'Nothing you can do,' said Death.

When I lived with Amy, I hadn't yet grown a hard outer covering. Affection burst out of me like water from a spring. I told her I loved her on countless occasions, and meant it. This is more than I can claim for the relationships which eventually followed.

After she left, I surrounded myself with a carapace which shielded me from intimate personal contact with other human beings. If I met a stranger, I withdrew into it; if I met a potential lover, I stuck out my head. But I never abandoned the shell completely, because I didn't want anyone to see the pink and quivering thing which inhabited it. The only trouble was, even if I *wanted* to expose my deepest self, the shell prevented me.

With one exception.

On the night I died, I was standing in the bedroom of Amy's apartment, delaying my exit because I wanted to be with her so desperately for just one more second. Without warning, my shell cracked open.

'I love you,' I said.

'Don't be ridiculous,' she replied.

Pestilence spat out a gobbet of something that could have been flesh, fruit, cereal, pulse, vegetable or dairy product. Its true identity was masked by a thin film of greenish mould darkened by saliva.

'Something wrong?' asked Skirmish innocently.

'This food,' he grimaced, 'it's . . . *fresh*.' He retrieved further remnants of breakfast from his teeth and flicked them onto his plate, shaking his head. 'Are you trying to poison me?'

Skirmish's denial and Pestilence's repeated accusations sparked a squabble which continued until Death stood up, beckoned me with a long white finger, and led me to the office.

'I'd like you to do me a favour,' he said. 'I've got a ton of paperwork to catch up on and we need to collate some information before tonight.' I nodded. 'I don't have the time to do it myself, so if you could read up on a couple of files—'

'Which ones?'

'The Life File, naturally . . .' He rummaged through his papers for a note on which he had scribbled the name of today's client, then handed it to me. 'And Machines. Mechanical Accidents, specifically. Procedural details, that kind of thing. I can remember most of it but I'll need you to fill in any gaps.'

'Where can I find them?'

'I think they've already been transferred to the Chief's office on the second floor. Here's the key.' I was about to leave, when he added in a whisper, 'One more thing. You asked me about Hades the other night . . . All I can say is – watch your back when War's around.'

Where's the Chief?

I opened the white door on the first-floor landing to find the cast-iron spiral staircase I'd seen yesterday. It coiled upwards into darkness. I groped along the wall to the right of the doorway, found a timer switch and pressed the button. Weak light from the head of the stairwell glimmered through the helix of black steps. I climbed the spiral slowly, turning through two revolutions, conscious of the sharp sound of each footfall. The naked bulb at the top swayed slightly, silently, and cast a dim glow on a low, wooden door ahead.

I knocked lightly.

And waited.

And waited.

There was no response so I knocked again, firmly. I waited as a corpse waits: quietly, patiently, passively. When I was convinced there would be no reply, I turned the handle, unlocked the door and stepped inside.

The Chief's office was a long, low attic framed by stunted walls and sloping roofs. Two dormer windows opposite the door provided the only source of natural light. The room was empty apart from a writing desk, several armchairs and (curiously) a tombola drum. Everything – furniture, walls and carpet – was white.

On the writing desk a mass of plain paper lay scattered, along with a small computer and laser printer, both switched off. Behind the desk was a fireplace, still smouldering from a recent fire. Nearby was a column of files, similar to the documents I'd seen in Archives on the ground floor. There were no other signs of life: no filing cabinets carelessly left open, no dog-eared books, no food, no drink.

The column contained about fifty rectangular document wallets, all the same shade of grey. I removed each one carefully, searching for any

147

reference to the subject or name Death had given me. Almost immediately, I discovered a wallet marked *Mechanical Accidents*, a heavyweight collection of files tied together with string. I spent two hours reading and trying to memorize every sheet, increasingly conscious that the Chief might return at any moment. At first I was simply curious to know how he might look. But the idea possessed me, and made me ever more nervous, until I was so afraid and resentful of the authority he wielded that my hands shook and I could no longer concentrate on anything but the fear of waiting.

But the Chief never showed up – and my scrutiny of the files yielded only a single passage devoted to procedure:

PROCEDURAL RECOMMENDATION:

To ensure successful execution, the client must be followed at all times. The recommended pursuit window is between 2.1m and 9.8m. Intervention, which should be kept to a minimum, will take place at the Agent's discretion.

I continued the search. Sunlight funnelled through the windows, a transparent tunnel of heat and dust terminating in a small white rectangle on the carpet by the desk. Apart from the sporadic creaks and sighs of slow-burning wood in the fireplace, the room was silent. And I was completely alone.

The Life File lay two-thirds of the way down the column and consisted of one hundred and twenty-six pages of detailed information. I discovered the average length of our client's facial hair (4.6cm), the distance from the bottom of his right earlobe to the dimple on his chin (12.3cm), the size of his left thumbnail (1.08cm × 1.2cm), the length of his penis erect (14.9cm) and relaxed (4.4cm), the average number of freckles per square centimetre on his right shoulder (7); and so on. The file also included data I could make no sense of: the colour of his skin (49), the shape of his head (2677), his behaviour pattern

(823543), his body type (343). Then there were pages of psychological profile, life history, character analysis, intelligence assessment; and numerical evaluations of abstract concepts such as love, hatred, courage and cowardice.

After a while I tossed it aside in frustration.

My own life can be mapped out in numbers, too.

I had nine lovers in all. The longest relationship I had, with Amy, lasted for thirty-five months. That's about one hundred and fifty weeks, or eleven hundred days, or twenty-five thousand hours. The shortest relationship I had was with a woman who was freaked by the revelation of one of my fantasies. This lasted nine days, or just over two hundred hours.

I had a favourite number, too – seven. I believed it to be magical and sacred. I believed it would bring me luck.

What is more pointless than faith?

As I sat by the fire, staring into the embers and considering the data from the file, something strange happened. I briefly turned my back on death and remembered what it meant to be alive.

This was a significant swing. As I've already explained, a zombie is neither alive nor dead, but exists in a kind of existential purgatory – a state correctly referred to as *undead*. More specifically: one broad definition of a Lifer is *someone who can fully interact with their surroundings*. Should they choose to do so, they can walk between two points, talk to each other, swim in the sea, fill in wall charts, fly kites, read news-papers, go fishing, have sex, play games, punch objects, light matches, climb trees, open doors – and on and on. Cadavers, on the other hand, know they are dead because of one simple fact: *nothing happens, nothing will happen.*

A zombie is a tightrope walker between these two poles. He has the potential to feel, but can't see how to achieve it. He has the ability to say anything he wants, but too often finds himself dumbstruck by his surroundings. He can survive amongst the living, but prefers the safety of his own room. A zombie is a corpse with certain limited privileges.

And right now I was sensing the expansion of those privileges. I felt free, for instance, to sit in the chair at the Chief's desk and read the Post-it note stuck to the computer: *1/12 of Batch 03/99 still missing. Strongly suspect S. – P.* Free, also, to switch on the computer and watch it boot up, ignoring all the rules about privacy I had learned in the soil. Free to place my hand on the mouse and move the cursor over the options which appeared on screen:

CODES

CONTRACTS

LIFE FILES

REPORTS

TERMINATIONS

My hand wondered how much it could explore. My brain replied: *as much as you want.* So I clicked on the first category, and was surprised by the computer's speed. It loaded a database program and revealed the contents almost immediately:

TERMINATION CODES VER. 08/99

CODE 1:   A Lifer whose termination has been carried out successfully in accordance with the methods detailed in Terminations.

CODE 2:   A Lifer terminated accidentally during the successful termination of another Lifer. *Recommended solution(s):* immediate resurrection.

CODE 3:   As in 2, above, but where the normal termination process is unsuccessful. *Recommended solution(s):* at the Agent's discretion, the relevant Life Files should be amended appropriately, or a Code 2 solution implemented with an immediate second attempt to complete the original termination successfully.

CODE 4:   A Lifer whose termination, accidental or otherwise, cannot be *immediately* reversed due to unforeseen circumstances. These include:

     4.1:   Cremation.

     4.2:   Transplantation of organs or loss of vital limbs immediately following termination.

     4.3:   Other kinds of physical disassembly (explosion, excessive mutilation, termination by wild animals, exposure to vacuum, acid, lime, etc.).

     4.4:   Loss of appropriate files.

     4.5:   The corpse's right to refuse resurrection.

All such cases will typically suffer a loss of memory and/or co-ordination, proportionate to the degree and nature of the disorder sustained. *No recommended solution.* For a complete list, see Appendix A.

---

save   print   copy   next page   prev page   search   exit

None of this made any sense – but my brain, which only four days before had been about as useful as a jellyfish at a rodeo, suggested I explore some more. I scrolled through the next five pages, then exited and clicked on the second option: CONTRACTS. A different database loaded, and a sub-menu offered me a bewildering series of choices. But one word caught my attention, having been mentioned both by Death and Skirmish: *standard*. I clicked on it, and read:

STANDARD CONTRACT

Standard Resurrection Covenant, legally binding between the Agency and the deceased, hereafter referred to as [...............] or as 'the deceased'. The Agency agrees to engage the services of the deceased as an apprentice Agent for a seven-day trial period. This period provides guaranteed employment, protection, sustenance and all other rights afforded to apprentices in accordance with the appropriate Termination Codes; in return, the deceased will forfeit his/her interment rights and remain the property of the Agency for the duration. The Agency agrees to undertake an assessment of the deceased's performance at the end of the trial period, at which time the deceased, if his/her work has proved satisfactory to his/her superiors, will be offered a permanent Agency position, the nature of which to be determined; failing which, the deceased must choose one termination from a short list of seven to be witnessed during his/her apprenticeship, which will be enacted on the evening immediately following the Agency's decision. All data and all files concerning the case are to be returned to the Chief by Monday morning at the latest.

N.B. This contract is subject to the usual terms and conditions offered by the Agency to its clients. Due to the special nature of certain Termination Codes some clauses may prove unworkable. The deceased has the right to refuse resurrection but should state this intention clearly and unequivocally before signing this contract. Should the deceased fail to choose a method of termination at the end of his/her apprenticeship, the Agency will

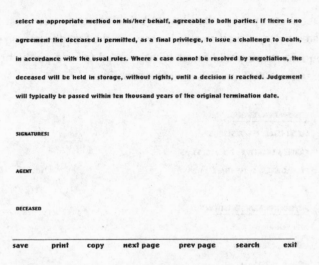

My body reacted to this new information by pumping out adrenaline. The adrenaline told me that I had discovered something important, but my head couldn't work out what it was.

So I thought about it. I remembered that during my adult life I often sought excuses for my behaviour. I convinced myself that circumstances were in control of me, that I had no choice but to do what I did, that I never had time to step back and consider my actions. I argued that because there was no time to consider anything, I couldn't be held responsible for my actions; and if I couldn't be held responsible, I could do what I liked with impunity. I was so stupid back then, I might as well have been a corpse lying in a coffin, knocking out idiotic messages to its neighbours.

My adrenaline was merely reflecting the fact that every action has consequences; and that, in signing the contract on Monday without considering the alternatives, I had behaved like a complete airhead. But even as my confusion and humiliation reached their peak, a small voice in my brain was whispering that in the details of the contract, there might yet be a way out of this mess.

I exited twice, clicked on REPORTS, then on the first directory in each subsequent menu until I found what seemed to be a pertinent file-name: FALLING–08/99.TR. This is what it contained:

TERMINATION REPORT

CLIENT CODE: F-S/F/5139857

INCIDENT LOCATION: 2-30-35/53-35-41

BURIAL AREA: 2-29-48/53-34-28

PHYSICAL CHARACTERISTICS:

M/F: Female

AGE: 366,961.58hrs

HEIGHT: 167.75cm

WEIGHT: 49,847g

SKIN: Colour 107; Area 14,317sq cm

BLOOD: Type A; Volume/Weight: 3,561 (ml/g)

FAT: 15%; Water Content: 19%

MUSCLES: 639 (intact); Weight: 19,939g

BONES: 206 (fractures: multiple)

VISION: 18.9L/18.6R

HAIR COUNT: 3,109,682

ACTIVE NERVE CELLS AT TIME OF TERMINATION: 11,876,954,117

FOOD/DRINK CONSUMED: 27,540,031g (F); 26,316,794cc (D)

BREATHS: 291,865,117

HEARTBEATS: 1,723,968,007

MEMORY: 71.4% intact

DISTINGUISHING FEATURES: Scars: left knee, 3cm; left wrist (4 × 6cm)

MAJOR RECYCLABLE MATERIALS:

WATER: 29,908ml

CARBON: 8,307g

ADDITIONAL SUBSTANCES: Lime, phosphorous, sulphur, iron, etc. (usual trace metals and minerals).

AGENT:

Death, assisted by apprentice Agent.

INCIDENT SUMMARY:

☠ Termination by Falling from a Great Height. No unusual features.

☠ See files: Falling (etc.), Suicide, Life File.

save   print   copy   next page   prev page   search   exit

It took me a moment to associate this data with the woman who had committed suicide on Monday, but the realization was far from comforting. It only accelerated the sickness rising within me, and the more I flicked backwards and forwards through the menus on screen, the more I felt like a creature from another planet.

In the blackest moments of depression following my breakdown, I regarded the world as an enormous filing system. I saw it as an infinitely large room filled with great, grey cabinets, each cabinet with billions of drawers, each drawer containing numberless folders, each folder holding countless documents and sub-documents. I perceived a labyrinthine network of cross-references so complex that no-one could possibly understand how even one single part interacted with another. How could they? The subject-range contained information from the smallest subatomic particle to the universe itself.

And though individuals might claim to be separate from

this process, they were integral to it. They were either its administrators, responsible for labelling, classification and control; or they were nothing more than anthologies of statistics, stacks of useless documents crammed into cabinets of skin and bone.

I must have been crazy.

In the corridor below, the door to the stairwell opened and the push-button timer clicked on. I turned off the computer, stood up quickly, and tipped the chair backwards. It struck the column of document wallets, which toppled over. Some files spread over the carpet; others slid close to the fire. I panicked and scrabbled around trying to reconstruct the pile, ignorant of the original order, but indifferent to the possibility of replacing documents in the wrong wallets.

Steps tapped heavily on the iron spiral staircase.

One of the wallets was smoking. I had to decide quickly whether to place it back on the pile and face the consequences, or to trash it. I threw it into the embers and poked it until it caught fire. I couldn't tell what was inside – I had no way of knowing whether it contained my contract, or a Life File, or the Chief's shopping list – but I took the risk and did it anyway. The destruction of information gave me an immense, and surprising, sense of relief.

The footsteps stopped at the top of the stairs.

I heaped the remaining documents onto the column, keeping only the Life File. I studied it casually as the door opened.

'Hello,' said Death, surveying the desk, the column of files, the now blazing fire. 'Where's the Chief?'

'I don't know.'

'Have you finished?'

I nodded. 'But nothing here makes any sense.'

'Tell me about it,' he said flatly.

Crackers

Amy returned the video (but not the equipment) a couple of weeks after I'd set the whole thing up. By this time I'd already discovered and documented enough evidence against Ralph to complete the case. It was possible that he saw me a couple of times – one afternoon I'd noticed him casually looking around as he turned a corner, and on the previous weekend he'd used his rear-view mirror far too frequently – but in less than a month I'd recorded or photographed bullying, black-mail, a mistress, a lot of unfriendly persuasion, and that little spot of torture down by the railway. It wasn't much, but it was enough.

But it was the video I was really interested in. My desire repelled and excited me in equal measure, but could not be resisted. It gave me back some of the control I'd lost during the breakdown; and I wanted to see how Amy had changed in the last seven years, whether her tastes were still the same. I wanted to know, too, if she had found the excitement she was looking for. I had so many questions.

She sent me the answers in a brown padded bag, unbroken, unedited, uncensored.

White noise, a blurred pink-and-white image, then her hand retreats from the lens. Her face is pale but her expression is neutral. The fear only shows in her eyes, which are wide and black. She is fully clothed.

'What the fuck are you doin'?'

She turns around and walks slowly to the bed.

'Get lyin' down, you dizzy cow.'

It's a four-poster bed. The curtains at the foot are drawn back. Red curtains. They look to me like labia. She climbs onto the bed, as if penetrating her own genitals, and lies on her back with her crown pointing towards the camera.

'You wannit this way round tonight, doll? 'S'fine by me. Whichever.'

She lies motionless for several minutes, not even turning her head to see what Ralph is doing. But I can see. I see a small, muscular man stripped to the waist, revealing a chest covered in coils of black hair. His face is not unattractive, but it's unbalanced by the long scar and twisted nose. His voice is strong. I watch as he admires himself in the mirror, combing his black hair, scratching his chest. I see him take four lengths of rope from his pocket and toss them onto the bed.

She flinches, slightly.

''Ang on. Forgot the fuckin' tape.'

'Don't,' she says as he leaves the room; and she lets the word hang there, as if to say any more might bring him back.

But he returns anyway, and sits on the bed next to her, and strokes her face. Then he produces a roll of white insulating tape from behind his back, and grins, and she says for the benefit of the camera or simply for herself,

'You don't have to do this. I don't *want* you to do this.'

And he says nothing as he takes the rope and ties each of her limbs to the four posts, and tears off a length of tape and winds it three times around her head, covering her mouth, lifting her crown gently each time. When the work is finished, he takes her cheeks in his hands and says quietly,

'I'll do what I fuckin' like.'

She moans as he exits again; but then falls silent, stays still.

Five minutes pass. Nothing happens. Another five. She remains motionless. After a quarter of an hour she turns her head, so slightly that the camera barely registers it.

'Keep fuckin' still. If I want you to fuckin' look, I'll tell you.'

He waits for another minute, then returns and sits at the foot of the bed, level with her shoulders. He kisses the tape over her mouth with short, stabbing movements like a bird pecking at seed. He repeats the action on her wrists and ankles, where the rope bonds are tightest. The blood rushes to her arms and legs as though he's transmitting some disease through his lips, through the tape, and she writhes a little, and he notices, and he stops.

'Fuckin' bitch.'

Another fifteen minutes pass, maybe more. Sometimes he approaches her but doesn't touch. Sometimes he places his hand on her face, or her breasts, or her legs. When she responds with any sound or movement, he interprets it as desire. *You wannit, don't you? You like it*. When she doesn't respond he calls her *fuckin' cold bitch*, and he says *who else is fuckin' you?* and *Not good enough for you? You won't get better while I'm still breathin'*, and he presses a little harder against her face, or breasts, or legs, until she moans with pain. Then he stops, and strokes her hair over and over, and says robotically, *Sorry, doll, sorry, doll, you know I don't mean it*. And he leaves the room like a little boy, with shoulders slumped and head bowed. She wriggles against the bonds when he's gone.

When he returns, he is carrying a small, white plate. The plate contains crackers and butter, and a sharp knife. He sits on the right edge of the bed and eats the crackers greedily, spilling the crumbs on her clothes, stopping only to abuse her verbally, or to pat her on the arms and legs, like a man joking with his friends in the locker room. Sometimes he breaks a biscuit over her body and rubs the crumbs into her clothes, laughing, telling her how stupid she looks; but when she writhes or moans or shakes her head, he stops again and repeats the mantra of apology.

When the crackers are finished he uses the knife.

'I don't love no-one but you,' he says. 'I mean it. No-one else.'

And he runs the blade of the knife around her breasts and down to her crotch, pausing at places that suit him; then along her legs and arms, slowly, carefully. And I can't see if the edge makes contact with her skin, or if he holds it a millimetre above her, the millimetre that denies her the relief of safe contact and threatens her with visions of short, downward stabbing movements. At last he holds the knife to her face, and now I see that the blade doesn't touch her skin, but is suspended an inch above her eyes.

'If you leave me, I'll fuckin' kill you . . . You say *anythin'* to *anyone*—'

He waves the blade over her mouth, the point close to her nostrils. One brief contact, and the blood will flow. But he doesn't touch her. He waves it more violently, to demonstrate his intention, then flicks the knife up in the air like a baton, and catches it by the handle.

'You're a fuckin' borin' cow anyway. No bloke on earth could get a stiffy lookin' at you. An' if you leave, I'll make sure no bloke does look at you.'

And it might all be over. He cuts the cords tying her to the posts, and she curls up into a ball, her body shaking with inaudible sobs. After a while, when she considers it safe, she gently removes the insulating tape from her mouth, whining with pain when it tugs at her hair. But he has one final desire to fulfil. He pulls down his tracksuit pants to reveal a pair of black Y-fronts, then takes out his flaccid lump of flesh and waggles it at her shivering back, taunting her like a child: *It's your last chance to see it. Won't get another.* And when she continues to ignore him, he shrugs his shoulders and starts to piss on the bed by her head, so that the drops splash against her hair, onto her neck.

She pulls away violently and stands up, enraged.

'You're fucking *mental*.'

''S'way you like it, doll.'

'Fuck off.'

'When I want to.'

'Fuck off *now*.'

He recognizes that he's lost control of her, of the situation, and the humiliation prevents him from apologizing or remaining. He directs the rest of his stream onto the carpet, tucks away his penis, pulls up his pants, and leaves – pausing briefly in the doorway to reassert his authority.

'Get a cleaner to sort it out. Tomorrow.'

As soon as he's left the room, she dry-retches against the bed, gathers up the sheet and uses it as a towel to dry her hair. She scrubs her head for a long time, but is never satisfied, trying again and again to remove the stain and the smell. Then, as if she has suddenly remembered she is being watched, she drops the sheet and walks quickly towards the camera. Her eyes are red, her face sags with disgust, but her mouth is twisted into a peculiar smile.

Her hand approaches the lens, becomes a blurred pink-and-white image, then white noise.

The rattling cyborg

It took fifteen minutes to walk from the Agency to the fair at St Giles, retracing the course we'd taken on Monday morning. The difference was, today we were dressed as paramedics. Death had selected two pairs of bright green overalls from the Stock Room and filled a small black medical bag with a variety of non-medical equipment. As we turned onto the road leading to my old burial ground, I revealed my feelings about some of the things I'd seen in the Chief's office.

'All those people reduced to forms and files and numbers...' I began. 'It's so depersonalizing. If everyone is reduced to a set of facts, and you can't distinguish one set of facts from another, then life means nothing.' Death studied me intensely, and I felt uncomfortable and embarrassed, so I wound up the speech quickly. 'I don't remember much about who I was when I was alive – but those memories I *do* have still mean something to me, even now. I'm more than a statistic.'

'I agree,' he said, nodding in sympathy. 'What's more, I find the detail of what we do to our clients increasingly repellent . . . Tonight's client is a perfect example. His termination just seems unnecessarily gruesome.'

A yellow glow hung over the houses as we approached the graveyard, and grew brighter as the crowd grew denser. People jostled for space or gathered in clumps of conversation, but all were sucked into the strobe-lit vortex possessing the main square; and we were dragged helplessly along with them. At the corner, the helter skelter loomed ahead of us like the spire of a sunken church. The wooden slide coiled from heaven to hell, carrying its helpless human freight endlessly downward. The owner, a walnut-faced, liver-spotted old man, innocently entreated passers-by to *have a spin*.

'Keep your eyes open,' Death advised. 'He could be anywhere.'

I scanned hundreds of unfamiliar faces in the hope of recognizing only one. Some disappeared into *The Famous Rotor-Disco*, a two-storey mincer which processed individuals into a single writhing unit of flesh. Up on the viewing gallery, a circle of abusers – made devilish by multi-coloured lights, thick puffs of steam and a hammering disco beat – gathered to bray at the bouncing bodies below. Other people were kidnapped by the scooping buckets of the big wheel, spinning and arcing away into the evening sky. Their desperate screams were softened by the juddering whine of an old generator, the murmur of the crowd, the incessant music. Still more were sucked into the Waltzer, a dizzying, shuddering maelstrom of light and sound. Hired hands whirled the seats at random, snapping necks, squeezing lovers together, making people sick with pleasure.

And at last, in the chaos, I saw him. A tall, tub-bellied, bearded man in a pink T-shirt and floppy green shorts, standing by a mobile snack bar, exercising his mouth on a steaming hot dog.

And the data from his file came to life in my imagination.

It's 1969. He is two years old. He is resting, half-asleep, on his father's lap, watching black-and-white images flicker on the television screen. The pictures show a space ship that looks like a metal octopus, and two snowmen running in slow motion over a dark grey desert. The snowmen are talking, but their lips don't move and their voices are unclear, like when the boy's father speaks to him on the telephone from a long way away.

But he is not interested in the pictures, or the sounds they make. He is not even interested in the thought that two men are walking on the bright circle that shines in the night sky. He just likes to stay up so late, and to lie half-asleep on his father's lap.

'That's him,' I said, watching the father stroke the boy's head, as my mother had once stroked mine.

'What's the recommended pursuit distance?'

'Between two-point-one and nine-point-eight metres.'

'Minimal intervention?'

'So I'm told.'

The snack bar adjoined a huge diesel-powered wind organ, decorated with rough representations of square-jawed heroes, Amazon women, giants, unicorns, elephants, centaurs – all protected by a thick, yellow coat of varnish. The organ grinder stood idly by, as old and yellow as his whining machine, grinning toothlessly at his audience; a grizzled black bull mastiff guarded his feet, its body bloated by scraps from passers-by. As the music wheezed and groaned, animated toy soldiers crashed cymbals and bashed drums out of time. Our client and his hot dog had come to rest here, listening, watching.

Death instructed me to wait and observe, then headed for the snack bar himself, barging his way through the crowd and giving dissenters the evil eye. He disappeared briefly, and the next time I saw him he was standing at the front of the queue. The assistant who served him was dressed in a mauve and white striped blazer with matching straw boater. He stood out like a rat at a cat convention.

'Yes?'

'I'll have one of those.' Death indicated something behind the counter.

'A doughnut?'

'No. The round thing on a stick.'

'Toffee apple?'

'Uh-huh.'

'Pound-fifty.'

Death patted the pockets of his paramedic overalls before producing a ragged note, then left before the bewildered assistant could hand over his change. When he returned, I asked him why he had bought the apple, suspecting that it would play some vital role in the success of our mission.

'I was hungry,' he replied.

He is twenty-one years old. He is tall and handsome and proud of his new wife sleeping in the hotel bed next to him. She is already pregnant with their first child, a girl who will live for five years before leukaemia wrenches her from their lives. He strokes his wife's belly as she sleeps, as his father had stroked his hair on the night of the moon landing, and he thinks of the child growing inside whose sex he does not know, whose future he has already planned, who will one day grow up to be as tall and handsome as him.

He strayed from the wind organ, paused at a prize booth, then slipped into the crowd. We caught up with him again at the ghost train – a giant, black shed, drably decorated with puny fluorescent ghosts, pathetic pastel-coloured monsters and grandmotherly witches. The sidecar-sized carriages that clattered through the exit doors invariably carried laughing customers, and as the trains rolled to a halt on the narrow track a skinny actor in a black-and-white skeleton suit hammed his way through a moans-of-the-undead routine. He began to lose heart even as we waited, his shrill whines and violent gesticulations downgraded to disconsolate murmurs and a listless shaking of the arms.

The bearded man passed through the entrance and climbed into the front carriage of the next train. Death bought a couple of tickets from a man whose face resembled an Arcimboldo painting, and we pushed through the turnstile and settled at the rear. A sharp jolt set us in motion: I turned around to see the skeletal actor recovering from the push. He stepped backwards casually, then set about disturbing his audience once more. The train rolled forwards and banged through a pair of black wooden doors, which pincered the carriage as we passed.

Light snuffed out, sound muffled. Faint, strange echoes of music and voices, wheels rumbling and screeching. I'd anticipated rubber skeletons rattling in cages, severed heads dripping fake blood, Frankenstein's monster, leering vampires, howling wolves, revolving tunnels – even the odd joke corpse. But I saw only this emptiness, heard only this stifling silence broken by the train wheels and the far-off fairground attractions.

I waited for something to happen.

The train snaked to the right, turned left, rumbled straight ahead, turned left again, rolled right – then squealed to a halt. I heard nervous laughter from the carriages ahead.

Silence.

Quick footsteps in the darkness. A hand slapped my cheek, then something soft, stringy and damp brushed against my forehead. I flinched, but it was over as soon as it had begun. The train moved forwards, squeaking, grumbling and twisting along the track towards the exit. The leading carriage banged into a second set of doors and forced its way into the light. I turned towards Death to avoid the glare.

His seat was empty.

Travelling from light to light through darkness. Waiting for something to happen. Muffled echoes of life.

This is what it means to be dead.

A terrifying scream rose from inside the ghost train. Our client, who had been climbing out of the front carriage, stopped and turned around. He and the other passengers left slowly, turned sporadically, gazed quizzically at the swinging exit doors. They watched, half-hoping that the source of the scream would reveal itself, until they were absorbed into the body of the crowd. I followed them, still wondering about Death.

He was standing on the other side of the gate.

'You took your time.'

'Where did you go?'

He shrugged. 'I just gave them a lesson in how to *really* scare people. It's the only fun I'll get all evening.'

It's 1982. He is standing by his grandfather's bed, fighting back the tears that seem to begin in his throat and push upward in hot, stinging waves to his eyes. The grandfather will not live to see his great grandchildren.

'Happy birthday,' the old man says. 'How does it feel to be fifteen?'

The teenager shrugs, choking on his misery. He is trying to grow a beard, but at this moment the soft down on his chin and cheeks strikes him as pathetic. The whole world is pathetic and cruel.

The old man nods. 'Neither one thing nor the other, is it?'

And I could not distinguish my memories from his.

The sun cast long shadows on the few unpopulated patches of ground. The light was faltering, throwing the multicoloured fairground bulbs into sharper focus. The sky had deepened to a rich, dark blue. At length Death stopped me with his hand, indicating a ride we hadn't yet encountered. I heard the whining of a generator, the groans of onlookers, the shrieks of victims. I saw light reflecting from spinning metal cages, I watched our client join the queue.

'This is the machine that will kill him,' he said.

It was a hideous, rattling cyborg. Its non-human components consisted of a dynamo, a strong metal web supporting a latticed steel tower, and a central revolving spar at the ends of which two cages spun freely. Its non-mechanical components comprised a live human being willingly restrained inside each cage, an operator, and two hired hands. The twin elements of metal and flesh were mutually responsible for the successful functioning of the apparatus. When the device moved, the caged people cursed, screamed, gesticulated and groaned, committed to their part in the performance. Once the ride was over they were free to leave, their roles readily filled by new players.

Death squinted at the signboard advertising the ride.

'The Voyager,' he read. 'A one-hundred-and-eighty degree vomit comet. Tasteful. No wimps allowed.'

'Are we going on?'

'No.' He sounded disappointed. 'But he is.'

Only two people were permitted per ride, and the queue shuffled forwards slowly. Our client was third in line. He seemed apprehensive, surveying the surrounding crowd and seeking approval of his daredevilry. As we watched the Voyager's spin slowed to a stop. The cage doors were opened, two satisfied customers staggered free, and a new couple climbed inside. The hired hands bound them tightly with leather straps and closed the doors. Soon the squealing occupants were tumbling over like amateur acrobats.

In the distance a bingo caller announced random sequences of numbers. Near by, a white-faced clown was selling helium parrots and foam lizards on wire leashes. I watched the crowd, catching indiscriminate phrases from passers-by until the ride came to an end. The rotating arm decelerated, the cages spun to a stop, the metal base shuddered with decreasing violence. The assistants prepared to unlock the cages. Our client rocked on the balls of his feet and whistled.

'Next.'

He handed over his money, passed through the gate and claimed the nearest carriage. The hired hands strapped him in, struggling to fasten the bonds around his chest, belly, thighs and ankles. Having mostly succeeded, they closed the door casually. The operator activated the revolving arm until the second carriage was level with the loading platform. The assistants secured the second customer as the bearded man swung idly in his suspended prison.

'Sit back, relax and enjoy the ride,' said the operator.

He switched on the machine. It began to rotate, slowly.

He is thirty-two years old. He looks through the café window and smiles as he notices his ex-wife sitting at their old table by the stairs. He enters, sits down, and places his hand on her shoulder.

'You're looking good.'

She turns and kisses him lightly on the cheek, and pulls a photograph from her bag. The photograph shows two children at a swimming pool. His eldest child, now dead, and her younger brother, who had just learned to walk. The boy visits him at weekends and during the holidays.

'I thought you might like to see this. I found it at the bottom of the suitcase. Do you remember?'

They talk about old times for an hour or so. They are still friends, and the fact that she holds his hand as they leave is, for him, a sign of hope. As he opens the door, he glances to his right and sees three people at the window table. Two of them – a pale, thin giant and a sickly individual covered in rashes – are engaged in an animated discussion.

The other man, who looks like a corpse, is staring at him sadly.

The revolving arm lifted its passengers high into the darkening sky and pulled them back down to earth, the cages describing circles in space. Our client groaned as he approached us and groaned as he left, his prison spinning like a propeller. His fellow convict screamed with pleasure and fear as the orbit accelerated. The metal base shuddered ominously, its rhythmic vibrations threatening to shake the apparatus apart.

The hired hands looked on coolly. The operator increased the speed.

The vibrations intensified, the shaking support hammering furiously against its foundations. The cages turned over and over like rolling stones. The revolving arm whirled like the sails of a windmill.

She handed him the photograph of their two children. *Do you remember?*

'The Chief took the liberty of removing a couple of important bolts this afternoon,' Death explained. 'It shouldn't be long now.'

'I'm not sure I can look,' I told him.

'Then turn away.'

But I watched.

A door flew open on one of the cages. It banged against the arm, clattered back against the lock, swung open again. The crowd gasped collectively; the bearded man, our client, screamed. The assistant nearest to the ride waved his arms wildly and shouted at the operator; but the operator reacted too slowly, his brain shocked by the failure of the machine under his control. His dysfunctional reflexes eventually moved his hands to the drive lever, pulled it into neutral, and switched off the power.

The rotating arm droned as it decelerated, but the broken cage continued to spin crazily, its rhythm broken. On the first revolution the open door crashed against the base, ripping against its hinges as the compartment reeled. It tore free from its housing and shot, rattling, clattering, beneath the webbed metal support. On the second rotation, the cage roll slowed, revealing our client with his head bowed, his body held in the compartment only by the loosening straps around his waist and ankles. He clutched feebly at the grip bars as the cage rolled forwards and backwards, out of control. On the third, the waist strap snapped and he fell out of the compartment, swinging freely from the opening, held only by the feet. As the rotating arm slowed to a halt, it dragged him through the web of metal and tore him apart.

The dance of Death

'We should hurry,' said Death. 'We need to take him back to the Agency. The Chief has something big planned for him on Sunday.' He opened his black medical bag and removed two green plastic refuse sacks, handing one to me. 'Reinforced. Triple strength.'

Time had congealed. In the dead, still air the sound of a thousand voices droned. Mannequin people gazed passively, trapped in mid-conversation, mid-laugh, mid-stare.

'What do I do with it?'

'Pick up the pieces. As many as you can find.'

Death pushed his way through the queue and slipped around the barrier, repeating the phrase: *Let me through. Medic. Let me through.* No-one challenged him, or the zombie in his shadow, and we reached the ride's revolving arm in seconds. The bearded man's battered cage swung idly at the base; the other was trapped at the apogee, its door perpendicular to the earth, its occupant staring emptily at the grisly scene beneath him and screaming. One of the assistants had turned away from the accident, his hands covering his face in disgust; the other crouched, staring, at the dismembered body. The operator's fingers still rested on the controls.

'Over there. *Quickly.*'

On the far side of the metal web, the bearded man's severed head lay face down on the pavement. I picked it up, turned it around: one dull eye, a crushed jaw, missing ears, smashed skull, skin and beard red and wet with blood. The face that had watched the men on the moon. I lowered it into the bag, then knelt down for a moment, feeling numb and weak, watching the dumb expressions of the crowd. Death moved in front of them like a giant praying mantis, stooping to pick up a finger, or an ear, or a clump of hair.

I returned to work. By the operating platform, pointing towards the assistant who was unable to watch, I found the hand that had stroked a pregnant belly. In the webbed metal base I saw his heart, broken for the last time. On the tarmac I discovered the remaining eye, now blind to his surviving child. I gathered all the fleshy, bony, bloody bits and pieces I could find and placed them carefully in the sack.

And then I threw up.

My throat and stomach burned with the violence of retching. My mouth and nose filled with the acid taste and pungent smell of vomit, spilling out of me like a pump. I had forgotten the colour and texture, and how uncontrollable the process was, how debilitating and humiliating. When it was over, I felt as if I had been scooped out. I had no desire to live.

I was still crouched in that position when Death knelt down, rested his hand on my arm and announced that we were leaving. I looked up. His bag was filled with broken and battered limbs, but he carried it over his shoulder as if it were a balloon.

'There are a couple of things missing,' he said, 'but it's all we can manage. The Chief will just have to put up with it.'

I nodded, wiped my mouth, and lifted my sack slowly. 'Where are we going?'

He pointed towards the helter skelter.

I focused on Death's bent back smeared with red stains and followed him through the crowd: past the ghost train, the row of prize booths, the wind organ and snack bars, the Waltzer, the big wheel, the Rotor Disco. At the helter skelter he turned right, negotiated the war memorial and advanced through the double iron gates into St Giles cemetery. He didn't pause until he was halfway towards the church, then he veered left through a clump of trees into a small clearing.

He dropped the sack, opened his black medical bag and removed the contents, nodding to himself. 'Parcel tape. Staple gun. String. Very good.'

I swung my sack onto the ground next to his, relieved to be free of the burden.

'What do we need those for?' I asked.

'Reassembly,' he said.

I watched as he emptied the sacks onto the grass, arranged the body parts in vague anatomical order, and proceeded to cut lengths of parcel tape with his pen-knife. 'You don't have to do anything,' he said at last, 'but helping me might help *you*.'

And, as it turned out, he was right.

We stapled the single ear to the head. We taped the head to the torso, the torso to the arms, the arms to the hands, the hands to the fingers. We stuffed his chest and belly with the organs we'd found, connected them crudely with string and staples, and sealed him up. We stapled his penis to his groin. We taped his torso to his thighs, his thighs to his knees, his knees to his calves and shins, these to his ankles, those to his feet. By the time we reached his toes our achievements were recognizably more accomplished. The head wobbled and grinned unnaturally, but the legs were perfect.

The reassembly was almost complete. We stapled his wounds, wrapped and knotted string tightly around each limb to aid stability, and stood back to admire our handiwork.

I found only one slight mistake.

'I think the right arm is out of line,' I said.

Death twisted it back into place.

'Lovely job,' he said, kneeling by the patchwork corpse. 'Now for the final touches.'

He pulled the last surprise from his bag: a pair of turquoise surfer's shorts in a Hawaiian design, a pair of red deck shoes with white laces, and a black T-shirt which boasted QUALITY COFFINS AT DISCOUNT PRICES, with a telephone number on the reverse. I helped him dress the corpse then sat down wearily. Putting the body back together had eased the sickness in me, at least.

But he hadn't finished: he pressed his lips against the cadaver's broken mouth, and breathed. The chest inflated like a balloon, stretching the string and tape bonds to the limit. Death breathed again, and the bearded man breathed with him. When he took his lips away the chest rose and fell naturally.

'Stand up.'

The corpse ignored his command.

'Come on. Get up.'

This time he obeyed, sitting up awkwardly, then rising to his feet groggily like a drunkard. Death pressed his fingers against the dead man's face and rolled open the eyelids. The corpse gazed passively at us both, but showed no interest in his surroundings. He did not ask about the noise from the fairground. He did not wonder why he was standing in a graveyard. He did not recognize his broken body. His death had been cold and unfeeling, as if the machine had studied him, analysed what he was, and then rejected him totally. I felt sorry for him, and patted him on the arm reassuringly.

'How are we going to get him back?' I asked. 'He's in no state to walk.'

'No problem,' Death replied. 'I'll just have to indulge one of my two weaknesses.' He smoothed his blood-soaked clothes, turned to the cadaver and took him by the hand. 'Shall we dance?'

'What's *dance*?' said the corpse, stupidly.

The Dance of Death: theory

RULE 1.   The Dance is for couples only. One half of the couple should ideally be Death, but any Agent of the Apocalypse will suffice. The other half should consist of a corpse, preferably recently deceased.

RULE 2.   Recommended dances include the galliard, the minuet, the waltz and the quickstep. The cha-cha-cha, lambada and foxtrot are forbidden.

RULE 3.   Within the limits prescribed in Rule 2, above, the couple shall engage in a random sequence of popular dance steps according to the prevailing mood.

RULE 4.   Music is permitted, but not mandatory.

RULE 5.   The Dance will be assumed to have ended when the destination is reached, when one of the couple is exhausted, or when an accident intervenes.

As he took our client in his arms, Death began to hum a tune which I recognized instantly: Billie Holiday's version of 'Cheek to Cheek'. He even sang a few of the words as he pirouetted out of the clearing, and kept to the rhythm as he swung onto the gravel path and glided away through the graveyard gates. He moved with a grace previously un-witnessed, skipping by every bystander on feet of air, touching no-one. The corpse fared badly in comparison, often stumbling and standing on his partner's toes, raising his taped arms at the wrong moments, or simply failing to catch the beat. But his motion required no effort. Death took the lead and the strain.

They squeezed together through the narrowest gaps, floating between people and traffic as if they didn't exist. They turned and whirled and twisted and leapt along the roads back to the Agency, the cadaver unsmiling, his partner's jaws fixed in a competition grin. It was all I could do to follow them, and when they finally stopped at the top of the slope a hundred yards short of home, I took a couple of minutes to catch up.

'He's falling apart,' Death explained. He tugged at the bearded man's wrists and thighs where the tape had come unstuck. The limbs were barely holding together.

'What's *dance*?' asked the corpse again, dimly.

Death ignored him. 'I think he's had enough anyway. Help me carry him.'

I supported our client's left shoulder, Death took the right. The corpse squirmed and wriggled, gibbered and cried out, but together we managed to bear him down the road and to the front entrance. We sat him on the pavement, then Death skipped down the steps, unlocked the cellar door and leapt back up. He wasn't even sweating.

'I'll take over from here.'

I sat on the wall, watching as he eased the load onto his shoulders and carried it down into the dark basement. The corpse complained a little, but fell silent again in the comfort of darkness. When Death returned, I asked him where he had deposited the body.

'Storage,' he said.

A lone candle burning

In the three years of my love affair with Amy, I felt more alive than I ever had before, or have done since. And when I told her I loved her, I meant it.

I meant:

I care if you live or die. I am interested in what you do. I trust you not to destroy me. I am attracted to you physically, mentally, spiritually, emotionally. I am proud when you meet the people I love. I will comfort you and care for you if you are sick. I will argue with you because you matter. I will value you above objects, plants, animals and other human beings. I will make no demands of you and set no conditions (within reason). I will sacrifice myself for you, if necessary, and whether you like it or not.

And I do not expect you to reciprocate my love.

At first.

The first time I told her was in the month before we decided to live together. It was spring, and we were standing together beneath an elder tree, by the river, sheltering from the rain. I couldn't stop myself. The drops splashing on the water, the sweep of rain on the trees – it was too romantic. I looked at her and thought:

She is a dark room in which a lone candle burns for ever. Her light shines like starlight, constant and miraculous and beautiful, but cold and distant. She is a hurricane blowing inside my head, a still centre waiting for me to find her. She is a deep, dark sea, and I will never dive to the deep sea-bed. But she will sing herself to me like a bird sings, and I will listen.

And I said it, as naturally as breathing: 'I love you.'

But everything fades, and nothing stays the same for ever.

It's seven years before my death, and Amy and I are sitting by the window in the Jericho Café, recovering from our long, cold walk back across the meadow. We have been together for thirty-five months. We aren't looking at each other, preferring the slimy grey pulp of snow and slush in the street.

'It just doesn't *feel* right,' she says, repeating herself. 'Not any more.'

I nodded. 'It hasn't felt right for a long time.'

'So what's left?'

'Why can't you just accept who I am?'

'Don't be sarcastic,' she snaps. 'Anyway, that's the point. Who you are just isn't what I want. It hasn't been for the last three years.'

'So what *do* you want?' I ask.

And I look across the table at her face, framed by long, black hair, slashed in two by a thin, inscrutable smile. At the same moment I know that I will always love her, and that our relationship is at an end.

Why am I telling you this?

Because a corpse does not love. He is incapable of it. If he should try he would almost certainly fail, because he does not understand the vocabulary, and he cannot interpret the signals. He can only ever express what it is like to be himself, and hope that this has meaning for those with whom he has contact.

And because love is part of the life I miss. A life that seems infinitely more real than anything I've experienced since.

Code 72

'To begin with,' said Skirmish, 'Hades is dead.'

We were talking in the bedroom late on Thursday evening, with only the crescent moon for company. Streaks of blood stained my slip-on shoes by the bed. I sat at the writing desk, my arms stiff from carrying the corpse in the cellar, the green paramedic outfit replaced by my familiar spangled suit. Skirmish was Barca lounging in a pair of burgundy pyjamas.

'Why wasn't he just resurrected?'

'No point,' he explained. 'Code 72: *An employee of the Agency terminated during his term of employment. Re-employment is not acceptable under any circumstances.* One of the Chief's more whimsical regulations. Anyway,' he added, smiling, 'his badge was missing.'

'Oh?'

He chuckled. 'Lose your badge and you lose your career.'

We fell silent for a moment. I ran my seven fingers over the typewriter keys, typing out the question which I subsequently asked.

'How did he die?'

Skirmish glanced towards the corner where the injured cactus flopped pathetically. 'No-one knows for sure. He liked to take a walk on Sunday mornings before anyone else was up. Trying to get rid of all that cake round his waist.' He laughed. 'We found him with his guts ripped out on Port Meadow. A gruesome sight ... Not that he was much to look at in the first place. Short, squat, flabby, beak-nosed, red-eyed, thin-lipped, *and* he combed his hair across his bald patch ... We were room-mates – *he* used to have the top bunk – but I never liked him. He was so ... unambitious.' He relaxed deeper into the chair. 'I should have had his job, too. I was counting on it. But Death had other ideas. He's spent the last six weeks hiring one crap corpse after another.' He raised his hand. 'No offence.'

I shrugged. 'I'm not sure I'll be here much longer anyway.'

He pulled a lever, flipped the chair upright, and stared at me.

'I mean,' I faltered, 'I don't think I'm doing very well. Nothing's been said, but I'd be surprised if I wasn't back in the coffin by Monday.'

He nodded. 'If you don't end up in storage first.'

I lay on the bed, gazing at the wooden slats overhead, wondering about my future. Skirmish was on the upper bunk, reading *The A–Z of Termination* by the light of a torch.

'You know,' he began innocently, 'if you're concerned about what's going to happen on Sunday – and I'm not saying you *are* – then I might have a solution.'

I wondered whether to answer, suspecting some kind of trap. But the truth was, I had no option, so I attempted to sound noncommittal. 'Uh-huh.'

'I've got keys for every room in this building, and I know pretty much everything that goes on.'

'Uh-huh.'

'And if I need something, I can get it.'

'Uh-huh.'

'And the thing is, I happen to know about something that, if you want it – and I'm not saying you *do* – could give you another option.' He paused, hopped out of bed, switched on the light, and headed for the table by the far window. 'In fact—'

There was a single, very powerful knock on the door.

'Who is it?' said Skirmish.

'War. Who the hell else?'

'Come in.'

The door vibrated violently.

'It's bloody locked.'

Skirmish tutted, shuffled to the door and turned the key. War entered, looking larger, redder and hairier than ever.

"Cking stupid rules.' He kicked the door fame, then slapped his assistant on the back. 'Get your clothes on. I'm taking you out.'

After they had left, I lay on the bottom bunk thinking about what Skirmish had said. But not for long. One of the first things you learn as a detective is not to attach much significance to anything anyone wants you to hear. However, his warning did focus my mind on whether or not being torn apart by a machine would be an acceptable exit on Sunday evening.

I processed the thought quickly – not in my head, but in my gut.

And my gut said: *no*.

FRIDAY

DEATH BY WILD ANIMALS

I forget the rest

When I awoke, the blood on my slip-ons had disappeared. Someone had entered the room during the night, removed my shoes, cleaned them thoroughly, and returned them before morning.

I had been woken up by Skirmish pounding the typewriter with heavy, laboured strokes. He said he was writing an abusive letter to a woman whose restaurant he had attempted to wreck the previous evening. He had been thrown out before he could overturn half a dozen tables.

'Where was War?' I asked sleepily.

'Trashing the place next door,' he replied.

Skirmish said he'd follow me after finishing his letter. As I was leaving he added that War was now stomping about in the Stock Room searching for equipment, and Pestilence was testing mid-flow vomit samples in the Lab, so neither would be at breakfast. I thanked him, and closed the door.

In the corridor on the way to the dining room, I was seized by a memory so powerful that it momentarily paralysed me. It was connected to the snow-white woman I had seen in the cinema foyer on Tuesday.

It is nine months before my death. I'm staring into the shadows at the rear of the Jericho Café, seeking a place to sit. I see a woman alone at the last table, her lowered face illuminated by a night-light. She is scowling at a cappuccino and poking a brownie with a fork. Since the café is full and no other place is free, I walk over and ask if I can join her.

'Do what you like,' she replies. 'It's all the same to me.'

Her bluntness feels like a challenge. I respond in kind, with the words which had once been my reward in a time of misery, and which I sense will provoke her now: 'Cheer up – it might never happen.'

She looks up and smiles sarcastically. 'It already *has*.'

And deep within my carapace, I feel the first churning feelings of love. I am falling for her dark, penetrating, melancholy eyes, for her tortured soul, even for the simple black clothes she wears. So I ask her innocently, evenly:

'What's the problem?'

Her name was Lucy, and my relationship with her was typical of all my affairs in the final two years of my life. I sought out the company of women in order to recapture memories of my mother, to disinter that sense of security. But security soon bored me, so I looked for risk: emotional, physical, and moral danger. But risk brought with it the threat of being hurt, so I nourished situations which allowed me to retreat. It was an unending cycle of failure.

I must have been sick in those last days. I wanted all my relationships to be like a contract, negotiated from the beginning with conversation, writing, expressions, gestures, touching. I wanted the terms of this contract to be so polished, so refined, so *safe*, that even before we first kissed, my lovers and I would be nothing more than mirrors to each other. We would never commit ourselves beyond any commitment already agreed between us; we would simply reflect everything the other said and did. And when a lover finally *did* kiss me I kissed her in return, with precisely the same intensity. If she told me she loved me, I parroted the reply.

But that kind of relationship is like a corpse: the longer you leave it, the less attractive it becomes. In an attempt to stop the rot, one or other of us would take the risk of renegotiating the deal: we would suggest new ideas, open ourselves up to the possibility of rejection, defend our position strongly. It didn't work: our affair became nothing more than a series of contradictory amendments and non-guarantees, reams of small print, a maze of linguistic tricks – until the contract itself became worthless.

I wonder now how I could have lived this way.

My zombie body, still paralysed in the corridor, suffered a violent spasm. I leapt forwards in time from our first meeting.

Lucy and I have been seeing each other regularly for some weeks – informally at first, then on the basis of an unspoken commitment. I arrive at the moment when I crawled out of my shell and said:

'I think I'm falling in love with you.'

'Me too,' she replied.

Another leap forward. Another spasm.

'I *love* you,' I tell her.

She smiles and says, 'Where are you sleeping tonight?'

And the memory of that question still burns in my zombie blood.

'Robots,' said Death, as I entered the dining room. He was eating while Famine watched. 'It's the Chief's long-term plan. Another couple of hundred years and they will conquer the Earth. Anyone who isn't killed will be enslaved; anyone refusing slavery will be killed. It's all part of his efficiency drive: he's aiming to cut our future workload by three-quarters. If you ask me it's a stupid idea. Ah – good morning.'

I returned his greeting, sat down and started to eat.

'What's happening today?' Famine asked.

I spoke between mouthfuls. 'I don't know.'

'Doesn't anyone ever tell you?'

'Not until just before we leave.'

'Don't you *want* to know?'

'Have I got any choice?'

'Of course.'

This was untrue. Since leaving the coffin, I had only been offered two kinds of choice: which method of death would be my reward at the end of the week, and which clothes I should wear on any particular day. Today's outfit, for example, consisted of the same jacket, trousers and shoes as yesterday, a pair of boxer shorts decorated with red roses, sea-blue socks embroidered with crimson octopuses, and a blood-red T-shirt proclaiming the lie: CORPSES DO IT LYING DOWN.

'No-one has any real choice,' Death argued gloomily. 'We are all the servant of someone.'

We ate our meals in reflective silence, until Skirmish barged through the door, grabbed a banana, and announced he was going to the post box.

Death nodded dismissively. 'Make sure you clean out the car before lunch. I want *all* the dog hairs removed. Not like last time.'

Skirmish slammed the door.

'So what *is* happening today?' Famine repeated.

'We're going on a nature trip,' Death replied. He turned towards me. 'Actually, I'd like to introduce you to some of my friends first. They're War's responsibility, but I borrow them when the Chief wants a clean, efficient termination.' He placed his hand on mine. 'The thing is, we'll need your help finding them.'

'What are we looking for?'

'A large, brown sack with a small, red letter on it . . .' He paused. 'Or a small, red sack with a large, brown number on it.'

'Which is it?'

Death stroked his beard between thumb and forefinger.

'You know – I *can't* remember.'

When I was alive, I was constantly tricked by my memory. I forgot things I wanted to remember and remembered things I wanted to forget. Sometimes I forgot that I was supposed to remember something, and only realized that I'd forgotten it when it was too late. I was never one of those blissfully self-deluding Lifers who could forget everything they didn't like and remember everything that pleased them. This often made me unhappy, particularly when I was thinking about Amy.

In an attempt to improve my memory, I read a great deal about how it works. I learned that everything received by the senses is translated into pulses of nervous energy. These pulses, and the pathways they create in the brain, can be recreated instantly to produce the effects of short-term memory. Long-term memory works by repeating the pulses and pathways often enough to create virtually permanent anatomical and biochemical channels, so that—

I forget the rest.

The red army

The door to the Stock Room was already open, and we found War chest deep in a heap of tiny, brown packages. He was cursing loudly.

Death coughed. War looked up irritatedly.

'What do you want?'

'We've come to give you a hand.'

'Hands I don't need. Eyes I do.'

'We have both.'

An awkward pause.

'I'm looking for a sack,' War admitted, sulkily.

The room was filled with sacks.

'What kind?'

'Large and red. I can't remember what's written on it.'

Death rubbed the palm of his hand across his chin and scanned the room. War, pouting like some gruesomely bloated child, returned to his search.

The Stock Room was filled from floor to ceiling with boxes, sacks, parcels and packages, devices, tools, gadgets and gizmos, contraptions, kits, pieces and parts. Everything appeared to support everything else: pull a tiny packet from a stack on one side of the room and a pile might collapse on the other; remove a bag from the top of a heap and the whole structure beneath might be fatally unbalanced. The walls and carpet were invisible beneath fragments of unidentified objects; four windows, obscured by cliffs and crags of jumble, failed to provide adequate light; and a door leading directly to the Diseases Department was blocked by a precarious column of cardboard boxes, all unmarked. It was the most cluttered, chaotic and confusing space I had ever seen. It was a smuggler's cave, a devil's workshop, a wizard's hut. It was a miracle that anyone could ever find anything here.

Death, for example, was having trouble.

'I can't move this crate,' he said to War. 'Have you seen the whatsit?'

'What's that?' War replied.

'The thingumajig. You know . . . The lever tool thing.'

'I don't know what you're trying to say.'

Death stood up, frustrated. He surveyed the room for the object of his desire. War shook his head slowly and stared at Death as if he were mad.

'Here it is,' He burrowed behind a heap of battered cartons and produced a small jack; then used the jack to lift the crate. He wedged his hand beneath the crate and pulled out a shrunken brown bag, 'What colour was it again?'

'Red,' said War. 'And it's about ten times larger than that.'

'What's inside the sack?' I asked.

'Equipment,' War replied. Then added, nervously: 'If you find it, don't shake it. It'll only bloody annoy 'em.'

Most of the jumble had no identity. There were no labels, markers, tags or stickers. I confined my search to the area to the right of the door, a windowed wall that faced the front of the house. At first I was careful not to disturb anything, but after half an hour of fruitless foraging I began to disentangle the jungle of rubbish.

'Have you found something?'

Death stood over me, looking weary. He was holding a large tin of dog food in his left hand. His right was covered in grease and grime. War was still burrowing eagerly on the far side of the room.

I shook my head.

He sighed and returned to a pile of sacks. All of the sacks were grey, empty and unmarked.

My mind back-flipped to the past.

Amy and I are sitting in the Jericho Café, gazing at the rain through the window. It's half an hour after I told her I loved her in the shelter of an elder tree, nine years before I will speak the same words to Lucy at the same table. Our clothes and hair are damp. We are sharing a cappuccino.

191

'Do you really love me?' she says.

I love her irresistibly like a wave hissing against the shore; irreversibly, like a comet caught in the gravity of a star, instinctively, like a dog relishing a bone; possessively, like a comedian protecting a joke; naively, like a child excited by a present; hopelessly, like an idiot coveting genius; comically, like a foot drawn to a banana skin; aggressively, like a fist striking an enemy's face; desperately, like a starving man longing for food.

I love her less than I can, but much more than I have ever said.

And time passes.

'Yes.'

And time passes.

'Found it!'

Death waved a red sack above his head, grinning like an infant.

'Be careful,' War cautioned. 'It might not be tied securely.'

Death ignored him, whirling his prize high into the air before throwing it into the centre of the room. The bag was about the size of a sheep, and bright red. It flopped and quivered like a jellyfish. An enigmatic message was crudely printed in brown ink on the front: *A. A. Qty 10,000. Handle with care.* In frustration, War kicked out at a stack of packing crates he had been investigating. The stack wobbled, but did not fall.

'What exactly is it?' I asked.

'Today's mission,' Death replied proudly, picking up the sack again. 'These are the friends I was telling you about. Ten thousand ants.' He untied the cord and peeked inside. 'Army ants, to be precise. They devour anything in their path. And they *obey* their queen.' He smiled at War.

Momentarily abandoning his sulk, War also peered into the bag. I expected a swarm of insects to spill from the sack and wreak havoc on the neighbourhood, but he mumbled some placatory incantation as he peered through the open end, and intercepted any sign of activity.

'What are you saying?' I asked him.

He looked up. 'You wouldn't understand.'

My zombie brain was filled with rubbish. One minute it was love, the next a bunch of useless facts from my favourite trivia encyclopedia. As soon as Death mentioned the word *ant*, it set to work thinking of the key differences between an ant and a corpse. I couldn't stop it. This is what it came up with.

An ant can lift fifty times and pull three hundred times its own weight. A corpse cannot lift or pull anything, because it is dead.

Ants have five noses. A corpse has one (and eventually none).

Ants have been used to cure diseases. A solution combining ants' eggs with onion juice is said to cure deafness, and the fumes from mashed red ants are reputedly a remedy for the common cold. A corpse, on the other hand, is rarely anything other than the result or cause of disease.

Some ants burrow eighty feet deep in search of water. Corpses never travel further than six feet below ground.

An ant is much smaller than a corpse.

What use is a brain like that? And why was it doing this to me?

The Rorschach Test

The night I collected the recording equipment from Amy's apartment was also the night I died. So far, the images associated with this memory have been no more coherent than arcane graffiti, the sounds no more meaningful than loops of jumbled messages. But I feel confident of the sequence now. I *know* how I died.

It was a humid evening in late summer, seven weeks after Amy's first phone call. She had contacted me a couple of days earlier, informing me that it was safe to collect the video recorder, and asking for a progress report. I told her my work was finished, and that she could be more than satisfied with the results.

In the previous fortnight I'd watched the video of her husband's perverted power game half a dozen times. My need for repeated play-back, and my unwillingness to admit the reasons for that need, convinced me of something I had long suspected: I was human vermin. But it didn't stop me, of course. I can't say I was excited by anything I saw – I'm not even sure prurience was my main motivation – but I was too close to understanding the desire for my own comfort. In the end, and against all principles, I broke open the plastic case, ripped out the magnetic tape, and burned the evidence.

But I couldn't forget that final image of her mouth twisted into a smile. Why was she smiling? The video was hardly conclusive proof of abuse: a legal eye could see it as a simple case of S&M role-playing gone too far. Was it, then, a sign that she had exercised some form of control over Ralph? By exposing one of his secrets to an outsider, and poten-tially to a much wider audience, she had wielded some retaliatory power. But how much would he care? He was much more likely to be concerned by the other evidence I had gathered.

So was that smile meant for me? It was a narcissistic thought . . . but perhaps some part of her was pleased at being able to show me just how far she had come; how far she had managed to push the limits of her desire. Perhaps, in some crazy way, she even wanted to remind me of who I had once been, and to make me jealous of what I had missed.

But I didn't feel jealousy. I felt self-disgust.

Amy was holding a half-empty glass of orange juice when she opened the door. Both rings were missing from her right hand. I walked into the living room and saw an open box of Ritz crackers on the coffee table. I turned around as she fastened the bolt, and noticed again the small depression in the skin at the nape of her neck. In my memory I felt its roundness with my forefinger, ran its tip down the ridges of her spine, explored a mirrored hollow in the small of her back. I saw her roll over, heard her say she loved me, felt her kiss . . . And I was still standing here seven years later, having already fallen so far into the abyss that no light penetrated the darkness.

I opened the French windows and stepped outside, attracted by the cold glow of the moon. The balcony was a small undecorated area with a low wall made of yellow Cotswold stone, overlooking the deserted square below. I kept well away from the edge. Only a thin layer of concrete prevented me from falling seventy feet to the ground.

I sensed Amy's approach as I leant against the door frame. I glanced sideways and saw that she was gazing at the street lights in the distance. She hesitated before she asked, afraid of my answer.

'Did you find anything else?'

'Enough,' I said.

'I'm disappointed.' She turned away and sighed. 'It's different when you know for sure . . . But thank you.'

I shrugged. 'It's why I'm here.'

'It's not the *only* reason.'

And I didn't know what that teasingly ambiguous phrase meant. It could have been an expression of desire, or a casual blandishment. Seeing the puzzlement in my face, she laughed bitterly and walked back inside.

It started to rain.

We were childhood sweethearts. We met when we were fifteen, were good friends until we left school, fell in love shortly afterwards. Our homes were only a couple of miles apart in Oxford, and I cycled over to see her almost every night. And I wrote letters, too – twice a week for over two years. Passionate letters, filled with energy, and desire, and joy.

Teenage romance!

'I've left the evidence in a locker at the railway station. There's a micro cassette in there, and some photographs.' I handed her the key. 'I've sealed the photographs in a plain brown envelope. You might not want to look at them.' I took a sheet of paper from my inside jacket pocket. 'Here's a list of everything I've found. Bare details – but it should be enough to convince him.'

'Thank you.'

She hid the key and the sheet in her wardrobe, and retrieved the recording equipment from beneath a pile of jumpers. I recognized none of her clothes, and felt the slightest stab of jealousy. There's no explanation for emotion.

'I'll send the bill next week – unless he opens your mail?' She shook her head. 'As soon as you settle, everything I've discovered is legally yours. You can use it before then, naturally . . .' She nodded. 'And if there's nothing else, I'll—'

'Didn't you ever miss me?'

Her question surprised me, but I tried not to let it show. 'Of course.'

'You could have called. Just once.'

'I . . . disappeared for a while.'

'I'm glad you're back.'

I felt my shell weakening. I was playing by *her* rules now. 'You could have called me, too.'

She laughed. 'You wouldn't have *satisfied* me. I bet you couldn't, even now—'

'That's not the issue.'

We stared at each other sourly, and fell silent, listening to the rain rattling on the roof of the round tower.

'Why did you marry him?'

'It's none of your business.' She shook her head, then sighed. 'It was a mistake . . . Though not at first.' She smiled. 'And I didn't know about his past. He didn't – *doesn't* – tell me.'

'But you weren't blind.'

'It was different back then. He was wonderful. Just what I needed.'

Silence and rain.

'How can you just lie there when he does those things to you?' My disgust was directed at myself, at my own desire.

'You've seen what he's like.'

'The whole thing makes me sick—'

'I'm not interested in your opinion.'

'I don't know what you see in him.'

'You have no right—' She breathed deeply, then suddenly reached across and clasped my face in her hands. 'Let's not talk about him any more. I don't want to hear it.'

She pulled me towards her, and we were locked in a kiss. We became one person, joined at the forehead, nose and mouth, at the arms, hands and chest, at the groin, thighs and feet; consumed and controlled by the kiss, worshipping each other so completely with our bodies and minds that we became one spirit, one ecstasy. The taste of her mouth was sweet, like an orange, and for a fleeting moment I imagined our tongues as the flesh, our lips as the soft, waxy rind. And as we stood there in the glow of a pink light bulb, my shell cracked open.

'I love you,' I said.

'Don't be ridiculous,' she replied.

We were lying on the bed when the buzzer rang.

'Oh shit. Oh *shit.*' She leapt up, rearranged her clothes quickly. 'It's him. I know it is.' She was already at the intercom by the time I reached the doorway. 'Hello?'

''S'me. I've lost my key.'

'Hold on. I'll come down.'

'Just open the door.' Then fainter: 'Stupid cow.'

She panicked. 'No. Let's go out tonight. Anywhere. Let's—'

'Look, 'ave you got some wanker up there with you? 'Cos if—'

'*No.*'

'Then *open the fucking door.*'

She pressed a small, black button on the intercom panel, and a moment later I heard a door slam far below.

'Hurry,' she said, pulling back the bolt on the front door. 'You have to go.' I straightened my tie, and listened for the sound I didn't want to hear. Sure enough, I heard it: footsteps from the stairwell. 'Take the lift.'

I felt violently sick. 'I can't.'

'What do you mean?'

'I mean *I can't*. Lifts. Not since my—'

'Well you can't stay *here*.' She looked around frantically. 'He suspects something. I can tell by his voice. He'll search every room in the house.'

Even if I'd agreed with her, any time I might have had to overcome my phobia was now gone. The lift was on the ground floor, and Ralph was ascending rapidly via the only other exit. He would arrive before the lift reached halfway. I suggested casually strolling down the stairs, meeting him on the way down. Amy shook her head and pulled the biggest surprise so far.

'I think he knows who you are. He's seen you following him.'

My only option was to remain where I was and talk my way out. I hadn't brought a weapon with me, and I knew from my observations that he always carried one wherever he went, so it was going to be tricky. But I could deal with it. I had done a couple of times before.

She killed the idea as soon as I suggested it.

'No. Please. You have to go. You don't understand.'

I closed the door and scanned the living room for anything which might help me, barely listening to Amy's desperate apologies. I couldn't leave, and couldn't conceal myself anywhere in the apartment. What *could* I do?

Rain pounded on the roof of the round tower in the far corner, drawing my gaze to a patch of light on the carpet near by – a pale rectangle created by the moon shining through the skylight. Within its borders curiously symmetrical shadows danced – water running over the glass above.

It was a moment of beauty in a time of terror. It was like a Rorschach Test, revealing aspects of your personality by inviting you to find meaningful patterns in abstract arrangements of inkblots.

And the only pattern I could see was the shape of my own doom.

Sex and Death

'Why do we do the things that we do?'

I sat in the rear of the car, gazing at the back of Death's head as he talked. Tentacles of black hair curled from the crown to the nape of his white neck. War's head was thicker and larger, but his hair had streaks of red like rust, and clumps of curls crowded his bovine skull like bedsprings.

'I told you. It'd be worse without us.'

Death stroked his beard absent-mindedly, the distraction causing him to veer towards a roadside storm drain. 'But how can I have avoided this question before now?'

'It's one of those things.'

'Yet it won't go away.'

He put an unlabelled tape into the cassette player, perhaps to drown his confusion. It was a pirated compilation by a band I knew well when I was a teenager: Joy Division. War informed us that it belonged to Skirmish, and speculated that he must have been playing it when he cleaned out the car. It took me barely a moment to recognize the unusually upbeat first track – 'Love Will Tear Us Apart' – but since it had no special emotional significance for me, I tipped my head back, stared at the sky through the rear window, and let my mind float away.

It drifted towards the decision I would be forced to make in two days' time: which method of death should I choose? At the start of the week I would have taken any option just to get back inside the coffin; but the more I experienced of life beyond the grave, the more I knew that my choice had to be right. None of the deaths I had witnessed so far was suitable.

And if I couldn't make a choice?

'Did you pack the ants?' Death asked War.

His question pulled me back from the future into the present. I was aware of the rough fabric beneath me, two bodies ahead, the light from a high sun, the hum of the engine.

'They're in the boot.'

'I didn't see you put them in.'

'You weren't bloody looking.'

'I was looking. I just can't remember.'

'Your Code Four was watching me. Ask him.'

Simultaneously, Death turned around, pressed his foot hard on the accelerator and swerved up a slip-road.

'Is is true?' he asked.

'Yes,' I said quickly. He faced forwards again, decelerated, pulled the wheel hard left, and narrowly avoided an ice-cream van in the inside lane.

Actually, I couldn't remember, either.

The needle on the temperature gauge rested in the red zone. Steam clouds swirled from beneath the bonnet, whispering, whistling, hissing. An acrid smell invaded the interior. The engine was still idling.

'Metros,' said War disparagingly. 'Bloody crap bollocks of a car.'

Death switched off the motor. 'It's taken us where we want to be.'

'It's a piece of shit.'

He climbed out and kicked the front passenger side wheel. Twice. Then he thumped the bonnet repeatedly, causing several minor dents. He calmed down briefly before launching an assault against the rear bumper.

'You should come back inside. Our clients will be along any minute.'
War capitulated and sat down sulkily.

We had parked by a gate on the edge of a green field. Ahead of us the land sloped downwards into a hollow and a clump of trees. To the right, on the rim of the depression and level with the car, a dark wood stretched as far as we could see. The words *Boar's Hill* appeared from somewhere inside my head. I had once brought Amy here. We had divided the time between talking about nothing and groping until the car windows steamed up.

'How many are there?' I asked.

'Two,' Death replied. 'A man and a woman.'

He explained that the woman was forty-two years old, the man forty-nine. I quickly calculated that, between them, they had experienced sixty-three years more life than I had. I would have gladly exchanged positions with either of them, just to taste another fifteen minutes.

They had known each other for nine months. They worked for a company which made polyextruded plastics. He was an accountant, she a project manager. In his twenties he had wanted to be a painter, but had been encouraged by his parents to pursue a financially rewarding career instead. In *her* twenties she had wanted to become a project manager, but had not expected to wait so long. They were both married, but not to each other.

They had been interested in each other since the first time they met. He was attracted to her impatience. She was attracted to his creative spirit. His creativity expressed itself most frequently in the sketches he drew for her, the notes he wrote and the jokes he made. Her impatience was familiar enough to tease him but not enough to annoy him.

Overt, uninhibited, mutual sexual attraction came later.

The office they shared was the same office in which Monday's client, the suicidal woman, had worked. They did not know her particularly well, but had attended her funeral on Thursday as a mark of respect.

The hearse was driven to the funeral service by the business partner of the accident-prone man who had been savaged by Cerberus on Wednesday. Apart from one of the pall-bearers stumbling and almost dropping the coffin, there were no unusual incidents during the ceremony.

The woman's seventh-closest friend was the bearded man who had been mangled in the fairground, and who now rested in storage back at the Agency. The woman ranked her friends using a complex scoring system based on general personality, sense of humour, intelligence, charisma, social skills, co-ordination, physical appearance, and bodily hygiene.

Neither of the lovers had any knowledge of the couple who may, or may not, have contracted a disease on Tuesday.

'How old are you?' I asked Death.

We were still sitting inside the car. It was thirty minutes since we had parked and I was trying to pass the time with casual chat. War was scraping his teeth with a Swiss Army knife.

'The question has no meaning for me,' he replied.

Two people approached hand-in-hand, the man grinning broadly, the woman laughing. Their conversation was too distant to catch anything other than its rhythm and tone. The man carried a Blackwatch tartan picnic rug. They glanced briefly, innocently, at the pale Metro as they headed for the dark wood, and only released their hands when they negotiated a stile. He climbed over first, then assisted her. She didn't seem to mind: as far as she was concerned, a bright sun shone between the twin moons of his buttocks.

Death coughed. 'We should follow them.'

They were fifty yards ahead. The man had medium-length grey hair, coarse like an old whippet. The woman's hair was blond, and curly like a West Highland terrier's. He had kept himself in reasonable shape for someone who was almost fifty, had led a sedentary life, ate, drank and smoked too much, took no regular exercise and had an underachieving destructive metabolism. She, too, was overweight.

War removed the sack from the boot and held it to his ear. 'I can hear their mandibles clicking. They must smell food.'

'Ants *can't* smell,' I told him. 'They use chemical trails to find—' I stopped, realizing I had missed the point.

We climbed over the stile and trailed the couple through the forest. The trees, mostly firs, were densely packed, forcing us to march in single file. We caught glimpses of our clients as they picked and skipped their way up a long slope, heard them laughing against the silence of the forest floor. It was cool and dark beneath the whispering branches.

'They'll be stopping somewhere ahead,' Death explained, his white worm finger resting on a map. 'There's a clearing near by.' He pointed vaguely to a patch of green between two grid-lines, where a big red 'X' had been scrawled with a crayon. 'When they reach the clearing they'll stop, kiss for a few minutes, spread out the rug, remove their clothes and have sex. At some point in this process we will release our friends here.' He indicated the sack. 'And when the ants have finished we need to collect every last one of them.'

We advanced deeper into the forest, Death at the head, War bringing up the rear. The laughter had stopped, and the only sound we heard was the rustle of our own footfalls. The light grew dimmer, the tree trunks more tightly packed. The cathedral of branches blocked out the sky.

'Damn blast sodding *hell*.'

I turned around. War had his hand over his left eye and was flapping aimlessly at a swinging twig.

'Bugger blasted lashing *thing*,' he continued.

'Are you all right?' I asked him.

'Just watch where you're going.'

He walked on with a hand covering the afflicted eye, leading the party at Death's invitation, dodging exaggeratedly the overhanging branches.

I avoided thinking about what we were doing. As we advanced further up the slope and deeper into the woods, my brain resorted to nonsense, as it had in the Stock Room. I tried to remember everything about sex I'd learned from my trivia encyclopedia, convincing myself that it would help with what we were about to do. All I could recall was a sequence of disjointed facts:

The female whale has nipples on her back.

Whalebone corsets were replaced by the brassière in 1914.

The fourth Mogul Emperor, Jahangir, had three hundred wives and five thousand mistresses.

Or was it the other way around?

The hyena, like man, does not have a penis bone.

Syphilis is transmitted from the genitals via the skin and mucous membrane to the bones, muscles and brain.

Cardinal Wolsey was accused of spreading syphilis to Henry VIII by whispering in his ear.

And in case you're wondering, there's only one kind of sex available to cadavers: necrophilia. But the dead, as everyone knows, do not copulate.

What would be the point?

I had just remembered that Donatien Alphonse Francois Sade was sentenced to death in 1772 for 'immoral behaviour' (which included describing six hundred different sexual techniques in his book, *100 Days of Sodom*), when we burst into a glade. Light from darkness, space from confinement, warm air from cool shade. It was a flat patch of land no larger than a small house, sparsely carpeted with grass and speckled with dry, brown needles from the trees. The overhead sun cast no shadows but enriched every colour, the intensity of the light drawing us in to the centre of the clearing.

The couple were already intertwined. Her hands clasped his neck, his hands clamped her waist. Their faces were connected, too. When they pulled away from each other their mouths closed like small, pink clams; when they came together their lips ripped apart at the seams. They spluttered through stuttering pneumatic kisses: glistening gums, flashing white teeth, spit-bright tongues dripping with the moment's release.

'It's disgusting,' said Death glumly, to no-one in particular. 'All that effort to avoid oblivion.'

'That's not the only reason,' I told him. 'Sometimes it just happens.'

'But it's so *meaningless*,' he countered. 'Individuals are just links in a continuing chain of life, a chain without pattern or purpose. Whether you exist or not – it makes no difference. Links will be forged elsewhere; the chain will continue to grow.' He picked up a dead leaf and tore it in two. 'Existence is so brief, so fortunate, so dependent on factors over which you have no control. It's nothing more than an illusion.' He tossed the broken leaf aside. 'I don't know how any one of you ever manages to smile.'

'There are some good jokes around,' I said.

'Look,' interrupted War, still holding his left eye, 'does anyone bloody care? The ants are getting ravenous.'

'A few more minutes,' Death replied. 'That's all.'

The accountant calculated that this was an ideal opportunity to spread the blanket on the forest floor. The project manager made a positive decision about the prospects of a meeting on a one-to-one basis. Refusing to delegate the responsibility of undressing to her partner, she removed her blouse, stepped out of her shoes and unfastened her skirt. Reckoning that he would profit by copying her clothing removal initiative, he slid out of his shirt, slipped off his slip-on shoes and slithered out of his slacks. After a mutually agreed pause, and without the need for arbitration or further negotiation, they tore off each other's underwear.

The groped and grasped, and groaned and grunted, and gripped and grappled, and grinned and grimaced, and grabbed and grafted, and gasped and gasped, and gasped and gasped, and gasped and gasped and gasped. They did not mention their dead colleague. They did not care about the roughness of the picnic rug. They did not mind the needles or the burning sun or the smell of sweat. They had no interest in any of these things because, for a brief, bright, blissful moment, they were alive.

Watching them, I felt myself salivating with a memory of desire, and sensed a vague stirring in my groin. But my physical deficiencies gave me no hope of relief: I was one stiff who couldn't get a stiffy.

'If we don't release them soon they'll cut their way through the 'cking sack.'

They struggled against the sapping midday sun, diminishing energy reserves and flagging mutual desire. Their groping, straining, gasping rhythm was slowing. The accountant's buttocks were almost luminously pink; the project manager's legs had trembled their last. Their activity was treading the borderline between ecstasy and chore.

'Maybe you're right.'

War rubbed his eye. 'You know I am.'

The slippery, skin-slapping frenzy slid to a soft, frictional stop. The lovers renegotiated their positions and concluded their meeting.

Over and done, over and out.

The spoils of war

They lay naked, rough, exposed. Watching the bright stillness of their connected living flesh, I saw Amy.

Her face is a moon with deep crater eyes. Her face is a child's dinner plate, a carrot for a nose. Her face is a rolled ball of snow, five shining pebbles smiling. Her hair is the darkness between stars.

Her body is a composition of denials: neither small nor tall, fat nor thin, beautiful nor ugly, smooth nor coarse. It is all these things; and it is wiry like an eel, pale like ashes, rounded like the stones on a beach. I smile at her thighs, zebra-striped with cellulite; her feet, flat and squat and funny; the finger-thick gap that divides her big toe from the rest.

She is the skin that covers her, the muscles that strengthen her, the bones that support her, the veins that drive her. And she is more than the sum of these impressions, more than the surface and the shadow it casts.

She is more, because she is someone I loved.

'Hold on,' said Death. 'They're starting again.'

The pink buttocks and the trembling legs were glued together once more, the adhesive made viscid by vigorous abrasion. I felt sickness in my stomach, prickling on my back, pressure on my lungs. I was afraid of my memories.

'It makes me ill every time I see it.' War shuddered. 'It's such a sodding waste of effort. I feel like kicking them.'

'Personally, I've often wondered what it would be like,' said Death.

'But why can't they go out and *fight* someone instead?'

Death shrugged.

War opened the sack.

I couldn't control myself. Breath quickened, blood rushed, nerves fired. My sluggish spine shuddered, my stomach churned, my shoulders shivered with pleasure. An aching memory of sexual feeling pulsed through me.

Sex was more than the sequence of events that defined it, more than conversation, eye contact, touching, kissing, clasping, penetration, pulsation, withdrawal, touching, kissing, separation. It was more than physical attraction, more than dilated pupils, open mouths, lubricating mucus, the unique ecstasy of pain, the relishing of creeping flesh, the comedy of bruised hips, sore lips, chafed skin. It was more than the chemical rules of attraction, more than the routine which smothered it, more than the growth and decay of love and the shifting of time.

It was one of the few reasons to live.

And in the last two years of my life, it was the means to erase the last traces of my innocence, by discovering the limits of my desire. It was revenge, too: on my parents for not preparing me for adulthood, on Amy for cutting me adrift, on myself for my naivety.

It was *revenge*.

*   *   *

A large army ant darted onto my left shoe, considered taking a diversionary chunk from my resurrected corpse flesh then scurried onwards to its main mission.

Ten thousand ants followed it.

I stepped aside. The bulging sack flattened as a red tide swept over the forest floor. A dark blanket of bodies picked its way towards the picnic rug, a sweeping, synergetic life form composed of prickling, acidic units. An advance party crept stealthily along the accountant's upturned sole, conquered the pinnacle of his heel, cut its way through the hairy forest of his calves and paused in the valley behind his knee. He reached out a hand to brush away a wayward insect, but barely broke his rhythm. The ants marched forwards, joined by reserve forces. They surmounted the great thigh plains, advanced over the buttock hillocks, ignored resistance from a low-flying hand, seized control of the small of the back and tore across the wide loins towards the shoulders. The army poured over him like treacle, dripped down his sides and settled on the woman's flanks: a rushing, tingling river of life, flowing outwards and upwards, spreading, swelling.

The accountant's cry of alarm and the project manager's scream which followed it went unheard by the advancing forces. A pincer movement reinforced the main thrust, reserves overwhelming their larger opponents with sudden strikes against the arms and neck. Ants prevailed over every inch of disputed territory: they filled the mouths and throats of their foes, ripped at their walls, seized their towers, desecrated their sanctuaries.

'Seems to be going well so far,' War observed blandly, scratching his temple. 'Some of them are getting a bit over-enthusiastic – probably the heat.'

Death hunkered next to him with a look of profound disillusion. 'I don't know what I'm doing any more.'

'Same as always. Breakfast, preparation, lunch, termination, dinner, sleep. What else is there?'

'There *must* be something.'

War changed the subject, bored with Death's angst. 'What's for dinner?'

'I can't remember.'

'Only I don't want chicken again.'

Death stared blankly at him.

The enemy had split into two factions: a walking, shouting carpet of ants (male) and a rolling, screaming carpet of ants (female). Both were doomed. The male carpet sprouted shivering arms and staggered towards the forest; the female carpet managed to crush some of the invaders but fatally opened her eyes to a roving squad of elite troops.

'Watch him,' War told me, indicating the accountant's progress towards the trees. 'Guide him back towards the clearing if he strays too far.'

'What if they attack me?'

'They won't touch you,' he laughed. 'You have completely the wrong *smell*.'

There was no need for concern. The accountant collapsed onto a bank of earth on the far side of the glade, his resistance crushed by the force of the onslaught. The project manager rolled through a couple of desperate revolutions before slumping to a stop at our feet. The enemy uprising had failed; the ants had secured a glorious victory.

They began to divide the spoils of war, allocating equal rewards to each combatant. Slowly, methodically, the army stripped away flesh and fat to reveal bloodied knots of muscle, stripped away muscle to reveal bones and internal organs, stripped away organs to reveal the skeletal core. The bones were picked clean of all flesh and blood until only a few, stray roots of hair remained.

Our clients were drained, hollow, scooped-out people. Frameworks, templates, blueprints of people. Memories, echoes, distortions of people.

'See,' War said. 'They're all the bloody same underneath. It's not the substance that distinguishes them. It's the surface.'

I answered him by throwing up. The burning, the acid, the pungent aroma again. The feeling of being drained, and wanting to die.

The second time in two days.

The frenzied consumption of flesh had ceased. The thick patterns of dark red matter dispersed. Some ants were already weaving rapidly towards the edge of the forest. I was wiping my mouth when War handed me a small, brown bag.

'Pick up the farthest ones first.'

Death moved to the left of the glade, I took the right. War ploughed straight ahead, stepping over the project manager's fresh skeleton. His collection technique consisted of using his giant hands to shovel as many ants as possible into the sack. Death plucked the ants individually, smiling at each one before tossing it into his bag, then resuming his expression of deep gloom. I combined the two methods, scooping only when I was confident that my resurrected flesh would not be stripped from my resurrected bones. And it was hot and hard work. Harvesting ten thousand wriggling insects is draining labour for anyone, but especially for the recently dead.

After ten back-breaking minutes beneath a burning sun, I sat down by the ex-accountant and rested my hand on his grinning skull.

Death approached with a weary smile. He continued to tease ants from the forest floor, picking them like wild fruit, talking to them; but when he reached me he sat down and put his arm around my shoulder.

'Having a rest?'

I nodded.

'Take your time.'

'Why do we have to collect them all?' I asked.

He smiled. 'Every single ant is carrying a small fragment of our clients, and each one is vital because it contains a tiny part of the whole. A miniature replica. Together they create a sequence of coded messages which fit together like a jigsaw. These messages will help us to recreate, if necessary, the couple that we disassembled.'

'But even if you do catch all of the ants, how are you going to remove the flesh they've eaten?'

'Micro-surgery,' he replied.

I resumed the clean-up operation, circumnavigating the glade in search of ant escapees. I stopped by the woman's remains and stared into the sapless sockets of her skull. Her head was as empty as a bucket at the bottom of a dry well; her barren, battle-scarred bones baked slowly in the sun. I knelt down and stroked her crown. An army ant crept from the corner of her laughing mouth and scurried across her cheek bone. I picked it up, watched it wriggle helplessly for a moment, then squashed it between my thumb and forefinger.

'How many have you got?' War asked Death.

'Fifteen hundred or so. How about you?'

'At least seven thousand.' He turned towards me. 'How many?'

'I don't know.' I glanced at the bag and shook my head.

'Let's have a look.' War snatched the sack from me, opened it and studied the contents carefully before delivering his assessment.

'Probably about three or four hundred.' His expression was sardonic. Sweat dripped from his dark curls, rolled down his red cheeks. 'They're all alive, at least.'

He emptied the bag into his own, then returned it.

Every ant I found from that moment on, I crushed.

It was late afternoon. The glade was shaded by trees and a cooling breeze blew fitfully. The intervals between discovering ants were growing longer. War's sack was swollen with life.

Memories swarmed over me, intangible, uncontrollable. I couldn't tell if they defined who I was or what I should become. Amy, Lucy, the decision I must make, my coffin existence – everything whirled by so fast and so frequently that it was impossible to focus on a single image, to separate it from the chaotic whole. These briefly bright flitting insects could not be caught.

'Have we got all of them?' Death asked, adding his ants to War's collection.

War shook the sack and turned to me. 'How many?'

'Four.'

'We're about twenty short . . . An ear's worth. Hardly worth bothering with.'

I gave him the remaining ants in my possession, failing to mention that they had all been squashed.

As we left the glade, Death stopped briefly and signalled for us to wait. He knelt down, plucked something from the grass, studied it briefly, then threw it away.

'Was that another one?' War asked.

'No,' he said.

Skylight

'There's a maintenance exit above the stairs in the next block. A manhole. It can't be more than a few yards along the roof. *Please.*'

There was neither time to think nor protest. He would be at the door in seconds. I hurried to the round tower, cleared several rows of pornographic videos from the free-standing bookshelf, tested the strength of the supporting brackets, and began to scramble upwards.

'Hurry. He'll go apeshit.'

As I climbed, my mind refused to think about practical considerations – such as what I would do if escape was impossible, or how I would negotiate the roof, or whether vertigo was preferable to assault and battery – and informed me instead that this was the first time I had ever heard Amy use that particular expletive.

I sat down on top of the bookshelf and glanced across at the skylight – two square panes of glass forming a single, rectangular opening the length of a small man. The catch was well out of reach, but before I could request assistance, Amy was below me, pushing against the window with a long wooden pole.

It opened three inches. I tried to widen the gap, but a pair of brass hinges prevented further movement.

There was pounding on the front door.

I had no choice but to break one of the panes. Gripping the top of the shelf tightly with my left hand, I pushed at the glass with my right, using the sleeve of my shirt as protection. The first attempt wasn't strong enough. The second was misdirected, and I struck the sloping roof instead, almost overbalancing. Amy saw what I was trying to do and gave the lower pane a tentative push, cracking the glass. She swore loudly and launched into a second, more violent attempt.

The window shattered.

Instinctively, I turned away to protect my face. There was a brief, surreal moment of silence between the shocking crash of the breaking window and the soft sound of splinters bouncing on the carpet below. The noise was answered with fists hammering against the door, and the same curses and threats I'd recorded on the micro-cassette now safely stored in a railway station locker.

Rain fell through the black, jagged hole. Amy smiled faintly at me and headed for the hallway, her shoes crunching against the glass on the carpet.

I pawed away the remaining fragments of the pane until a clear escape hole remained: a wooden frame two feet square. I felt a vague stinging sensation and examined my arm. There were a dozen tiny cuts on the back of my hand and some small fragments were lodged in the wounds. My shirt sleeve was shredded and stained. I ignored the tiny shards and concentrated on one large, irregular piece which had dug deep into the wrist. When I eased it free bright red blood, lurid in the moonlight, flowed over the wrist bone and down the side of my hand. The sight of it was nauseating, but I forced myself to ignore it. I raised myself into a crouch, shifted forwards slightly, then reached out to the wet, late evening sky until I caught the window frame. The rain turned the streaks of blood on my arm into pale, pink rivulets which dropped onto the carpet, but I was more alarmed by the sharp, persistent pressure of the water on my skin. I leaned further and poked my head outside.

A wet, tiled slope fell steeply from the skylight into the darkness. There, the gradient grew less dramatic until the tiles slanted gently to a thin, flat rim. I gripped the frame tightly, ignoring the spasms of pain shooting up my arm from the glass I hadn't cleared. As the key squeaked in the lock below, I launched myself forwards and swung free from the shelf. The frame sank into its closed position, almost shaking me loose – but with a quick push I manoeuvred the short, perilous distance through the gap and out onto the greasy tiles.

It was a cool, wet, windy evening. The sun had set, sinking the slant of the roof into deep, black shadow. I could barely distinguish anything in the gloom, and panic and fear welled up inside me, a dizzying combination of vertigo and blind terror. I took three deep breaths and eased myself down the slippery slope, holding onto the frame by my fingertips. Only when I felt secure did I look right to see where the round roof of the tower connected to the angled roof of the apartment. It was five yards, maybe more – and beyond it, a slightly greater distance to the raised aperture I hoped was the maintenance exit.

I felt sick. I knew that if I looked down, my head would spin, my grip would weaken, and I would fall. I realized only now, when it was far too late to change anything, that I had made completely the wrong decision.

I heard shouting from the apartment below.

'What the fuck happened?'

'A burglar,' Amy blurted, with convincing fear in her voice. 'He tried to—'

'Where is he? Did he touch you?'

Silence, broken only by the sound of sobbing. Whether she was indicating the skylight or not, my escape route was obvious.

'Did he have a gun?'

The weeping intensified. I guessed it was accompanied by a shake of the head, though a nod might have been more useful to me at that moment.

'I'll kill him.'

'No!' she cried. 'Call the police—'

'*Fuck* the police.'

The conversation stopped. I heard the bang of a door being wrenched open and slammed shut; then the sound of clattering metal. I pulled myself upwards until my head was level with the frame, and peeked inside. Amy sat cross-legged on the carpet, her face covered by her hands. Her body was shaking. Brightly sparkling shards of glass surrounded her. Bizarrely, I remembered that she always sat in that position when she was upset . . . I looked up and saw Ralph approaching with an aluminium stepladder, as if he was about to tackle some unfinished DIY. He saw me staring through the window, and though I didn't quite hear his words because of the rain rattling on the roof tiles, I managed to read his lips.

'Fucker,' he said.

I jerked my head away from the broken skylight, interested only in survival; but the sudden movement unbalanced me, and my hand slipped from the window frame. I started to slide, uncontrollably. Panic purged any remaining feelings of control.

I let out a long, loud cry of terror.

Famine

I finished my meagre dinner and put the plate back onto the tray. Death had invited me to eat in the breakfast room but I had refused, preferring to be alone. I had made myself a few slices of dry toast and returned to the bedroom, hoping the food would ease the sickness that swilled around inside me. But eating had only made me feel worse.

I moved the tray to the middle of the floor. The floor rose to meet it. Loud laughter echoed from the corridor. War's voice. On our way back to the car that afternoon he had bullied a small child into yielding a bottle of mineral water, which he had used as a temporary coolant in the Metro. The memory brought bile into my throat. I stood up, and the ceiling descended. I moved towards the wardrobe and four walls shifted slowly, inch by inch, pressing inwards; and before I could open the door to select my clothes for the next morning, I had fainted.

I was roused by a knock so weak I wasn't sure I'd heard it, until it was repeated a moment later. I didn't answer. I was lying on the floor in a foetal position. I had been dreaming briefly of today's deaths, and the memory lingered. I knew in my heart it would be an unsuitable climax to my employment with the Agency. My mind was whispering some vague, silly, metaphorical ideas about passion, and going over the edge, and self-destruction, but I had a much stronger reason for rejecting it. A powerful sensation that it was too similar to the way my life had actually ended many years before, and an overwhelming feeling that I didn't want to repeat the experience now.

A third knock.

'Who is it?'

'Famine.'

'Hold on.' I raised myself to my knees, then stood up slowly. 'Come in.'

He unlocked the door, opened it slightly and squeezed through the gap. 'Everything OK?'

'Fine.'

He responded with a pleasant smile. He looked like Nosferatu the Vampire on Prozac.

My childhood image of God was much like Famine. I refused to accept the classic picture of a senile codger with a fluffy white beard, wearing a long white robe and brown sandals. I preferred to think of him rather as a sophisticated, balding, intelligent gentleman with half-decent dress sense, a perverse sense of humour, and a slightly sinister side ... But then, I've always had my own view of the world, and been unhappy when anything contradicted it.

As I grew older my image of God changed. Gradually, the face was concealed behind a mask. The mask had a hard surface and a fixed expression, and it was as big and powerful as anything I had ever gazed upon. Then, when I was about fifteen, I realized that I could no longer see God at all – only his unyielding disguise. From that moment until my death, I was never certain whether he had ceased to exist, or whether he was simply playing some childish game of hide and seek. My idle faith remained, because the image of the intelligent gentleman was so strong. But it was vulnerable; it no longer mattered.

Well. You live, you die, you discover the truth; and the truth is, I still don't know. Like everyone else, the dead have to wait for proof of the existence of God. There *is* an afterlife, of course, but whether it eventually involves a beard in sandals, I can't say.

What an anti-climax!

'We'll be working together tomorrow,' Famine said at last. His face was so pale I suspected he applied white make-up to those areas which showed the slightest signs of rude health. 'Thought I'd come and say hello.'

'Uh-huh.'

'Haven't been properly introduced.' He reached over and offered me his outstretched fingers. His grip was so feeble it was like shaking hands with a glove. 'Truth is, I don't have many friends.'

'That makes two of us.'

He laughed, but it was a truncated, pathetic effort, more like a sigh. 'Hard being a zombie when you're used to the coffin.'

I nodded, and sat down on the bed.

'How're you settling in?'

'I don't know.' I fought off a wave of nausea. 'Everything seems so . . . perplexing.'

'Always happens. New apprentices. Understandable.'

'The thing I find most confusing is why I'm here. I mean – why *me*?'

'Pot luck,' he said. 'Unholy Tombola. Your number came up.' He licked his lips with a thin, pink tongue, like a snake's. 'And Hades, of course.' He studied me fleetingly, perhaps to gauge my curiosity.

'So I've heard.'

'Ripped apart. Guts torn out.'

'Sounds horrible.'

'Worse than that. One of the few ways an immortal can die.'

'Unfortunate.'

He agreed, and sat down on the edge of the Barca lounger. 'Suspicious circumstances, too. Looked like Cerberus' handiwork at first, but not so simple. Someone let him out.' He lowered his voice. 'Death disliked Hades. Hated him always following him around . . . Skirmish made poppy and honey cake the same morning. Smell still on his breath, maybe . . . War didn't come to breakfast until ten-thirty. Cagey about where he'd been . . . Pestilence playing with Cerberus in the garden at eleven.' He spoke normally again. 'Could have been anyone.'

'Couldn't it have been an accident?'

'Unlikely. Very few things are.'

I paused. 'What were *you* doing?'

'Preparing breakfast.' The question hadn't fazed him. 'Hades was neither my enemy nor my friend. Same as everyone else.'

I wondered if I would ever discover the truth about Death's former assistant. I had my own suspicions, but the precise manner of his demise was still something of a mystery.

'I see you've finished,' said Famine, indicating the tray. I nodded, and he picked it up. As he headed for the door, I felt an uncontrollable urge to share something with him. I sensed – without any logical explanation – a kindred spirit.

'Do you want to hear my all-time favourite joke when I was alive?'

He stopped. Smiled. 'Like jokes. What is it?'

'It goes like this.' I coughed. 'An alligator walks into a bar and orders a drink. And the barman says to him . . . *Why the long face?*'

I waited.

'What's the punch-line?' he said.

Seven eyes for seven udders

When I awoke I was an ant.

I had been released temporarily from my sack. For a period of seven days I was free to move within the strict boundaries of the forest glade. I performed the Agency's work under Death's supervision.

If I disobeyed, I would be crushed.

I dressed and scurried along the corridor to the dining room, feeling like Gregor Samsa in *Metamorphosis*. When I reached the door, I heard no conversation, no movement. I knocked lightly on the wood.

No response.

I opened the door. The dining room was empty. My breakfast of cereal and fruit had been left at Famine's usual place, and a half-eaten bowl of yoghurt lay next to it. Famine had been reading the *Daily Telegraph*, whose second-page lead blandly proclaimed *Calls for fairground safety to be improved*. The *Oxford Times* rested on War's chair, with an equally mind-numbing headline on the front page: *Disappearing body baffles police*.

'Hmm-um-*umm*!' a voice moaned. I leapt a couple of inches into the air, kicked over the chair, and landed badly on my three-toed right foot. When I looked around the room for my assailant, I was relieved to discover it was Skirmish.

I tried to sound calm: 'Sorry?'

He crunched twice on the apple he was holding, sucked once and swallowed. 'I said: Oh, it's you.'

'It is.'

'Sit down. Tuck in.' He gestured frantically with his arms, indicating my plate; then returned to the kitchen.

'Where is everyone?'

'Already eaten,' he answered laconically.

'Really?' I wondered what the time was.

He peered over the saloon doors, and smiled. 'Meetings start early on a Saturday.'

The fact that I had been invited to Wednesday's gathering but excluded from today's didn't particularly bother me. I was never one to feel instantly wanted whenever I received formal invitations; or to feel rejected when I didn't.

Amy saw things differently. She explained to me once that an invitation is a sign that you are known to someone else, that you aren't just an isolated mound of earth in an archipelago of five billion islands. She said that it momentarily contradicts what we are often told: that we are accidental life forms inhabiting an insignificant planet, which orbits an unspectacular star, on the outer rim of a galaxy containing millions of solitary suns, in a universe filled with friendless galaxies.

But I wasn't convinced. Even now, as a zombie, I am more comfortable with the attitudes of the dead. They welcome solitude because it is unavoidable. They refuse to worry about what they might be missing, thinking only about what they have.

If life is a party and they aren't invited, so what?

'Are they discussing anything important?'

Skirmish re-entered and sat down, clutching a bunch of baby bananas. 'Mostly business. Death's got last month's figures on the sales of Seven-Eyed Lamb merchandise. Confidential information – which is why I'm not invited.' He peeled the first banana by holding it upside down at the stem and quickly flicking his wrist. 'Though, if you ask me, they could *use* my opinion. All this apocalyptic shit, it's getting too heavy already. In a couple of years, it'll be dead in the water.'

I smiled inanely.

We ate in silence for a while. It was already a hot day, and through the open window I heard the intermittent noise of traffic. In between mouthfuls of cereal, I observed my room-mate forcing one fruit after another down his throat.

'Hey,' he said at last, 'you want to know something weird about the Seven-Eyed Lamb? Something John forgot to mention in Revelation?'

I mumbled an affirmative, scraping the last traces of cereal from my bowl.

'Well . . .' He shuddered. 'The thing is, it's got seven udders, too. Isn't that gross?'

I stared at him as he bit into his last banana, rubbed his belly, and belched. 'Do you know what I'm supposed to be doing today?' I said.

He smiled. 'You, D., and F. have got a P.B. on. Fam's coming along to help with the starvation side of things. Basic supervision job, really.' I had no idea what a P.B. was, but he pressed on before I could ask. 'Oh – and Death says he wants you to read the Life File in the Chief's office, like you did on Thursday. If that makes any sense.'

I nodded.

'He told me you can't miss it – it's on the desk.' He reached into the jacket pocket of his pyjamas, pulled out a small key and tossed it to me; then checked his watch. 'I should get dressed. War needs me to do the children's playground tour. Start a few Saturday morning fights. Maybe get some parents involved.' He rubbed his hands together and stood up, leaving a half-eaten apple nestling in the yoghurt bowl.

As he opened the door, I made an important decision. Unlike Gregor Samsa, I was determined to reverse my transformation. I couldn't remain an insect and live. 'Do you remember what you said on Thursday? That you might have something which could keep me out of the coffin?'

His expression was impassive. 'Of course.'

'I'd like to know what it is.'

'I'll talk to you tonight,' he said.

The empty dead

I unlocked the door to the Chief's office, and was about to enter when I heard loud voices from the Meeting Room. The temptation to listen was too strong to resist. Eavesdropping was the aspect of detective work which most interested me when I was alive, because you could always guarantee that suspects under surveillance would say different things to different people about their activities. And it was always a compelling moment when the deceiver was confronted with his deception. He would either struggle desperately to reconcile his conflicting statements, or deny ever having said one thing or the other, or simply give his accuser a broken nose.

I didn't fear any of these reactions now, but out of habit I checked the stairwell and the corridor before placing my ear against the door. Death's was the first voice I heard.

'. . . T-shirts and dairy products are up by twenty-five per cent, due to the weather. Sales of baseball caps, soft toys, tea towels, and mugs all remain stable. Hot-water bottle receipts, as we anticipated, are down. As for the future, market research suggests that a branded range of apocalyptic children's toys would perform well at this time. Something along the lines of a *Seven-Eyed Lamb versus The Beast* concept, or a *Seven Seals* RPG. The Chief suggests there might even be potential for Four Horsemen combat figures, with associated weaponry and side-kicks. Videos and computer game spin-offs will become viable once the principal characters have been established.'

'This is all very interesting,' interrupted Pestilence, 'but could we possibly move on? I've got some tests to run before lunch.'

'Really?' Death countered. 'How is the bruise coming along?'

'It's almost disappeared. Why?'

'So it didn't work?'

'I'm still at the trial stage. The initial results have been extremely positive. Better than any of us could have expected.'

'But it didn't work?'

'The spread was very impressive. Almost total torso cover. And extremely painful.'

'And then it disappeared?'

'Yes.'

'So it didn't work.'

'Not in a *final* sense, no.'

I turned away. The only trouble with eavesdropping is that, all too often, you hear nothing of any interest whatsoever.

I climbed the spiral staircase and entered the Chief's office. The morning sun dazzled through the dormer windows, and the paper-white brightness of the room caused me to squint. I headed for the writing desk, which today contained only the computer, printer, and a green document wallet. The fire in the grate was long dead. The column of files had disappeared.

The wallet contained the Life File. I opened it, studied three rows of figures, closed it again. I couldn't face reading another two hundred pages of arid statistics. I placed the document back in the folder, then wandered around the office for a while, thinking about nothing much, happy just to be alone. I turned the handle on the tombola drum and listened to the rumble of the balls. I lowered and raised the blinds on the windows a dozen times. I sat down at the computer, but felt no great urge to discover any more information about myself or my employers. I couldn't explain why. I felt listless and empty.

This is how the dead feel all the time: empty. Sometimes they want to scream about it, to terrify the living, to tear the world apart. But no-one can hear them. So they just go on feeling empty.

But this was different. It felt like the melancholy emptiness of being alive.

I lay down in a warm patch of sunlight on the carpet, closed my eyes, and drifted in and out of consciousness. I imagined myself as the dreamer in 'Pearl', a seven-hundred-year-old poem I'd read in the school library, in which religious and philosophical truths are revealed in a vision. I recounted the story of Lazarus to myself, substituting Death for Jesus, and myself for the old man. I remembered a character called Billy Liar in a book of the same name, who protected himself against unbearable reality with a vivid imagination. And inevitably, the flotsam of my own personal shipwreck rose to the surface.

I remembered the last occasion I had spoken to Amy as her lover. We were sixty-three miles apart at the time, because she had moved to London to take a job the details of which I no longer recall. We were talking on the telephone, and I hadn't seen her for two months, not since our terminal discussion in the Jericho Café. At the end of the conversation, I told her that our enforced separation had left me with an emptiness inside. Attempting to fill some small part of that vacuum, I added that I loved her.

'Why?' she said.

And I put the phone down, because I couldn't think of an answer.

I still can't, even now.

More flotsam, as I travelled further back.

Amy and I first spoke at a mutual friend's house. There was a big party for people in our class, and everyone was invited – even me. I remember an old stereo, and plentiful supplies of alcohol, and vomit on the bathroom carpet. About halfway through the evening I saw her, sitting on the floor, cross-legged, facing away from me. She wore blue jeans and a white T-shirt. We had noticed each other at school, but I had been too reserved to speak to her, and she had never shown much interest. She turned around and caught me watching her.

'Hi,' she said, smiling.

'Hello,' I said.

'I'm Amy.'

'And I'm . . . pleased to meet you.'

She laughed, though I hadn't intended to be funny.

Her laughter saved my life, because the previous day I had been contemplating suicide. This happens so often to teenagers that it wouldn't be worth mentioning, had it not been so serious this time. It wasn't just an absence of purpose, and a feeling that my future was drifting into chaos, and a sense that all the defined elements of my life had fallen apart – these things are commonplace. Instead, it was a sudden and overwhelming realization that existence was not the cosy, narrow prospect which my parents' example had encouraged me to believe in. I had a revelation: I saw my future not as the inevitable extension of my unconditionally happy childhood, with its clear moral boundaries and easy solutions, but as a terrifying hydra emerging from a thick fog. Responsibility, sexuality, self-consciousness, sophistication, power, self-determination, mortality: these words were no longer abstract concepts discussed in the books I'd read, but a single, vile creature with seven reptilian heads from which I would never escape. And the horror of it made me want to destroy myself. I remember walking to the bathroom, repeating *This is too much . . . This is too much . . .* I wanted to slash my wrists and melt into oblivion – in my mind I could already see the blood flowing. As it turned out, when I got to the bathroom I discovered my father had recently switched to an electric shaver, and I was forced to carry on living for one more day – a day which brought me Amy's laughter, and then her friendship, and ultimately her love . . . But from that terrible moment of revelation onwards I was always aware of the hydra lurking in the fog, and my happiness was always conditional.

I guess I was susceptible to suicidal tendencies because I was a loner. Throughout my teenage years I felt inadequate, inaudible, and invisible. I would often make jokes which nobody laughed at, get angry only to be mocked, make statements which no-one heard, wander in and out of rooms unseen. And I had no great talents. I was inquisitive and bookish, but not intellectually gifted; and because of my illnesses as a small child, I was never an outstanding physical specimen.

Old flotsam now. I was ill as a small child because my mother kept me apart from other children. As a result I had a negligible immune system, and when I attended nursery school I caught every disease going. I was in hospital every other month, and I almost died only three years after I was born – twenty-five years too soon.

And why was I born? the only answer that makes sense is: *because my parents wanted me*. Without that desire, I would never have been ill, or inquisitive, or suicidal, or numb, or happy. I would not have met Amy, or had lovers, or become an investigator. And I would not have been sliding down that wet rooftop in Oxford late one summer evening, screaming in terror.

The final logic is inescapable: I was destined to die only because my mother and father wanted me to live.

Is this all that existence means?

Up on the roof

I lurched forwards for the skylight, but my hands patted uselessly against the greasy paintwork. For the thousand moments contained within that single first second, I felt I could stop myself; but my body slithered down the roof with increasing speed, over the grey slates, the steep slope accelerating the slide, the wind and rain whipping into my face. I slapped my hands and feet against the wet tiles, hoping to gain a hold, trying to slow the descent, but the desperate ride continued.

Until my trousers caught on a raised tile.

My left knee jerked upwards as the trapped material ran up my leg. The edge of the tile scraped along my calf, grazing the skin; the rest of my body maintained its downward motion, forcing me into a crouch. I twisted sideways to avoid tumbling over, but this only caused me to spin around, until I was facing backwards down the slope. The tile came loose under the stress of my improvised gymnastics, and I felt myself sliding once more. This time headfirst, and on my back.

I screamed.

Even though I knew I was about to plunge eighty feet to the square below, my immediate instinct was to protect my head with my hands. I briefly struggled to create some friction with my heels, but the roof was too greasy, and my efforts only increased the feeling of falling, emphasized the helplessness. I closed my eyes and opened my mouth, like a baby – but no sound escaped.

The slope began to level out: the lower part of the roof pressed against the top of my spine. By the time I realized what was happening, my whole body had slipped onto the shallower incline. Immediately, I pressed my hands and feet against the tiles, gripping as tightly as I could. For a brief moment I was hanging between life and certain death, between renewed hope and despair, as my progress towards the edge slowed. I lowered my head onto my chest and watched the peak of the roof cone receding, until gradually, gratefully I came to a halt with my shoulders resting on the rough, angled rim.

I was so terrified I could hardly breathe. I saw the whiteness of my knuckles against the tiles, felt my feet arching inside my shoes. My clothes were drenched by the pouring rain, my thighs formed a black V against the sky. I relaxed a little, and lowered my head to ease a crick in my neck. But where I had expected to find the edge, there was only thin air; and a moment later, the tile I'd loosened with my trouser leg trailed me down the slope and struck me on the left shoe.

I panicked.

I cried out with surprise, and the effort loosened my body's grip on the roof. A moment later the tile struck my hand, and instinctively I pulled it away. With no firm hold, I twisted and slid sideways, shouting for help. In a last desperate attempt to save myself, I flapped wildly with my arms, looking for something to support my shifting weight.

I felt my whole body slipping over the edge. But the erratic swings of my arm saved me: my elbow caught in the gutter and provided just enough leverage to interrupt the fall. The pressure inside my chest and throat was so enormous, I felt it would crush me. Lowering my head again and looking down beyond my feet, I saw that if I had rolled another inch, I would have plunged to my death.

I tried to move, but my courage had gone. I had to do something, but every muscle in my body felt like water, like paper soaked by the storm. I felt as if the first strong breeze would peel me from my fragile hold and whip me over the side. Nothing in my body would obey the feeble commands issuing from my brain.

I closed my eyes and let the rain fall on my face, distantly aware that someone was watching me from the skylight, and laughing.

X-ray vision

It was the longest journey of the week. Only three or four miles – but to someone who'd been squeezed into a coffin for years, it might as well have been a trip to the moon. Death drove with the front windows wound down; Famine sat quietly in the passenger seat. I lay in the back daydreaming, thinking about my slumber in the Chief's office. I looked up briefly, and saw the cemetery where Wednesday's client had died.

'Where are we going?'

'Wytham Woods,' Death replied cheerily. 'A renowned local beauty spot. Personally, I prefer Boar's Hill – where we went yesterday – but the Chief claims this is much more scenic.'

Death was wearing a beige polo shirt with cream-coloured jeans and Caterpillar boots. Famine sported a moth-eaten black tank top with black jeans and pumps. Apart from my usual outerwear, I had chosen purple petunia boxer shorts, purple socks embroidered with sea-green starfish, and a purple top. Today's slogan was: MY FAMILY WENT TO HELL AND ALL I GOT WAS THIS LOUSY T-SHIRT.

As we headed west towards the ring road, I lapsed into a daydream again. Memories were colouring every waking moment now. I couldn't stop them. Nor did I want to: they made me feel more alive than at any time since I'd been woken up inside the coffin. And my desire to live was growing stronger by the day.

I closed my eyes and saw a line of thin, black trees.

Amy and I are walking in the snow on the west bank of the Thames, at the northern end of Port Meadow. Dark pines burst like huge porcupine quills from the white ground around us. The snow is shallow and crisp underfoot, untrodden, untouched. Golden evening light dazzles in the gaps between the trunks, sparkles on the ice in the swollen river.

'I just can't see how it's going to work,' she says. 'It doesn't *feel* right. Not any more.'

'How is it supposed to feel?' I reply.

'Better than this. This is not what I want.'

Once, we rose together like these trees, linking limbs, sharing light, spreading our roots until they coupled like clasped hands. When the wind blew, we were stronger. We were so firmly intertwined, nothing could touch us. But the trees grew taller and thicker, and their bark became old and gnarled, and the competition for sun and soil stifled their growth.

'What *do* you want?'

'Anything but this. *Anything*.'

On the edge of a black wood by the swollen Thames, we speak in a code created by our ancestors, without reference to words which might reveal precisely how we feel. I can still see Amy's sharp features frozen there in an expression of despair. I still hear her teeth chatter, briefly, comically.

I watch, as her black hair falls in front of her eyes.

And she brushes it aside.

'What d'you know about our client?' Famine said, turning around. With his tiny, bald head, bird-like body and scruffy black clothes, he resembled an ailing vulture. My mind was still full of snow, and I hesitated – before realizing that I didn't actually have an answer.

'Don't bother him,' Death interrupted. 'He's had a hard week.'

I was grateful for his face-saving intervention. Half an hour earlier he had discovered me lying, half-asleep, beneath the dormer windows in the Chief's office. He had been neither angry nor concerned, but had simply said:

'Finished already?'

I looked through the rear window and saw Amy in the shade of an elder tree.

* * *

We are standing together on wet grass at the southern end of the meadow, after a desperate dash to avoid the worst of a spring rain-storm. We are sheltering from the shower and laughing hysterically, uncontrollably, in great gasps and spurts.

We watch rain splashing on the river in front of us. It makes the water seethe and boil. We feel the drops as they drip through the gaps in the leaves. We listen to the sweep of the storm on the trees. Anything we say at this moment will have meaning: whether it interests us, whether we know nothing about it, it's all the same. We can fill the air with words of all shapes, ideas of all sizes, statements and declarations and intentions of all kinds.

'I love you,' I tell her, drawing her towards me.

'Me too,' she replies.

We embrace, and time collapses, and the world shrinks to a kiss.

We're running back across the meadow towards town now; back through the side streets; back to the café. We still can't stop laughing, and talking, and shouting, and people stare at us gloomily when we sit down. Amy sticks out her tongue at a scowling man as old as my father, then turns to me.

'Do you really love me?' she says.

'Yes.'

We watch the rain run down the window in rivulets, silent for the first time, as the light begins to fade.

'Why don't we live together?' she says, adding: 'Why don't we just do it.'

The rain has stopped, and we are back on the meadow, walking bare-foot on the wet grass. We kiss again, more passionately, wrapping ourselves around each other, needing the electric shock of each other's skin, wanting the pressure of atom against atom. And love infects us. It hijacks our blood cells, races to the extremities of our bodies, opens fire in the tips of our toes.

I look up briefly, and see the sun sinking slowly behind her – one of a hundred different sunsets we will share, a thousand different skies.

The Metro whined as we pulled off the ring road and struggled up a small, steep hill. At the top, Death turned onto a gravel car park and switched off the engine. We were surrounded by sloping woodland, descending behind us, rising ahead. Clumps of deciduous trees hissed quietly in the gentle breeze.

'Now,' he said. 'We've got a long walk to the river – where we *should* find a small mound of earth with a thin air-pipe sticking out.' We followed a short stony path over the brow of the hill and down a tree-covered slope, until the ground levelled by a line of weeping willows. 'I'm afraid I can't remember precisely where she's buried,' he announced, pacing back and forth on the path. 'So it would save us some time if we split up.'

He pushed his way through the willows towards the river. Famine struggled up the steep tree-lined slope for a better view. I headed along the path parallel to the bank for a while, then stopped. I finally realized what Skirmish had meant at breakfast when he'd referred to today's client as a P.B. Given the description of our destination, it couldn't have been anything other than a premature burial.

I shivered as a cold blast of air ran through me.

The blanket of snow makes everything we once knew unrecognizable. There are no signposts or landmarks – just crisp, white earth, a delicate sheet of fallen flakes. The air is bitterly cold.

'This was a stupid idea,' Amy says. 'I shouldn't have listened to you.'

'We can't go back now.' Behind us, the trees have moved together to form a wall of darkness.

'Why not? We're not getting anywhere.'

'When we find the other side we'll know where we are.'

'You're useless. You've never done anything right.'

The snow crunches and squeaks beneath our boots. Pine trees burst from the white ground like bristles on a giant's chin. Golden evening light dazzles through the trees like sunlight on water. We walk slowly forwards, unprotected, freezing in the face of an ice wind.

'What's the point in going on?'

'There's always a point.'

'It doesn't *feel* right.'

'How's it supposed to feel?'

I gaze at her, recording her face in memory. Raven's wing hair, knife-cut lips, witch's nose, brown dagger-eyes. Her teeth chatter. Her features are frozen. Her black hair falls.

I file the memory and turn around. I see a mound of snow through a break in the trees. It rises like a wave, like a dune.

'A bridge.'

She follows my pointing finger and nods, but the despair remains. We are individuals divided by time and space. She was a lone candle in a dark room, she shone like starlight, she was a hurricane blowing, she was the sea and the shore, she was birdsong – and I was all of these things to her. And I am an extinguished candle, a black hole, a weakening breeze, a dried-up riverbed, and a long, loud wailing.

And she is all of these things to me.

Famine's pale, sickly shape strode quickly through the snow in my mind. Dry pine needles covered his tank top. The sight of him surprised me. I stepped backwards and tripped over a root on the upland slope.

'Shouldn't be so jumpy,' he observed, offering me his hand.

'You shouldn't sneak up on people,' I countered.

'Found anything yet?'

'No.'

'Nor me.' He stopped and studied me briefly. Opened and closed his mouth like a fish. 'Haven't read the Life File, have you?'

I shook my head.

'No problem. Not really necessary anyway. It's a simple ransom job.' He smiled thinly. 'We're here to make sure it goes wrong.'

'I'm tired of all these deaths,' I complained.

'Never easy . . . But you get used to it.' He gestured for me to accompany him along the path. 'Today, for example, I have to supervise the starvation procedure. Ensure that the body has exhausted all stores of glycogen and fat. If client shows severe wasting, tissue proteins will be under attack. Good sign.' His yellow eyes rolled sideways, lizard-like, then flicked back. 'And I need to make sure she doesn't have water . . . And that she really *feels* hunger.' He stopped. 'Don't like any of it, don't *dis*like it – but have to do it. Chief's orders.'

'Death seems to feel the same way,' I suggested.

'Death's like me, perhaps worse. Tired of it all.' He paused, and sighed. We sat down on a patch of grass beneath a weeping willow. 'Working for the Agency isn't easy. After the first thousand years you begin to recognize patterns. Patterns that repeat, and repeat, and repeat in millennia that follow. Difficult not to become very bored.' He sighed again. 'All terminations different, but all essentially the same. Anything we achieve creatively is a bonus . . . But for Death, problem is more serious. Not just the detail of his job which bothers him, but the reason for it.' He scratched his hairless head with long, black nails. 'Pes and War different. Always take pleasure in their work. Don't stop to think.'

'What about Skirmish?'

240

'New. Still enthusiastic. Big ideas.' He smiled. 'Can be dangerous.'

We walked along the path, back towards where Death had disappeared.

'The Chief tries to make our terminations more exciting . . . But lacks compassion. No experience of dealing with Lifers face-to-face.' He frowned. 'Had you read today's file, as I have, you would've seen that today's termination is totally inappropriate to the client. Has not lived her life in a manner which *deserves* a death such as this.' We stopped at a shaded viewpoint overlooking the sluggish grey river. 'Feeling is that the Chief is *staging* terminations. Manipulating the data we've compiled to produce work which satisfies him on a personal level. Could have very serious consequences.'

'Why don't you speak to him about it?'

'Would like to. But have never spoken to him. Never even *seen* him.' He chuckled briefly. 'Sometimes doubt that he exists.'

I heard a shout in the distance: 'Over here.' Down the slope to our left, near the river.

Death was standing by an eroded stretch of bank, surrounded by trees. A slender, brown boomerang of silty water bent towards and away from us in a smooth arc, its ends disgorged and swallowed by the woodland. As we drew closer we saw the narrow, plastic air-pipe rising from a low mound of raw earth.

'Still alive?' Famine asked.

'Barely,' Death replied.

He reached into the front pocket of his jeans and produced three pairs of sunglasses, like the ones I'd seen in his polo shirt on Monday morning. He handed one each to Famine and me, and kept the last for himself.

'What are these for?'

'Try them on,' he suggested.

I studied the glasses in my hand. Thick plastic, black lenses. A simple frame. Nothing unusual. I shrugged and put them on.

I removed them immediately, afraid of what I'd seen.

'It's OK,' said Death, reassuringly. 'Everyone reacts like that the first time.'

'What happened?'

'Put them on again. Keep them on. You'll see.'

I tried on the sunglasses once more, and the gloom of twilight descended. Two grey aliens grinned at me in a dim landscape of ghosts. Everything was shadow, nothing had substance. I removed the glasses agitatedly.

'I don't understand—'

'They help us to observe,' Death explained. Both he and Famine were now wearing them, so that I couldn't see their eyes behind the black lenses. 'They're handy in cases like this, when you need to record the precise moment termination took place. But generally, we use them to check that we've found the right grave when we're digging people up. Look for yourself.' He pointed at the earth mound.

As I put on the glasses for a third time, the world lost its colour and slipped into a dimension of shimmering spectres. It was as if the top layer of existence had been peeled away to reveal the grim, grey structures beneath. I looked at the skeletal giant standing at the grave side. Diaphanous layers of changing patterns fluctuated over his entire body: sombre clothes shivered above ashen flesh, flesh slid over pallid muscle and fat, colourless organs hung inside string baskets of blood-less veins. A gloomy framework of pearl bones held the creature together.

'We've got a whole box of them back at the office,' he announced, proudly.

'How do they work?' I asked.

'Who knows?'

The figure standing next to the giant was tiny in comparison, but its translucent fragility was just as disturbing. It wavered before me, its mouth open in a toothy grin. The folds of its white brain and the feeble beating of its withered heart disgusted me.

'Shock, isn't it? Keep looking. Becomes routine.'

The landscape had no depth. Features were laid on top of each other in a series of overlapping planes. I turned around. The fish-speckled river was a dirty grey cloth sliding between two flat banks. I turned again. I saw a thousand feet of hillside and woodland, dimly floating in space. I looked down. I felt like I was walking on air. If I took a single step, I would fall to the centre of the earth.

The vision was clearer than an X-ray but darker than daylight. The further away everything was, the hazier it became.

It was like looking into the past.

I turned at last towards the grave. I saw the mound of earth, six feet of soil, the wooden coffin walls. I saw seven feet of black plastic pipe stretching from the head of the casket to Famine's skeletal feet. I saw the body of a tall, young woman, the clothes that covered her, the panic on her face, the pounding of her dark heart through the watery bars of her ribs. I saw her hands coiled into fists. I saw grey worms burrowing in the soil beneath her, waiting.

And through all this confusion of skin, and soil, and skeleton, I realized, with horror, that I knew her.

Snow White and the three Agents

My zombie brain refused to deal with this information, and reverted to trivia mode again. It reminded me that I'd once had a paranoid fear of premature burial, because it was one of the few forms of death that offered no chance of escape: those who bury you assume they have good cause, and don't normally dig you up every fifteen minutes to check if they've made a mistake. I wasn't the only one afraid of this fate, either. I knew of over twenty patented devices designed to avert the annoyance of accidental interment.

I could never understand those lunatics who actually requested to be buried alive for the sake of some record. Such people exist. They've even devised two strict rules to ensure that they are as uncomfortable as possible during their subterranean confinement:

The coffin should lie at least two metres below ground and have a maximum capacity of 1.5 million cubic centimetres.

To keep the contestant alive, a communication and feeding pipe with a diameter of no more than ten centimetres is allowed.

Just before I died, I read that the longest documented voluntary interment was one hundred and forty-one days.

Beat *that*.

'Let's get on with it,' said the tiny skeleton.

'I agree,' agreed the giant skeleton.

I knew who she was. I had seen her, still alive, on Tuesday. I had been paralysed by the memory of her yesterday morning. It was Lucy. And I couldn't restrain my imagination: I remembered again the moment when I emerged from my shell at the Jericho Café.

'I think I'm falling in love with you,' I said.

'Me too,' she replied.

When I first met her, I thought she was the kind of person who would throw you a conversational rope and use it to drag you down into the mire of her own misery. When I tried to speak to her about anything else in those first few weeks she suffered from temporary deafness. She hardly ever listened to anything I said and often completely ignored the questions I asked her; even when she did answer, her reply betrayed a profound misunderstanding of the question. It was a challenge simply to communicate – a challenge I found irresistibly attractive.

But after that moment when I first crept out of my carapace, I discovered that she could also be the funniest and most charming person anyone would wish to meet. She told me jokes like my father's: inoffensive, surreal and short. She once made me laugh so hard that I had stomach cramps for an hour. These are the kind of memories a zombie treasures.

And we became lovers. We wanted to, because we were so happy. But it was a mistake, and it only lasted nine days. I didn't claim, as Amy had once said to me, that it just didn't *feel* right. I didn't look for incipient signs of rejection in Lucy, as I had with others, which would convince me that I should leave before I was kicked out. I didn't even pick on something trivial, such as powerful body odour and bad breath (the kind of combination that, were he not dead already, a corpse would die for). Instead, and without knowing it – without even consciously intending that the end should come so soon – I found a different echo of my relationship with Amy.

Our entire affair was spent in bed together. Eating junk food, sleeping fitfully, having sex often. Every suggestion Lucy and I made to each other, we acted on. We seemed totally compatible. And I recall every detail of her room, from the hills of soft toys in every corner to the leopard-print duvet, from the white shagpile carpet to the Artex ceiling. I remember lying half-awake on the morning of the last day and gazing up at the frozen patterns of stalactites, like little white stars clustered in crazy constellations. I even recall the patterns I saw: animals, and food, and faces, and the chaotic spinning of suns. I was comfortable and relaxed, and free to imagine everything or nothing, as I had often been in my father's study so long ago.

Our relationship felt so open and natural, I thought I could suggest anything to her; and lying there on the bed, gazing at the ceiling, I had an idea. Normally, I would have waited several weeks before mentioning some of my more unusual sexual preferences, but my fantasy fuelled my desire, and my desire had to be satisfied. I pulled back the duvet and stood up.

'I've got a surprise for you,' I said.

She smiled sleepily.

I left the bedroom and drifted into her kitchen, where I repeated the game Amy had once played with me. I found a plastic shopping bag and a large elastic band. I returned with both to her double bed, slipped the bag over my head and pulled the elastic band over my neck. I felt myself growing very excited, and sucked the plastic into my mouth as I spoke.

'Take it off when I start to pass out,' I said.

But she didn't reply – and a moment later I removed the bag and the elastic band and tossed them aside. I saw that she was standing up, with her back to me. She had begun to dress.

'What's wrong?' I asked, breathing deeply, feeling my face redden.

'You're fucking sick,' she replied.

And I couldn't see why. I had buried the corpse of my past. So I simply told her what I had often told myself, believing it to be true, hoping it would help:

'How do you know what you want until you've tried it?'

She wouldn't listen. And I amplified this minor incompatibility between us until it became an excuse to end our relationship. Like all the others, it decayed to a pile of dry bones and a handful of dust.

Safe again.

Pathetic.

'What are you doing?' I asked the tiny skeleton. His white teeth were fixed in a grin over the end of the grey air-pipe.

'He's making her feel hungry,' the giant skeleton replied.

'Very hungry,' confirmed the tiny skeleton.

'Why?' I asked.

Both skeletons turned towards me and, as well as skeletons are able, stopped grinning.

'Chief's orders,' they said in unison.

I didn't need to look at the grave to describe Lucy – a tide of random memories washed over me. She was six feet two inches tall. Her face was angular, but not bony. When she moved, her limbs resembled an octopus waving half of its tentacles. She despised onions; she had thousands of friends; she loved sex, and gave it freely. And now she had a dark bruise on her right cheek, and a red cut on her lip – both, presumably a gift from the man with the deep, black eyes. I remembered him watching me. He didn't seem the tolerant type.

'What are you thinking about?' the giant skeleton said. His tone was sombre, but his skull was laughing.

'I know her,' I told him.

'It often feels that way when you've read the Life File.'

'No – I mean, I've seen her before.'

He nodded, but still misunderstood. 'Tuesday was an unfortunate day for meeting future clients.'

When he wasn't breathing into the pipe, the tiny skeleton hummed a melody I didn't recognize. I watched his small grey lungs shrinking and expanding inside his grey chest. He breathed, and he hummed, and continued to breathe and hum in an irregular pattern, repeating the

247

same tune against the background of birdsong and the rolling river, until his breathing and humming irritated the hell out of me.

'What's the music?' I asked, trying to break the cycle.

'Funeral march from *Akhnaten*,' he said, turning towards me. 'Philip Glass. Seems appropriate.'

And he started to hum some more.

I desperately wanted to speak to Lucy again. Just a few words: *It's not so bad*. Or maybe a reassurance: *Don't be afraid. Dying is the worst part.* Just to talk to her. But I didn't want her to die like this. I glided over to the graveside. The skeletons glanced at me then continued their work: the giant skeleton supervising, the tiny skeleton breathing.

'Is there anything I can do?' I asked.

'You can watch,' suggested the giant. He reached out with his double-boned arms to touch my shoulder, but I backed away in fear. I still wasn't used to the reality the glasses were showing me.

I looked down, through the bones of my feet, through the soil. Above the faint whiteness of her skull and below the shadow of the coffin, Lucy's grey face was frozen into a grimace. Her arms and legs were quivering. Her white eyes were wide open. I sensed something was wrong, and the tiny skeleton confirmed it by abruptly ceasing his inane humming.

'Know those days when everything goes right? When you feel proud of your achievement? When you just *know* you've done a good job?'

The giant skeleton sighed. 'Uh-huh.'

'This isn't one of those days.'

'What's the problem?'

'*That* is.' The small skeleton pointed at a dark grey blockage about two-thirds of the way down the air-pipe.

'What is it?'

'Blockage.'

'I can *see* that. What's causing it?'

'Leaf, maybe. Can't tell.'

The giant tapped his bony fingers against his skull, and looked as depressed as any death's head can. He stared at the grave, and at both of us, before announcing his decision.

'Nothing we can do,' he said.

I removed my sunglasses and put them in my pocket. The world re-assumed colour and three dimensions. The skeletons fleshed out, became Death and Famine. Both were standing by a mound of earth from which a yellow plastic pipe rose like a periscope. I could no longer watch my friend dying. I was glad not to see the terror on her pale face, or the involuntary spasms of her limbs.

'She's not getting enough air,' Famine observed, staring at the ground.

'But she's still breathing,' Death said. 'I suppose it would be kinder if we blocked off the supply completely; but it's a couple of hours too soon. I don't know what the repercussions would be. The Chief said nothing about this.'

I felt nauseous. I remembered the warmth of her body against mine. I could trace every inch of her with my hands, even now. I remembered the sweet taste of her mouth, the cute angles of her crooked teeth, the deep blue sparkle of her eyes. I could still hear her laughter; and when she laughed, her mouth opened like a flower, revealing everything that she was, inviting you inside. She didn't want to know you, but it didn't matter.

You're fucking sick.

I stared at the mound and imagined her deep in the soil below. Her face stretched tight, turned blue; her mouth gaped wide as she gasped for air; her hands curled into claws, twitched. I didn't need to picture any more details: Death and Famine provided a running commentary.

'Struggling for breath,' said Famine, unemotionally. 'Chest heaving.'
'Good.'

'Veins swelling on neck. Starting to writhe. Should speed up the process.'

I couldn't move. I stared at them, flicking back and forth between the two. I had to do something. Do something now. Just *do something*. Move. At least move. Just an arm, or a hand. A finger. Some evidence that I lived and breathed and *could* move. My gaze froze, fixed on Death. I couldn't move. I couldn't decide what to do. Death looked mournful; Famine waited impassively. She was suffering a slow, suffocating end. And I couldn't move. She didn't deserve to die this way. She had no enemies, she'd done nothing wrong. *Move*. Could she believe what was happening? Or was everything drowned by the terrible, wheezing, wasted agony? I knew her agony. Just the tip of a finger. Her breath was being endlessly reprocessed. She was inhaling the past, exhaling the future. The more she wanted the less there was. And I couldn't move. The more she wanted the less – I *couldn't*. The more the less. I wanted to move, scream, move, shout, curse, move, move, *move*.

You're useless, Amy said. *You've never done anything right*.

'Knocking on the coffin lid,' Famine observed nonchalantly. 'Using her knuckles. All classic signs.'

I listened. It was all I could do. I couldn't even watch. Through the pipe I heard a faint rapping sound, rapid at first, then rapping more softly, more slowly. The feel of her skin beneath my fingers. My mouth opened. The way she could make anyone laugh with a single word. My tongue sank to the base of my mouth, receded. Her eyes. I felt a tightening in my throat.

'Can't?' I gasped.

Death turned towards me, puzzled.

'Can't you help her?'

He removed his glasses and placed his hand over the pipe.

I wanted to free her from the terrible moments of dying. I knew her. I could still feel her. Some residual memory in my nerve endings. A distant pulse from a well-worn pathway. I wanted to scrape at the ground with my hands, scoop away the soil, dig her up. *You're useless.* But only my eyes responded. *Fucking sick.*

'She's bleeding,' Famine announced, indifferently. 'Only the finger-nails – but a start. Scratching at the wood. Slapping it. Head rolling.'

I couldn't listen and couldn't act. I wanted to tear the bank apart. Whirl against it like a terrible storm. And dig down into the warm earth. Bring air, like a gift. But I was a zombie, still clinging to the corpse within me. The dead have no desire, and do nothing. And there was a terrible deadness inside me. *Useless.*

'Stopped pounding,' Famine said. 'Tearing at herself now. Typical behaviour. Clawing at her face . . . Arms . . . Stomach. Hitting herself on the chest.' He paused. 'Biting has started. Chewing at the back of her hand.'

I shook my head involuntarily. I could move to shake my head, to deny. I was only capable of denial. Not one positive movement escaped me. I had to move, or I would break.

'Thrashing now.' His speech quickened. 'Not much air.'

I shook my head. I imagined her, flipping like a beached fish, straining for breath, finding none.

'Bruises on her face. Cuts on her neck and arms.'

I shook my head.

'Stopped breathing.'

I shook.

'Unconscious.'

Death knelt down next to the mound and pulled hard on the pipe until the entire length was removed. It looked like a scythe without the blade. He tossed it into the water, watched it float gently downstream, then spoke to me.

'In seventy years the river will erode the last traces of soil on this part of the bank. What remains of the coffin and her body will be exposed. No-one will know that the man we saw on Tuesday buried her here, or why he did it. He will not be punished for his crime, or any others he commits. It's not our business to judge.' He turned towards Famine. 'Is the heart still beating?'

'For now.' Famine looked at me. 'Suffering is over.'

'How long?' I whispered.

'Varies. Any time.' He studied the mound of earth. 'Heart is . . . slowing. Faltering.' He waited with an open mouth. 'Slowing.' I heard birdsong in the trees, the soft slaps of the river against the bank. 'Stopped.'

'Are you sure?' Death asked, checking his watch.

Famine nodded.

I couldn't move. My eyes were hot, my throat tight. Something was irritating the skin on my face, on both sides of my nose. *Move.* I raised a hand to scratch the itch, then pulled it away, surprised. The tips of my fingers were wet.

I was crying.

The last thing I saw

Lying on the edge of the roof, I opened my eyes and squinted against the rain. I avoided the temptation to turn my head and look down, but tried to imagine the precise shape of everything around me. I was several yards below the skylight, on the rim of the round tower. Behind me, the wet, black tiles curved away until they joined the main roof of the apartment block – a steep, straight, sloping section of tiles incorporating the maintenance exit.

I moved my right arm further away from my body for greater balance and, using my feet, pushed myself a couple of inches towards the relative safety of the main building. My left arm was twitching erratically, but I managed to control it long enough to shift my elbow along the gutter, first sliding the raw, rough skin along the trough of slime, then pressing down hard to gain a hold. I arched my spine and slithered backwards with the rest of my body. I repeated the process – balancing and gripping with my right arm, pulling with my legs, sliding with my left arm and moving the bulk of my weight with my back – until, inch by terrifying inch, I was wedged in a small trough between the base of the main roof and the cone of the round tower.

'Well fuckin' done.'

I turned my head to the right and saw a dark shape against the brightness of the skylight. I couldn't distinguish his features clearly, but I had his picture in my jacket pocket – the photograph which Amy had given me seven weeks ago.

'Let's see how far you get.'

'Help me,' I said.

'Help your fuckin' self.'

I turned my head back slowly, and caught a glimpse of the fall that awaited – my first mistake. The rain guided my gaze downwards, every drop dragging me to the square below. I closed my eyes and waited for the weakness in my limbs to pass, waited for the spasmodic shivers to cease. It was a long time before I raised my head, forced my eyelids open again, and scanned the rest of my rooftop environment.

The gutter that had saved my life was a plastic half-pipe. Apart from a wedge of black slime, it contained the loose tile that had almost killed me. Behind me the main roof sloped upwards, gently at first then at a frighteningly steep angle, until it reached a raised maintenance exit below the ridge. In front of me I saw the nose cone of the tower, and the skylight from which I'd emerged a few minutes before. Even if I'd had the courage to make such a journey again, it would still have been a terrible mistake. Below me, to the left, the pale expanse of the square, luminous in the light of the moon and the storm, seemed tiny. And it was deserted.

'Nowhere to go . . .' He laughed. ' 'Cept down.'

'I can't move,' I said.

'Better stay where you are, then.'

He disappeared from the skylight.

The rain lashed against my head and bounced off my wet clothes, driven by sporadic gusts of wind. The noise of the storm was echoed by shouting from within the walls of the tower itself: Amy's voice, somewhere between pleading and self-defence. I realized that I would have to do something.

The alternative was unthinkable.

I rolled onto my front and raised myself slowly into a squatting position. Then, without giving myself any time to ponder, I stood up quickly and ran a couple of yards up the greasy slope of the main roof. Almost immediately, I felt my grip slipping, and threw myself flat against the tiles. My heart was beating rapidly, and I could barely see through the driving rain. I couldn't do it. I would fall. *You're useless*. But I didn't want to die.

Slowly, and without once looking down, I inched upwards. When I raised my head I could clearly see the maintenance manhole, only five yards away. I clawed with my hands, pushed up with my knees, gripped with the sides of my shoes, trying not to breathe too hard in case the movement of my chest unbalanced me. But the closer I came, the harder the rain seemed to fall, and the more unreachable my goal seemed.

Three yards. I was a long way from the edge of the roof, but any slip, however slight, would be fatal. My clothes had saved me before, by slowing my descent from the skylight; but there wasn't a single dry spot on my body now. I felt as if I was holding onto the steep incline by my hands alone.

One yard. The angle of the roof was greater than forty-five degrees; the rain and the wind tried to prise me off the slope; the tiles seemed to be covered in a thin, black film of oil. I couldn't move any further. I wouldn't make it. I reached out briefly to grab the metal handle of the manhole, but pulled back when I felt myself beginning to overbalance. I couldn't do it. But I crept upwards, more slowly than before, shifting in eighths of an inch, realizing that I had no choice but to try and survive. I saw only the wall of slate in front of me; imagined nothing but the final slip, and the fall that would follow.

I almost made it. My head was level with the exit. I was clinging to the roof with the tips of my fingers and the weight of my body. I had one chance to grab the handle and pull myself upwards. I wasn't sure if I had the strength to do anything other than hang there, delaying my fall – but I knew I had to try. How could I die so young? It seemed so random, so stupid, so unlucky.

And I wouldn't let it happen.

I felt sick with fear. The borderline between life and death was so fragile. It depended on the tiniest adjustment, the most minor co-ordination skills, the speed of movement of a hand. It depended on the people around you, on the impulsive decisions you made, on a sequence of circumstances so commonplace that no-one could predict the outcome. It depended on the stupid games my father played when I was a child, and on the career he had chosen. It depended on an old love affair, and a chance encounter. It depended on the weather.

I tried to imagine reaching for the handle, grabbing it, pulling myself up.

But the manhole opened before I could make the attempt.

*   *   *

It was the first time I'd seen Ralph face-to-face. His photograph had flattered him, the video had smoothed out his rough edges: a thick neck red with rage, square jaw tightly clamped, slick black hair spotted with rain. The scar running from his left ear to the corner of his mouth was pink and gruesome. His broken nose was bent at an unbelievable angle, as if he'd been struck sideways with a mallet. And in his small, deep-set eyes I saw nothing but hatred and triumph.

He grinned, flashing me a gold front tooth.

'Goin' somewhere?' he said.

And I fell.

I slipped down the slope, kicked against the tiles, rolled sideways. I screamed with terror, lashed out with my arms for one last hand-hold . . . But nothing could stop me falling. I experienced an instant of bliss when the roof ended and there was only air beneath me: a powerful and liberating sensation that I could fly. But it was only fleeting – and the last thing I saw before my death was the green-and-white striped awning of the bus station café, rising rapidly to meet me.

The magic potion

I sat at Skirmish's writing desk, staring through the window at the street below. There were no houses on the opposite side – just a brick wall and a towpath running along the canal. Every organic and in-organic surface reflected the yellow glare of the street lamps. I stretched forwards and peered to the right, where the road crossed a long bridge over the canal and railway line, before petering out into the dry, stony track which spanned the meadow. It was the same route I had often followed with Amy – and presumably the same one Hades had taken on a bright Sunday morning seven weeks ago.

I had wept uncontrollably on the walk back to the car. I hadn't cried for so many years. Not since my mother had found me at the restaurant, two years before my death. And the misery had returned in short spurts and sobs throughout the return journey, until my face felt like a swollen water bomb, ready to burst at any moment. I could still taste the salt on my face, feel the heat and wetness. The experience had left me drained.

Death had escorted me back to the room, but hadn't locked the door; as if he'd sensed my new mood. I wasn't going anywhere, of course – but I no longer felt the corpse's need for confinement.

I'd been staring through this window ever since, observing the darkening of the sky, watching the lamps fizz and glow, following idle passers-by with my gaze. In truth, I saw very little of what was happening outside. I was too busy contemplating my future.

I knew that death by premature burial would not be my preferred exit tomorrow evening. It's true that in the corpse community it's one of the most highly regarded ways to end your life. A cadaver who claims to have been buried before his time – especially if he still occupies the coffin in which he was originally interred – commands respect from everyone. It's almost as if he's been chosen. But for me, it was deeply unattractive. In fact, I could think of few worse ways to die.

More importantly, I had a single, overpowering wish which rendered all other decisions irrelevant; a wish that had caused me to sit here for the whole evening, wondering how I could achieve it.

I wanted to live.

But I couldn't see a way out. I was bound by contract and the options were clear: apprenticeship (unlikely), termination (undesirable), or storage (unknown). For four hours, I'd been trying to think of a plausible alternative. But there wasn't one.

Skirmish was my last hope.

*　　*　　*

There was a polite knock on the door.

'Who is it?'

'Pestilence.'

'*And* Skirmish.'

I remained seated. At the bottom of the deep well inside me, a drop of water fell. *If you can't move, open your mouth.*

'Come in.'

The door opened. Pestilence entered, supporting War's assistant by the arms. Skirmish looked slightly drunk, heaving into the room and flopping onto the lower bunk, laughing all the while. It was only when he finally managed to keep still for a couple of seconds that I saw the huge, strawberry-coloured abscess on his forehead.

'My friend here,' said Pestilence slimily, 'has been helping with a little experiment. He should be fine by the morning – though you can never be sure, of course.' I had a question gnawing at the back of my mind, but it refused to emerge from its hiding place, and I decided it could wait until tomorrow. 'It's a new range of boils,' he continued, 'caused by a new strain of staphylococcus. The details are absolutely fascinating – but I'm afraid I don't have the time to discuss them right now.'

He stared at me briefly, perhaps anticipating that I would ask him anyway, or (better still) beg him to tell me. When I offered no response, he tutted loudly, turned sharply, and left.

'He's an idiot,' said Skirmish, when the door closed. 'They all are. People's lives are in the hands of morons.'

'How are you feeling?'

'Like shit pushed through a mincer.' He touched the boil and winced. 'He sneaked up on me in the office. I was on level nine on Tetris, so I didn't pay him much attention. Bastard stuck a needle in my arm, and then apologized. Said the element of surprise was vital.' He stroked his forearm absent-mindedly. 'Worst thing was, I'd almost beaten my high score.'

I stood up, walked to the table by the rear window, looked down at the canal. I couldn't wait any longer. 'Do you remember what we were discussing this morning?'

'We talked about a lot of things.'

I turned around. His face was serious. I couldn't decide if he was being deliberately obtuse, or had simply forgotten.

'I need to get out of here,' I said.

He smiled, approached the table, and for one brief, bizarre moment I thought he was actually going to kill me. Instead he asked me to stand aside, picked up the blue glass ornament in the shape of a swan, and turned it over. With his thick thumb and forefinger he reached into the hollow base and plucked out an ampoule of clear liquid. He placed it on his palm and offered it to me.

'What's this?'

'Batch zero-three-stroke-ninety-nine.' He closed his palm, teasingly. 'I borrowed it from the Lab a few weeks ago. It's powerful stuff.'

I looked at him questioningly. 'And?'

'It's the Chief's finest achievement. Just one drop will kill anything – alive or undead – in seconds.' He tossed it into the air over his shoulder, and deftly caught it behind his back. 'We mainly use it on our own Agents. Sometimes they get rebellious, or start itching to live again, or they just turn bad and go on the rampage. There are many temptations when you're out in the field.' His expression turned sour. 'But the consequences can be disastrous for the Agency. And rogue Agents need to be put out of action.'

'I don't see your point.'

'Of course not.' He smiled wryly. 'Let me make it clear. What I'm asking you for is . . . a favour. And in return, I can do one for you.' He opened his palm again, this time letting me take the ampoule. I realized, belatedly, that it matched those I had seen on Tuesday in the Lab. 'Tomorrow, when Death delivers his appraisal of your per-formance, he'll share a drink with you. It's tradition.' I studied the liquid: it looked completely harmless. 'All you need to do is break the seal, empty a little liquid into his glass, and you're free.'

I couldn't believe what he was implying. I stepped away from him, dangerously close to the damaged cactus.

'Are you saying what I think you're saying?' He inclined his head slightly in what may, or may not, have been a nod. A flood of adrena-line surged through me. 'What about the consequences? What about the future?' And a small, selfish urge surfaced: 'What about my contract?'

'No-one has seen your contract since Wednesday morning. Perhaps you've been lucky. Perhaps it's been lost . . .' he added suggestively. He offered to take back the ampoule, but I held on to it. 'Besides, the Agency will have more pressing things to do than launch a zombie hunt . . . And I can always *swear* on my badge that Death put you back in the coffin before he was killed.'

I doubted this, but I could find no holes in his argument. Besides, I didn't have much choice.

'What's in it for you?'

'Immediate promotion,' he said simply. 'With both of you out of the way, I'll be in line for a senior position.'

I turned to the window again, clinging to the magic potion in my hand. The drop of water dripping into the well inside me became a trickle, became a stream, became a flood.

'I can't do it,' I protested.

He placed a sympathetic hand on my shoulder. 'It's the only solution, if you want to get out of here . . . I wish there was a better one.'

SUNDAY

DEATH BY THE SCYTHE

Damned if you do

This is the corpses' creed:

I am nothing. I have nothing to offer, I have nothing to say. I define myself with silence, by inaction, through hopelessness. I will restrain every pointless atom of my being until I achieve permanent paralysis and sterility. I will do nothing, think nothing, believe nothing; and I wish only for the continuation of this powerless condition.

I mouthed these words as I examined myself in the mirror on the back of the wardrobe door. Skirmish was dozing peacefully on the top bunk, undisturbed by my activity or the pale dawn light filtering into the room through the open curtain. I hadn't slept much, having spent most of the night considering his offer very carefully. The silence and darkness had focused my mind, but I'd failed to reach a firm decision.

I am nothing.

In the mirror I saw a man. He was naked. He stood on two clumsy wedges of flesh, terminating in eight skinny toes. Bony shins bent outwards from the ankles to the knees; thin thighs bent inwards from the knees to the waist. The pale skin of his pin-cushion legs was stitched with coarse black hairs, running upwards to the pubic triangle, in which a loose, useless stump of a penis nestled. The withered belly was a mouldy grey fruit of flesh in which his navel, that mocking reminder of his birth, was nothing more than a shadow. Above it, the wasted chest was a deflated life-belt punctured by dozens of cactus wounds, and adorned with two small, white nipples like plastic mouth-pieces. Hard collar bones curved against the slope of drooping shoulders, forging a triangle of skin below the scrawny neck. From an ape's hairy arms a pair of slender, blue-veined hands hung, lacking two fingers and a thumb. The entire body was criss-crossed with thick, black surgical thread, disguising a network of angry red scars arranged in bite-shaped arcs.

I am nothing.

His face was sad and weary.

I am nothing.

The man moved closer to the surface of the mirror. His head was deathly grey. The chin was unshaven, and disfigured by a raw, red wound at the centre. The lips were pale and thin, and broken by creases and cracks. The nose was sharp like a rat's, cratered with pores, blemished by bruising. The eyes were reptilian creatures cowering in caves of bone. The man's ears clung to the side of the head like rock-climbers, one higher than the other. Scattered patches of short, black hair crept up to his crown like iron filings drawn to a magnet.

On the left side of his neck, a number was stamped: 7218911121349.

I am nothing.

After showering and disposing of my body's waste, I selected the last remaining clothes from the wardrobe: boxer shorts decorated with pink roses, pink socks with a grey porpoise motif, and a plain pink T-shirt with the slogan DAMNED IF YOU DO printed on the front, and DAMNED IF YOU DON'T on the back. I put on my blue suit and white shoes, popped Skirmish's ampoule into my inner jacket pocket, and checked the mirror for the final time.

I saw a zombie. I saw me.

On the way to the breakfast room I was surprised to find Pestilence walking towards the front door. Seven white cardboard boxes were wedged between his hands and his chin, and he was stepping very carefully.

'Love to talk,' he said, teeth clenched, 'but can't stop.'

'What's in the boxes?' I asked.

'New virus. Batch zero-nine-stroke-ninety-nine.' He lifted his head from the uppermost package, balancing the column against his chest. 'That's better. I can speak properly now.' He jiggled his lower jaw to prove it. 'It's based on the contusion experiments I conducted earlier in the week. I think we've finally found the right formula. Massive bleeding . . . Rapid spread . . . Potentially fatal . . . Probably as many as one in a hundred cases . . .'

He continued in this vein for several more minutes, until I remembered the question I had wanted to ask him the previous night.

'What happened to the disease we released on Tuesday?'

He frowned, annoyed at the interruption. 'A complete and utter *failure*, I'm afraid. Our clients remain sickeningly healthy.' He gave me a look of contempt. 'Pity, really. The Chief had been working on it for years. It would have been a truly spectacular way to start the next millennium.'

'Nothing you can do,' I said.

'Indeed.' He lowered his chin again. 'Now, would you be so kind as to open the door for me?'

I squeezed past him and complied with his request. Pale sunlight broke through the doorway, intensifying the contrast between the pallor of his complexion and an overnight onslaught of acne. He looked terrible, and I told him so, intending it as a compliment.

'You look as bad as I've ever seen you,' I said.

'You look like Death warmed up,' he replied.

No-one else was awake, and I ate breakfast alone. I found a couple of brown bananas and a half-opened carton of yoghurt in the fridge, and devoured them eagerly whilst standing at the window. Apart from

Pestilence and a couple of early-morning joggers, I saw no-one.

I was about to return to my room when Death walked in, wearing his grey kimono and velvet slippers.

'Hello. You're up early.'

'I couldn't sleep.'

'Uh-huh.' He stared intensely at me. 'How are you feeling?'

'Fine.' I meant it. 'What time do we start?'

He didn't answer immediately, but went into the kitchen. I heard him mumble something excitedly, as if he was speaking to a child. He was answered by high-pitched squeaks and the rattling of cage bars. A moment later, he appeared behind the saloon doors, only his feet, chest and head visible.

'I've been thinking,' he said slowly. 'Today's client . . . it's a pretty gruesome affair. Don't ask me *why* it has to be that way – we *could* arrange for him to pass away peacefully in his sleep. But the Chief wants something special.' He shook his head. 'I'm told it's the person who saw Hades being killed two months ago. The Chief says his termination will solve some problems and tie things up neatly . . .' He lowered his voice. 'Anyway, this is all irrelevant. My thought was: why don't you have the day off? I can easily handle things on my own.'

We discussed it a little more, and I briefly considered what effect it would have on my slim chances of continued employment, but in truth I was glad. It was increasingly likely that I would finish the day back in the coffin, and there were a couple of things I wanted to do first:

I had to discover whether my parents were still alive.

I needed time to think.

After explaining my plans to Death I returned to the room, where Skirmish was still in bed, snoring quietly. His diagonally-striped duvet had ridden up his legs.

I poked his arm. He grunted, and turned over.

'I'm going for a walk. Can I borrow your front-door key?' I whispered.

He grunted again – a sound which was far from an agreement, but even further from a denial. Since I didn't have time to probe further, and since I probably wouldn't be seeing him again anyway, I took his answer to be a *yes*. The key was lying on the desk.

I glanced back at him as I left. In the darkness, and in the way he slept so peacefully, I had a brief vision of him as a tiny baby, held in his mother's arms.

Tales from Tomb Town

I left the Agency and headed back to St Giles cemetery where, until recently, I had been comfortably buried. I wasn't afraid to walk around alone. I'd found some blusher and concealer on Pestilence's desk, and applied them to my face using the bathroom mirror. My general appearance wasn't a problem, either. Over the past week I had learned to walk upright, stop shuffling, and keep my mouth shut. I had even managed to control the bug-eyed stare that all zombies have.

On the way there, my brain untangled the mystery surrounding Hades' death. I would never know for sure, of course – I was no Sherlock Holmes, and I couldn't prove anything – but I had a clear picture in my mind of what happened.

It's late Saturday evening. Skirmish has just finished making a small poppy and honey cake. He leaves it to cool overnight on a wire rack, knowing that his roommate will find it the following morning . . . And he's right. Hades, always first in the kitchen on Sundays, is attracted first by the smell, then the texture, and finally the taste. He can't resist one bite, then two – then the whole cake is gone.

With the sun rising behind him, he sets off on his weekly walk across the meadow, bloated but satisfied. Skirmish, watching him from the rear window, waits until he's halfway towards the river then quietly opens the bedroom door. Careful not to wake anyone, he leaves the house through the rear exit and pushes his way through the tall grass in the back garden. Arriving at the kennel, he opens the door and frees Cerberus.

Maybe the hellhound hasn't been fed in two days, and it snarls at him from hunger. Maybe Skirmish sprinkles a few drops of water on its back to enrage it further. Maybe he's even removed an article of Hades' clothing from the wardrobe they share, and rubbed a little honey into it; and now he hands it to the dog and watches as the animal sniffs, then growls, then tears it to shreds. Whatever: he unlocks the iron gate, encourages Cerberus onto the street, and smiles as the dog's three heads turn towards him for instructions.

'Go and find him, boy,' he says.

It seemed plausible. Who would suspect Skirmish? Even if they did, and they managed to connect him with the events I imagined, he could easily claim it was an unfortunate accident. Cerberus was the real killer, after all.

I tried not to imagine Hades' face as he saw the animal bounding towards him, knowing that he had the smell of poison on his breath. I tried not to feel his terror as he realized that his end had come. I tried not to hear his screams as those razor teeth sank into his belly.

But it was impossible. Your mind does what it wants to.

*   *   *

I was so absorbed in this speculation that I briefly forgot who and what I was; but the few people I met on the way to St Giles didn't give me so much as an interested glance, let alone the terrified scream I had feared on Monday. Their indifference made me feel alive again.

I crossed the main road, turned into the narrow paved walkway running alongside the church, and entered the cemetery. I was searching for my parents' graves, though my hope was that I wouldn't find them. The thought that they might still be living somewhere was a source of joy to me – but I needed to know for sure. All I had was a memory of the burial plot they had purchased, somewhere near the junction of the south and east walls.

I followed the narrow sandy path towards the iron gate at the far end, walking slowly, absorbing the rich and varied greens of the trees and plants, imprinting the colours of flowers on my memory, memorizing the rows of tombstones arranged like crooked teeth. But I didn't have the courage to head straight for the plot. Instead, I sat down on the damp grass a few yards from the clearing where Death and I had reassembled Thursday's client – the bearded man who had been mangled by a machine. I listened to the breeze, the cars passing, the distant sound of ringing bells. I heard a bird singing.

And I saw my father.

He pulled hard against the oars of a wooden rowing boat, drawing us away from an island into a broad lake below a weir. His arms were leathery and thick, like the African snakes I'd seen in books. He was laughing.

'Tell me,' he said.

He let the oars drag in the water and began to rock the boat. Gently

at first – but when he saw I was refusing to play the game, he caught
the rhythm of the undulations and rocked it more violently, and for
longer.

'*Tell* me,' he repeated.

I couldn't swim, but I wasn't afraid. I knew he would rescue me
if anything happened; and he knew how much I enjoyed it. I watched
the muscles rise in his left arm as he pushed down on the left side;
in his right as he swayed in the opposite direction. The oars chafed
against the rowlocks and slapped against the water, sending sparkling ripples towards the bank where my mother stood watching
nervously.

'No more!' I squealed.

'Then tell me.' He let the boat settle and looked me straight in the
eye. 'What do you want to be when you grow up?'

And I gave him the answer I had always given. The truthful answer.

'I want to be like you,' I said.

The sun burned above the dark green trees, and the heat of the day
dried the grass even as I sat upon it. I peered into the shadows beneath
the chestnut tree, hoping for some sign – an absence of gravestones,
or an undisturbed patch of ground. But the whole corner was locked
in darkness. I could barely see my own grave lying between the two
thick roots near to the wall.

I would have to move closer.

'It's all right. Come over here . . . Sit down.'

I did as my mother asked, but perched cautiously on the edge of the bed, level with her feet. I had just cycled back from Amy's house, and the room was bright with moonlight. My mother sat up in her dressing gown, drinking a cup of chamomile tea, a white pillow supporting her back. A bloated hot-water bottle lay beside her, like a stranded puffer fish. I wondered why she needed it on such a warm night.

'There's something I want to say to you.'

'Mum—'

'It's important.' She reached over and touched my hand with her own, resting her fingers on my thumb, stroking it gently. Embarrassed by the attention and physical contact, I stared through the window at the clear, black, night sky. 'It's about you and Amy.'

'Nothing's happened,' I lied. 'We're just friends.'

'That's OK.' She nodded. 'But if something does – if you think you might actually live together . . .' I laughed embarrassedly '. . . just make sure you love her as much as I love you.'

Her words were excruciatingly personal. I had once adored her voice, the rising and falling tone, the emphases that made her unique. The sound of her had been as familiar and necessary to me as the rise and fall of my breathing, or the beating of my blood . . . But time shuffles the deck, and I couldn't bear to listen now: I was too old, too grown up. I wanted my feelings to be a secret.

I turned around, wanting to leave, and saw that my mother was gazing at me intensely, with the same powerful, unwavering love I had perceived as a child. And in the darkness of her pupils I saw the half-moon reflected, as I would see it reflected in Amy's eyes ten years later.

271

I stooped beneath the branches of the chestnut tree, noting that the mound of earth by my grave had already been replaced. The moss-covered headstone still remained, even though the corpse to which it referred was now walking amongst the living. The feelings of nausea and dislocation this provoked surprised me. It's hard to stand at your own graveside and remember the way things used to be.

I glanced across at my neighbour's grave on the far side of the tree. His stone rested at an odd angle to the ground, probably disturbed by a root. He'd officially died of natural causes, but had always maintained that his doctor had poisoned him. I think he was just trying to show off. Of the two people buried behind me, one had committed suicide, the other had been killed in a road accident. Par for the course. All three occupants of the plots to my left had been killed in war time: a bullet wound, a plane crash, a bomb. I knew nothing of the corpses immediately outside this tiny ring of satellites.

I knelt down and scraped the moss away from my headstone, but the inscription was too worn to decipher my name or discover any significant dates.

It was as if my whole life had been erased.

It was Christmas, and we were staying at a seaside hotel. My father and I were in the lift, travelling from the ninth floor to the lobby where my mother was waiting. I was seven years old, slowly emerging from the fantasy phase of childhood, learning not to believe everything he told me. But about halfway down the lift stopped, and before I could even begin to wonder what had happened, my father started to panic.

'Oh God,' he shouted, 'we're going to fall.' He paced from one wall to the other, then banged loudly on the doors. 'Let me out! Somebody. Help!'

His terror communicated itself to me very quickly, and I began to cry. But he ignored me. He just paced back and forth, and banged on the door again, and punched all the buttons, and stamped on the floor, repeating over and over how we were going to fall and die. But I knew that he liked to play games with death, and after a few minutes I began to suspect that he was only teasing. I stopped crying, and sat down in the corner, watching him, admiring his acting. And sure enough, when the lift started moving again, he calmed down. He noticed me sitting on the floor, wiped the sweat from his brow, and knelt down to pick me up.

I laughed.

But he wasn't smiling, and it only took me a moment to realize he hadn't been joking after all. It was the first time I had ever seen him so upset, and a creeping tide of dismay swept over me. And in that moment of cold terror, I received three priceless gifts: a fear of falling, a horror of lifts, and a sense of panic in enclosed spaces.

I stood up. In the corner of the graveyard, in the shadow of the wall, I saw a single, white headstone above a fresh mound of earth.

I was a child when I left home at eighteen, though I believed I was an adult. I was still a child at twenty-one, when Amy moved to London. I was a child when I wandered the streets, and cleaned toilets, and swept roads, and waited on tables. I am still a child now, long after my death.

And I was a child when my mother walked into the restaurant where

273

I worked, five years after I had last seen her. I was so childish, I didn't know who I was. I needed help – but I couldn't help myself, so I turned to everyone around me for the answer. But no-one else could help me, so I turned back to myself. But I couldn't help myself. And so I went on, whirling from one moment to the next, and never stopping. I'd spent half a decade trying to forge my own identity, but all I'd created was a stupid spinning top.

When my mother shouted my name across the room, I stopped moving. All the bonds that had been burnt or severed were renewed and reconnected; and as she grabbed my hand and gently rubbed my thumb, I knew who I was again. The feeling didn't last long – when I became a detective and moved into my own flat, I spun more wildly than ever – but for those few precious moments I felt that I had finally come *home*.

And when I looked into her eyes, I saw a look of such compassion that I couldn't speak, and I waited for her to break the long silence between us.

'I thought you were dead,' she said at last.

The inscription told me that my parents had been buried within a year of each other: my mother first, my father nine months later. I don't know the details of how they died. It could have been an accident. It could have been one of those emotive terms which are so common but so imbued with fear: cancer, stroke, heart attack. It could have been natural causes – they would have been nearly sixty when they heard the news of my death, and a few years had passed since. It could have been none of these. The only certainty was, there were no flowers on the grave, fresh or otherwise, and apart from their names and dates, there were only six other words carved on the headstone:

I GIVE IN! I GIVE IN!

My father's parting joke.

I spent an hour at the graveside, digging up more fragments from the past, and considering why I'd felt the need for this visit. I eventually realized it was because I had wanted to say something to my parents which I hadn't had the chance to express while I was still alive. It wasn't that I loved them (love is no use to the dead); nor was it a desire to tell them I was alive again (they couldn't do anything about it, after all). It was just a single word.

I said it as I laid some wild flowers on their grave, which I'd plucked from the soil by the wall.

Goodbye.

In Corpse Code: a long, slow scratch.

Claustrophobia

Few people know when their life will end. Some prepare for it too soon, so that their minds give up long before their bodies. Some don't prepare at all, and are amazed to discover they aren't going to live for ever. But no-one gets it exactly right. I, for example, was absolutely convinced I was going to die when I fell from the roof and saw the ground rising to meet me; and I was utterly certain the agony would last for only the briefest of moments.

I was wrong on both counts.

The green and white awning of the bus station café broke my fall, along with my left arm. And that minor piece of luck kept me alive, and in severe pain, for another two hours.

When I consider what followed, I wish the fall *had* killed me. I remember nothing of the landing – I've always assumed that the awning saved me, but it could easily have been a misguided angel or a bored demon – but I do remember waking up some time later, unable to move, with violent stabbing pains in every part of my body.

I was in a warm, dark, vibrating place. I couldn't see anything, but I heard a low, muffled hum. My hands were tied behind my back with rope; my legs were tied to my hands. My mouth was stuffed with a rag that tasted of oil and grease, sealed in place by insulating tape. The tape wound three times around my head, biting into the skin on my face and neck, tearing my hair when I moved. Sweat rolled into my eyes, ran down my cheek, dripped onto the warm, dark, vibrating surface beneath me.

I thought I had been buried alive, so I screamed for help. But with the rag, and the tape, and the low, muffled hum, no-one could hear.

Even as I was crying out, I realized that the details didn't fit. If I was buried, why was I bound and gagged? And there was something soft pressing against my eyes – a blindfold. Why would anyone blindfold their victim before sealing him in a coffin? It didn't make sense. I briefly wondered if the shock of the fall was causing me to hallucinate, but the oily taste of the rag stuffed into my mouth was too persistent, and the pain in my limbs too real.

I had no choice but to lie there, and continue screaming.

Somewhere behind my blinded eyes, behind the pain pulsing through my body, behind the knowledge that something terrible was about to happen to me, I saw Amy's face. It wasn't the image of her, pale and weeping, sitting on the carpet in her apartment in a shower of broken glass – though that picture returns to me now. Nor was it the incredulity which greeted my last profession of love, or the desperation as she tried to break the skylight window.

It was the memory of the last time we had met in the Jericho Café, seven years earlier. We were sitting by the window, recovering from the long, cold walk back across the meadow. We weren't looking at each other, preferring the slimy grey pulp of snow and slush in the street.

'It just doesn't *feel* right,' she said, repeating herself. 'Not any more.'

I nodded. 'It hasn't felt right for a long time.'

'So what's left between us?'

'Why can't you just accept me for who I am?'

'Don't be sarcastic,' she snapped.

'I wasn't being.'

She changed course. 'Anyway, that's the *point*. Who you are just isn't what I *want*. It hasn't been for the last three years. And I just can't stand it any more . . . You keep telling me how much you want a relationship like the one your parents have, but you don't think about what *I* want. It's too much *pressure*.'

'So what *do* you want?' I asked.

'That's my business!' she shouted. She looked around the room, embarrassed. The café was empty, but she still lowered her voice. 'Look – I'm sorry – but I don't think this is ever going to work out.'

The skin on my back shivered, as if a soft carapace were taking hold there.

'Thanks for telling me,' I said.

'We're just not the same people any more—'

'Fuck off.'

'Don't be *stupid*.'

'Get away from me.'

'Who the hell do you think you are?' She stood up, furious. 'Look . . . It's not my bloody fault you can't loosen up. I can't solve that one for you. And you can't keep blaming me.' She collected her purse from the table top. 'I'm too young. I want to experiment – enjoy myself while I can . . . If I don't, I'll never know what I've missed.' She bent down to kiss me on the forehead. 'You must see that?'

*　　*　　*

And I *do* see it now.
  But now is too late.

The vibrating, humming, pain-racked terror returned. I understood, at last, where I was: imprisoned in a car boot, with no idea of the destination.

It felt like an hour before we stopped. I can't say for sure, but knowing where we ended up, an hour is about right. The crunching of tyres on gravel softened as we rolled the few yards to our final resting place. The humming of the engine grew quieter, then cut out. The random vibrations of the suspension ceased. The oily rag was making me delirious. My heart beat furiously.

I heard whispering voices, then two doors closing. Footsteps, coming closer. A key turning in the lock, then the boot opening.

'Give us 'and, Ron,' said Ralph.

'Right you are, Ralph,' said Ron.

Death by description

I returned to the Agency, my mind preoccupied with my parents – but when I reached the front door, I discovered that the key I had borrowed from Skirmish didn't fit, and that I was locked out. Make-up or no, I didn't relish the thought of watching the world go by until someone arrived with the right key. Fortunately, Death answered my pounding just as it was becoming frantic. He opened the door and ushered me inside.

'Knock any louder and you'll wake the dead,' he said.

He invited me into the office, where Famine mumbled a barely audible hello from behind a tall column of paper.

'Where's War?' I asked him.

'Still asleep,' he muttered. 'Late night. Sore head.'

'Come and look at this,' said Death. He showed me his typewriter, which contained a Termination Report like the one I'd seen in the Chief's office on Thursday. It was a description of my friend, Lucy, but the details bore no resemblance to the person I'd known when I was alive. 'I'm just about to send it upstairs. Is there anything you want to add?'

I shook my head; then thought better of it. I borrowed a pencil from War's desk and scribbled this simple, three-word message at the bottom of the page:

Life is luck.

'So what exactly *are* you doing today?' I asked Death.

'A skinning,' he groaned.

'Live or dead?' Famine interrupted.

'Alive. Fully conscious. Introductions, explanations – the lot. Then it's down to business.'

'Carving knife?'

Death shook his head and pulled an elongated black briefcase from beneath his desk. He paused, then flicked open the catches and lifted the lid. The contents shocked me.

'That's sick,' I said.

'Someone has to do it,' he replied.

The case was lined with a moulded plastic insert. Lodged in the insert was a single tool comprising nine parts: eight interconnecting poles made from polished bone, and a single, shining scythe blade, three feet in length. Each bone was embossed with a small black skeleton. The blade was carefully wrapped in cellophane.

'Nice piece o' kit,' said Famine, who had slithered unnoticed from his desk.

'And brand new,' Death commented wearily. 'Seems a pity to get it dirty.'

He removed the bones from the case and carefully screwed them together to make the shaft; then slotted the blade into a narrow groove in the top piece, securing it with a metal clasp. He stood up and posed briefly with the assembled weapon. It was at least eight feet long.

'Magnificent,' Famine observed.

'Frightening,' I added.

'Gratuitous,' Death sighed.

The scythe was disassembled and repacked without further comment; but the sight of it had unnerved me a little. I patted the ampoule of liquid in my jacket pocket for reassurance; but it was beginning to feel increasingly like a burden. How could I use it on someone who had been nothing but helpful to me? Then again, as Skirmish had already pointed out, what other options did I have?

Death checked his watch, breathed hard, and turned to me. 'It's time,' he said. 'I'll be gone for most of the afternoon. There's a good deal of preparation, and once the first blow has been struck, the skinning itself involves – well, you don't want to know the details now . . . I'll pay you a visit when I get back, and tell you how I got on. In the meantime, you should find the door to your room open – if not, go and see the Chief.'

He picked up his briefcase and left without fuss. I was about to follow him when Famine stopped me.

'Good luck,' he said, his bony hand resting on my arm. 'This evening. Your appraisal.'

I thanked him. 'I'll let you know what happens.'

'Unlikely,' he replied. 'Very busy today. Going abroad for three months tomorrow. Leaving after breakfast . . . You can read my postcards – if you're still here, that is.'

The door to my room *was* unlocked, so I was denied yet another opportunity to meet the Chief. I was seriously beginning to doubt his existence. Perhaps I'd been around Famine too long – his paranoia was contagious.

Yet the more I thought about the situation, the stranger it became. As I replaced Skirmish's key on the writing desk, I realized that I didn't even know if the Chief was a *he*, a *she*, or even an *it*. For all I knew, the attic room's sole occupant could have been a feathered creature with the body of a fish, the legs of an elephant, and the head of an axolotl . . . But most likely there was nothing suspicious about our never meeting. It was just bad luck.

Whatever. I lay down on the bed, closed my eyes, and spent the next seven hours thinking: about everything that had happened to me, and about the terms of my contract. I didn't stop to eat or drink, and barely paused at all until I heard a knock on the door – by which time my head was aching. I'd long since forgotten what Death had said to me earlier that morning, and I was genuinely surprised when he entered. I was even more surprised to see that he'd lost his briefcase and was grimly clutching his scythe in his right hand.

'What happened?' I asked.

He sat down in the Barca lounger, slipped into recliner mode, and told me the whole story.

'I should begin by telling you about skinning – so that you know from the start I've got nothing against this method *per se*.' He propped his scythe against the wall almost as an afterthought. 'It's actually got all the elements I used to relish in a termination . . . For instance, there's a lot of detailed planning, involving the isolation of the client, finding the right moment to strike, the time allowed for cleaning up, and so on. Then there's the formal requirement of an efficient skin removal – a major challenge in itself. Within *that* you have plenty of scope for creativity. Do you start with the head or the feet? Which part of the blade should you use? Do you hack out pieces patchwork-fashion, or cut a long line down the back and peel the torso like an orange? I'm being simplistic, of course: it's actually quite a wrench to tear the flesh from . . .' He faltered. 'Is this too much for you?'

I shook my head, frantically searching for some trivia to distract me. But my brain refused to comply. It clearly had its own agenda, because the only message it fed me was: *Grow up. Deal with it.*

'Fine . . . So you've got satisfaction in the planning and execution stages, and then there's plenty of work in the aftermath. For example, it's *vital* to clean the blade as soon as you've finished, otherwise the metal will rust. The reason why I've been using a new scythe is because I let Skirmish borrow the old one a few weeks back. Don't ask me *what* he used it for – the point is, he didn't return it for days. And when I challenged him, he said he'd lost it – but do you know what?'

'What?'

'He'd kept it in his room all along, stored under the bed. The handle was covered in blood, there were traces of fat and flesh on the blade, and he hadn't even wrapped it up again. I watched over him while he cleaned it. He spent hours and hours scraping away every last mark, and I wouldn't let him go until I was satisfied. You could barely see the damage once he'd finished. But I knew it was there, and it never felt the same after that . . .'

He gazed wistfully at the implement leaning against the wall. All the talk of administrative matters had briefly animated his blank features, and even caused a few short-lived smiles to illuminate his grim face; but the mention of his old scythe sent him back into a silent depression. I tried to relieve his mood by changing the subject.

'What was your client like?'

'Deeply unhappy,' he sighed.

'Why?'

'He was convinced that life had betrayed him. He'd always tried to be as honest as possible in everything he said and did. He felt that nothing should be hidden below the surface, that everyone should be open. A completely stupid idea, of course – and he paid the price. He could never keep friends for more than a few months.' He laughed bitterly. 'Everyone he met he offended, sooner or later, and always without meaning to.'

Two years of private investigation taught me that people have an ambivalent attitude towards honesty. They like it, they hate it, they want it, they don't. Sometimes they believe it's best not to know, then they complain that they haven't been kept informed. They despise ignorance, but don't like turning over rocks to see what lies underneath.

My years underground taught me a different lesson. The dead accept that there are things that are known, and things that are unknown. This is why corpses are so stupid.

Sorry for the interruption.

'What did he do for a living?'

'He worked in an abattoir on the southern edge of town.' Death stared at the ceiling and breathed deeply. 'But, look, I should finish this story off. It might help me understand why I did what I did at the end.'

I nodded, and made myself comfortable. He flicked a switch and eased the Barca lounger back into armchair mode before continuing.

'Imagine this. You're on a two-lane road bordering farmland. You drive over a low, hump-backed bridge spanning a canal and turn left into a slaughterhouse yard. The Metro's air-conditioning sucks in the sweet smell of boiled bones and blows it around the interior. You get out and scan your surroundings: a plain, two-storey brick building with a sloping slate roof, four small windows, a narrow front entrance, and a cobbled courtyard. There's a tall, grey chimney rising from an extension on the right and several metal pipes protruding at odd angles from the walls. This is where I found myself at ten-thirty this morning.

'There was no-one else around. I got out, put the briefcase on the bonnet, opened the catches, lifted the lid. I took the bones and screwed them together, then removed the blade from the cellophane and attached it to the shaft. I closed the briefcase, and approached the main building, entering through the narrow doorway. The Chief had arranged a meeting with the client inside. I was about ten minutes early.

'The interior was gloomier than the exterior. I passed through a dark corridor with offices on either side down to a bare, blood-stained room that stank of powdered bone – a large, open space filled with animal pens, tool cupboards, and overhead poles lined with hooks. And there was a steel-fenced channel at the centre, used to direct animals from the pens to the slaughtering racks: this was where the termination was due to take place. On the far side of the channel, there was a second door leading to a cold store, which I explored while I waited for my client to arrive. I felt a little restless, so I picked up half a dozen gambrels, placed them between my fingers like extended metal claws, and scraped the walls for a while. Then I found a captive-bolt pistol, put it to my head, and pressed the trigger. Naturally, it wasn't loaded – not that it would have made much difference.

'But something strange occurred. All the doubts I'd been having this week – the same doubts I've been having for years – suddenly made sense. In fact, they made much more sense than what I was about to do. I looked around at the abattoir, and thought about my client, and it all seemed so stupid. And I distinctly remember saying to myself, over and over again: *No-one gets skinned alive any more. It simply doesn't happen.*'

He paused, the memory evidently reverberating through his mind. I walked over to the rear window and looked out beyond the canal, across the railway line, to where the green meadow stretched towards the early evening sky. I imagined myself striding along the path towards the river, sitting on the bank beneath the burning sun, lying on the brown earth.

'Things got even stranger,' Death continued. 'My client was late. I didn't feel comfortable admitting it, because the implications were disturbing: either I'd been given the wrong details, or he simply wasn't going to show. Either way, the Chief had made a mistake. I rehearsed the movements I'd have to make when he finally did appear, but my heart wasn't in it . . . I just kept hearing this circular argument inside my head: *Life has no meaning, because everything a Lifer does is swallowed by time. Nothing they achieve has ultimate value. And if their* existence *is insignificant, then it follows that* my work *is insignificant, too – because my work is precisely what makes life meaningless in the first place.*'

'I don't follow,' I said.

'It doesn't matter. The point is: standing there, swinging my scythe downwards into an imaginary chest, I finally understood that everything I did was pointless. And I also realized that the only meaningful act I could perform was to— Well, I don't want to spoil the ending . . . I waited for four more hours, with the same thoughts turning over in my head, and I was just about to put the whole day down to a misunder-standing, and be grateful that I didn't have to answer all those awkward questions, when the client finally walked through the door. A tall, wiry man with greasy black hair. Wearing a clean, white apron.

'"Who the fuck are you?" he said.

'"The Grim Reaper," I told him, without much enthusiasm. "Your time has come."

'And he just collapsed on the floor in the middle of the fenced channel, and started writhing around, begging for mercy. I stood over him for a while, the scythe raised above my head, ready to strike – but I realized I couldn't do it. I *couldn't*. So I just walked out, got in the car, and drove back here ...' He smiled thinly. 'It felt like such an anti-climax – and there'll be hell to pay, of course – but, I tell you, sparing one man's life has given me more satisfaction than anything I've done in the last millennium.'

Sensing a momentary weakness in his position, I blurted out a question I'd been considering asking for the last few days.

'I don't suppose you'd be willing to spare my life, too?'

He looked at me sympathetically. 'Against the rules, I'm afraid. I'm in enough trouble with the Chief as it is. I left my briefcase behind at the abattoir, too. Very bad.' He stood up, shaking his head; and when he spoke again his tone was as business-like as it had been seven days earlier, when he pulled me from the coffin. 'Meet me in the cellar in an hour. We have some things to discuss.'

Ralph 'n' Ron

Life is luck, and my luck was out.

I'd been trapped in Amy's apartment because we'd once loved each other. I would have escaped but for a childhood phobia about lifts. I suffered from vertigo, and my only outlet had been a wet roof eighty feet from the ground. The fall hadn't killed me, but my rescuer was a psychopath. And the psychopath, who had driven me in a car boot to a mysterious destination, had brought his sidekick.

'Grab 'is 'ead, Ron,' said Ralph.

'Right you are, Ralph,' said Ron.

I felt strong hands pulling at my ankles and neck. I remember shouting and writhing around, but the sound was muffled, the movement was futile, and they ignored me anyway. I was carried less than ten yards before my feet were dropped onto the gravel path.

'I'm forgettin' myself,' said Ralph. 'I 'aven't introduced the two of you . . . Ron, this is the git who's been followin' me and pissin' about with my wife for the last seven weeks.'

'Pleased to meet you,' said Ron, lowering my head gently to the ground. His voice was shifty and obsequious like a weasel who'd learned to talk. I remembered the short, balding, stocky man I had seen from the warehouse roof; and recalled him beating his victim's naked feet with an iron bar.

'And this is Ron,' said Ralph, kicking me on the foot. 'Ron's a keeper in the Alligator 'Ouse.'

'Reptile 'Ouse,' Ron corrected.

Ralph ignored him. 'Been 'ere since 1968. Knows all sorts of interestin' stuff about animals.'

'My Dad worked 'ere in the thirties, when they built the Penguin Pool.'

''S'right, Ron . . .' He kicked me again. 'So you're in good 'ands.'

As if to prove it, the two of them lifted me up again, and carried me without rest for another ten minutes, dropping me only twice, and politely apologizing on both occasions.

If I hadn't already guessed from their conversation that they'd brought me to London Zoo, the distant sounds of roaring, chattering, howling, squealing and shrieking would have told me. At the end of the walk, they left me lying on a grass verge, and had a brief discussion before opening a door somewhere ahead. They picked me up again and carried me inside, where the atmosphere was cooler and more humid, and where the air bore the salty, fishy stench of an aquarium.

''Ere we are,' said Ralph. 'Easy does it.'

They lowered me onto a cold, concrete floor. Every part of me was in pain, and the oily rag in my mouth made me want to vomit. I started to writhe again, and shouted for help as loudly as I could. My muted cries were answered by a long and horrifically loud bellow only a few yards to my left.

'That's Gerty,' said Ron. 'She's a bit tempera . . . temper . . . She's a bit *mental*.' He laughed. 'Like the wife.'

'D'you know you can 'ear the call of an alligator a mile off?' said Ralph. 'Tell 'im, Ron.'

''S'true.'

'And d'you know *alligator* comes from a Dago word meanin' lizard?'

'I *did* know that, as a matter o' fact, Ralph.'

'I was talkin' to 'im.'

In the back of my mind, far away from the horror, I couldn't help thinking that Ralph and I had a lot in common. Amy, a love of trivia, perversion, dishonesty . . . The more I thought about it, the more I realized we weren't so different after all. So I screamed again in the terror and darkness, further infuriating the reptile waiting for its midnight snack.

'Keep quiet, will you, mate?' said Ron. 'There's eight thousand animals in this zoo. You're upsettin' every one of 'em.'

'Best way to shut 'im up is to get it over with,' said Ralph.

And that's how it ended. After a short-lived argument about who would take the feet and who the head, Ralph and Ron picked me up and swung me into the alligator pen. The landing winded me, and every nerve along my spine and neck sent worthless warning messages of agony to my brain. But the pain didn't continue for long, and the last thing I remember, before waking in the coffin, were two huge, powerful jaws crunching on my right leg, and a deafening, primeval roar that turned my blood to ice.

How I got sewn back together is a mystery I'll never solve – and why the alligator ate nothing of me other than six minor appendages, is equally puzzling. Perhaps it just didn't like the taste.

The annoying thing is: if I'd known in the grave that this was how I died, my neighbours would have treated me with a lot more respect.

Storage

After checking I still had the ampoule, I opened the bedroom door and headed for the rear exit; but as soon as I turned the handle I heard a loud moan from the corridor behind me. I turned around and saw War staggering out of his room. He was holding his head and beckoning me towards him.

'I thought it might be you.' He massaged his temples as I approached. 'This bloody, buggering headache.'

'What happened?'

'Thrown out of a second-floor window last night . . . Bunch of 'cking comedians.'

He groaned again, and knelt down. I glanced over his head into his room. Almost everything was blood red – bed, bedspread, carpet, light bulb, ceiling, two cupboards and a desk. The walls were lined with red bookshelves containing defence manuals, weapons catalogues, histories of world conflicts, photographic records of battle and pocket guides to strategy. The only non-red item in the whole place was a huge, two-handed sword to the right of the door.

'Nice colour scheme,' I told him. 'It suits you.'

'Thank you . . . But it's bloody awful when your skull's splitting.'

He continued to rub his head.

'I haven't seen you for a couple of days. How's your eye?'

'Fine.' He groaned a little more at the memory of the twig.

'Did you want me for something specific?'

He raised a stubby thumb to his hairy chin, and scratched. 'Not really . . . I just thought I'd wish you luck. You'll need it.'

He offered me his hand. When I took it, he crushed my fingers.

I descended the stairs to the cellar: seven steps to the garden, reverse direction, seven more to the basement. I opened the door, and a pungent smell of mould and decay filled my nostrils. I coughed, and groped along the wall for a light switch, touching several cold, clammy objects before finding a cord-pull.

I tugged, my resurrected heart pounding.

And there was light.

Rows of pale white feet protruded from wooden shelves on all four walls: sallow cadavers, stacked seven high in orderly lines. Hundreds of legs – some rotting, some fresh; some with stumps, some with five toes; some covered with skin, some with only the bare bones remaining. Ranks of dead flesh, luminous and eerie in the yellow glow from the lone bulb.

'Who is it?'

The speaker's voice was toneless, like a duck call. It came from one of the shelves on the right, close to the front entrance.

'A friend,' I said. 'Where are you?'

'Over here.' In a gloomy corner, three rows up, two white feet twitched. 'What do you want?'

I ignored the question, but skirted around a table and two chairs in the centre of the room in order to reach him. I noticed that every shelf was divided into separate sliding units resting on runners, one per corpse. I grasped the end of his shelf with both hands.

'What are you doing?'

I pulled. The runners squeaked.

'Leave me alone.'

I slid the body out into the light.

It was our client from Thursday evening again. He was lying on his back, wearing the clothes we had given him. His flesh was still quite fresh – white, cold, few signs of degradation – but he smelled awful, like old sweat. His face was drawn in the wide-mouthed leer of a sexually deviant clown, but his eyes were closed.

'What do you want?' he repeated. Though his lips moved, his grin remained frozen.

'I want to know what it's like.'

'What do you mean?'

'This,' I explained. 'Being here. In storage.'

'What's storage?'

I paused. He seemed contented enough. What business did I have disturbing him?

'Can you remember how you died?' I asked.

'Heart stopped,' he replied.

'How long have you been here?'

'I don't know.'

'When are they releasing you?'

'I don't know.'

'Don't you know anything?'

'No. Just put me back. *Please.*'

I slid him back into place. Talking to him reminded me of the interminable, mind-numbing tedium of eternal rest. And I briefly saw my own future: lying amidst all this rotten flesh, cadavers pressing down upon me, reaching up to touch me, crawling all around me. A writhing mass of quiet agony from which there would be no escape.

'Am I interrupting anything?'

Death stood at the bottom of the steps, holding a bottle of wine and two glasses. He was smiling.

'I was just talking to one of the corpses.'

'Don't worry about them – they don't worry about you.'

He slapped our former client on the soles of his feet. The dead man grunted, twitched, then settled into his previous position.

'What will happen to them?'

'Who knows? We've been trying for a thousand years to set aside time to sort out their future. But there's always something more important to discuss.' He led me over to the table, and we sat opposite each other as he removed the cork and poured out the wine. 'It could be worse, though. Before we thought of storage, we had no choice but to set our problem corpses free and let them wander the Earth.' He took a sip from the glass. 'There are still over a dozen stumbling around right now – and the majority are pretty annoyed. All they want to do is find somewhere to rest, but they're driven out of town wherever they go.' He frowned, finished his wine in one gulp, then stared at me. 'But I believe we have some business to attend to.'

I nodded, but said nothing. He poured himself another glass, pulled a crumpled sheet of paper from the pocket of his chinos, and flattened it on the table in front of me. It listed the six termination methods I'd witnessed this week along with Death's failed attempt today – making seven in all. There was a tick-box to the right of each, some illegible small print at the bottom, and a space for my signature.

'The thing is,' he continued, 'and I might as well get to the point – you aren't quite what we are looking for in an apprentice.' I shrugged. It was no surprise. 'Please don't take it personally. If it was up to me, I'd sign you up straight away. But the Chief doesn't think you're capable ... And I think you'll agree that throughout the week, despite your best efforts, you've been unable to—'

I waved my hand dismissively. 'So you want me to select the manner of my own death?'

'As your contract demands.'

He handed me the novelty pen he'd bought on Monday. It was orange, with a repeated pattern of tiny green alligators running down the shaft. I looked at him, wondering if it was just a coincidence, but in his deep-set, drain-dark eyes I saw only the reflection of my own smiling face.

'I've decided', I said at last, 'that I don't want to die by any of the methods you've shown me this week.'

'In that case, there is space on the reverse for you to fill in a method of your own choosing. And if I might make a suggestion, a lightning strike is an excellent way to go. It's my own personal favourite: the hum, the electrical charge in the air just before it happens, the violent blue flash ... The precise moment is always a surprise, even when you know it's coming.'

I raised the glass of wine to my lips. It slipped sweetly over my tongue, down my throat, warm into my stomach. And it gave me the courage to speak unequivocally.

'To be honest, I don't think I want to die at all.'

'You do understand the importance of your decision?' said Death. '*All* of its implications?'

I nodded. 'I have to remain in storage.'

He gazed mournfully at the table, collected the paper and pen, and stuffed both into his pocket. He took another drink, swallowed hard, and sighed.

'But before that happens,' I added calmly, 'I believe I still have the right to issue a challenge . . . How about a game of chess?'

His manner changed abruptly. He smiled broadly, clapped his hands together like a child, and leapt from his chair. He looked as if he was about to embrace me, but thought better of it, ran across the cellar, pushed open the back door, and scurried up the stone steps to the ground floor.

In his absence, I seized the opportunity to remove the ampoule from my pocket, break off the tip, and squeeze a drop of poison into his glass.

What choice did I have?

The dark river

Death returned a couple of minutes later with his portable CD-player, the same black and gold chess board I had seen on Monday, and a small, brown box containing a set of Staunton pieces.

'I don't know why I didn't think of this myself,' he said, panting. 'It doesn't give you much of a chance, I admit – but it's worth a try. And perfectly legal.' He put the CD-player on the ground by his chair and switched it on. The dramatic opening to an unknown classical piece blasted from the speakers. 'Berlioz' *Symphonie Fantastique*,' he explained, turning down the volume. 'I like to listen to it while I'm playing. It's a little cheery to begin with, but there's a nightmare movement later on called "March to the Scaffold".' He opened the box, removed a couple of the pieces, then held out his fists. 'Now . . . left or right?'

I tapped his right hand.

'Lucky you,' he said, revealing a white pawn.

As he placed the board on the table and set up the game, I realized that I had no prospect whatsoever of winning. On Thursday, when I'd discovered in the small print of my contract that a challenge was possible, it had seemed a credible option; but at the very moment I suggested it to Death as a concrete proposition, I knew it was futile. That was why I had poisoned his drink as soon as he'd left the room: I was desperate. It was my life all over again – I had acted on a whim, and because I could think of nothing better to do.

I'd told him on Tuesday that I had never explored chess in any depth, and at the time I'd believed I was being modest; but when I looked at my opponent I knew I had actually overstated my abilities. Compared to him, I was little better than a novice, with only a rudimentary knowledge of tactics and no grasp whatsoever of strategy. If I was fortunate, I might last twenty moves.

'This is pointless,' I said. 'I don't stand a chance . . . Why don't you just finish your wine and get it over with?'

'I never drink during play,' he replied. 'Bad for the concentration.'

I stared blankly at the thirty-two chessmen facing each other across the battlefield, and finally understood the awful significance of this one game. The pieces were no longer simple wooden figures, but representatives of a symbolic conflict which had become terrifyingly personal. The more I considered the consequences of failure, the more I recognized what was truly at stake in the next few minutes: my feelings, my freedom, my future, my existence.

I began to wish I'd taken the poison myself. Even if Death eventually took a sip from his glass, and Skirmish's plan worked in precisely the way he had predicted (which I doubted), I knew that my liberty would be destroyed by a terrible burden of guilt. But if I didn't finish the game, my options would be even narrower.

I made the first move, my hand shaking: e2–e4.

Death answered immediately: e7–e5.

We avoided each other's gaze – but in the middle of the board our pawns were locked in an eyeball-to-eyeball confrontation.

As I contemplated my next move, I attempted a crude diversionary tactic.

'If you don't like what you're doing, and everything you do is meaningless, why don't you just resign?'

'How can I?' he replied, focusing intently on the centre squares. 'I'm Death. It's a huge responsibility. I might be unhappy, I might even be disillusioned, but I couldn't possibly trust anyone else to do the job half as well.' He looked up briefly. 'I'm trapped . . . Just like you.'

'But if you *could* leave . . . if you could do anything else – what would it be?'

He turned his attention back to the board.

'I'd go surfing,' he said at last. 'And, please – stop trying to distract me.'

I moved my bishop on f1 to c4. Death mirrored the manoeuvre by advancing *his* bishop on f8 to c5. The two men of God smiled obsequiously at each other, face-to-face on the c-file.

'But if I beat you at chess,' I continued, ignoring his request, 'right here and now, in this game . . . then I can forget my contract and carry on living?'

'In the unlikely event that you manage to defeat me,' he said, frowning at his position, 'you're free to leave here and take your chances . . . But *living* isn't quite the right word. You're a zombie, so the best you can hope for is to remain *undead*.'

'Better a zombie than a corpse in the coffin,' I replied.

I marched my queen from d1 to h5, where, in alliance with my bishop, she threatened one of the pawns guarding black's king. It was a naive mode of attack and Death's response was instantaneous – but also profoundly stupid. Maybe the music had affected his judgement; or my conversation; or the client he hadn't killed. More likely his problems with the Chief had distracted him: it was the end of a week in which he had continually ignored protocol, been criticized for his performance, and questioned the very meaning of his work. Whatever: in a moment of absent-mindedness or shameless generosity, he advanced his knight on b8 to c6. I didn't hang around: my queen captured the pawn in front of the powerless king and, supported by the bishop, forced check-mate.

He realized his mistake immediately, but seemed more embarrassed than surprised. His butter-bean complexion glowed a kidney-bean red.

'Scholar's Mate,' he said. 'What a bummer.' He shook his head, bit his lip, and stared at me. 'I don't suppose you'd let me take back that last move?' I politely declined. 'How about best of three?'

'I don't think so.'

'But I just don't *understand* it.'

'Shit happens,' I said.

'I need a drink,' Death said, raising the glass to his lips.

I had to think quickly. If my idea of poisoning him had plagued my conscience before the game, now that I'd won it would be nothing less than a disaster. I had to stop him, but I didn't know what to do.

'How about a toast?'

He smiled. 'Anything in mind?'

I poured myself some more wine, and considered the options.

'To life,' I said.

As our glasses touched, I knocked the poison from his hand. The wine sprayed onto the chess board and Death's polo shirt; his glass shattered on the stone floor.

'I'm so sorry,' I said. 'I've been having accidents all week.'

I cleaned up as much of the debris as I could, the fragments of glass which caught in my hand reminding me of the broken skylight in Amy's apartment. When I'd finished, I carefully scraped the shards into a small pile on the table. Death, not wanting to be deprived of his drink, accepted the offer to finish mine, then petulantly threw the chess pieces back into the brown box.

'I just have one more thing to do,' he said resignedly. He removed a small, scythe-shaped silver badge from his chinos: the same design as the gold one pinned to his shirt. 'This is the symbol of my authority. If your apprenticeship had been successful, you would already be wearing it. As it is – which corpse were you talking to before?'

'Over there.' I indicated Thursday's client.

'Seven weeks of trainees is enough for me. It's time to make a decision.' He strode to the corner and slid out the shelf containing the bearded man. 'I have a suspicion that this was all part of the Chief's grand plan anyway . . . It's certainly the most efficient selection method.'

'Who's the Chief?' said the corpse.

Death ignored him, but pinned the silver badge on his T-shirt, just above the word COFFINS. The cadaver had a voice, but made no complaint; he heard what was happening, but didn't open his eyes to see. His employer slapped him affectionately on the left shoulder, and ordered him to stand up.

The Agency had a new Agent.

Death opened the front entrance to the cellar and indicated that his assistant wait outside. The corpse wandered idly by – his mouth open, his eyes staring into space – then collided with the stone steps, and tripped over.

'I can't say I'm sorry to be leaving,' I said.

He shrugged. 'Have you decided what you'll call yourself?'

'What do you suggest?'

He tapped his chin. 'Pestilence would insist on Antonius – after Antonius Block in *The Seventh Seal*. But that's a stupid idea. War would undoubtedly suggest one of the great generals, such as Alexander.' He looked me up and down, shaking his head. 'It doesn't suit you. You look more like one of the great losers. Famine would probably recommend something short and to the point – which happens to coincide with my own preference . . . How about Bill? Or Ted?'

I remembered *The Maltese Falcon*. 'How about Sam?'

'Perfect,' he said. 'I'll amend the files first thing tomorrow morning.'

We briefly discussed what I would need to survive in the outside world: a job, a supply of make-up, maybe even some corrective surgery. Death said he'd talk to the Chief and sort things out.

'And you're welcome to visit us any time you like,' he added. 'We'll take a stroll in the garden, and we'll talk, and you can say hello to Cerberus again.' He nodded, pleased with the idea. 'We've got another ten years on the lease before we have to move on. I can't say I'm looking forward to it . . .' He glanced around the cellar and grimaced. 'The worst part will be shifting all these bodies.'

Outside, a warm breeze was blowing: the heat of the day dying, the cold of the night beginning. I felt a shattering, shimmering starburst of freedom – as if I had swallowed the future, and let it filter through the walls of my stomach into my bloodstream.

I walked towards the emerald meadow in the twilight. As I crossed the canal, I briefly wondered how long I had left to live. At the railway bridge, I asked myself what I would do next. But as I moved further away from the Agency, all the questions disappeared, and I picked up pace, and started to run.

I ran towards the dark river on the horizon, where I lay down on the bank, and gazed at the emerging stars, and thought of nothing.

It wasn't you

It was Monday morning, seven weeks and a day since Hades' murder. In the dining room War, Pestilence and Skirmish were eating their usual breakfasts as Famine watched dolefully. The newspapers were late, no-one felt like talking, and nothing at all remarkable occurred, until – at nine a.m. precisely – Death breezed through the door and announced a hearty hello. He was followed by a sickly and rather clumsy companion, dressed in surfer's shorts and a T-shirt.

'Who the bugger is that?' said War.

'This is Hell,' Death replied, pushing the corpse into the room. 'He's my new assistant.'

'Oh dear,' said Famine.

'This *is* something of a surprise,' Pestilence added. 'I presume you cleared it with the Chief?'

Death ignored him. He seemed to have more pressing business with Skirmish, to whom he spoke firmly: 'I'm afraid you're going to have to eat elsewhere from now on . . . Until we find a larger table, of course.'

Skirmish, too shocked by Death's continued existence to argue, picked up his food and retreated to the corner stool, where he spent the rest of his meal scowling and sulking.

Hell was invited to sit down in his place; and after a little confusion and a great many questions, he did so. Death selected a white mouse from the customary trio and offered it to his assistant. Hell seized it by the tail, positioned it carefully on his plate . . . and began to stroke it softly.

Then he fell off his chair.

Over the next few weeks, the new Agent's intelligence and co-ordination skills showed no signs of improvement. During several meals he was observed playing with the saloon doors, walking into walls, and trying to eat his plate. In the office, he managed to knock over every column of paper on three separate occasions, and put his elbow through the window twice. Taking Cerberus for a walk on the meadow, he annoyed the animal so much that it savaged him – and he had to be reassembled again, this time with stitches.

Most importantly, during working hours his good-natured incompetence caused many of Death's clients to cheat their fate, at least temporarily ... And for a very short while, a very few people lived a little longer.

But it didn't last.